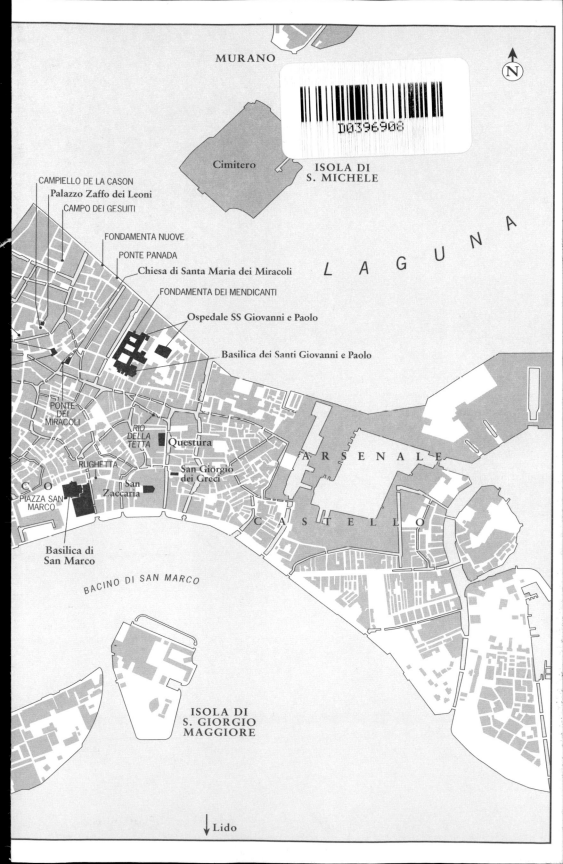

MURANO

ISOLA DI
S. MICHELE

Cimitero

L A G U N A

CAMPIELLO DE LA CASON
Palazzo Zaffo dei Leoni
CAMPO DEI GESUITI

FONDAMENTA NUOVE

PONTE PANADA

Chiesa di Santa Maria dei Miracoli

FONDAMENTA DEI MENDICANTI

Ospedale SS Giovanni e Paolo

Basilica dei Santi Giovanni e Paolo

PONTE
DEI
MIRACOLI

RIO
DELLA
TETTA

Questura

San Giorgio
dei Greci

RUGHETTA

San
Zaccaria

C O

PIAZZA SAN
MARCO

A R S E N A L E

C A S T E L L O

Basilica di
San Marco

BACINO DI SAN MARCO

ISOLA DI
S. GIORGIO
MAGGIORE

↓ Lido

N

So Shall You Reap

Also by Donna Leon

Donna Leon

So Shall You Reap

Atlantic Monthly Press
New York

Originally published in Great Britain in 2023
by Hutchinson Heinemann, an imprint of Penguin Random House.

Published simultaneously in Canada
Printed in the United States of America

First Grove Atlantic hardcover edition: March 2023

Typeset in 12/16.45 pt Palatino LT Std
by Integra Software Services Pvt. Ltd, Pondicherry

Library of Congress Cataloging-in-Publication data is available for this title.

ISBN 978-0-8021-6236-6
eISBN 978-0-8021-6237-3

Atlantic Monthly Press
an imprint of Grove Atlantic
154 West 14th Street
New York, NY 10011

Distributed by Publishers Group West

groveatlantic.com

23 24 25 26   10 9 8 7 6 5 4 3 2 1

For Cecily and Johannes Trapp

Oh, fatal consequence
Of rage, by reason uncontroll'd!
With every law he can dispense;
No ties the furious monster hold:
From crime to crime he blindly goes,
Nor end, but with his own destruction knows.

Saul Act II, 68
Handel

1

On a Saturday in early November, Guido Brunetti, reluctant to go outside, was at home, trying to decide which of his books to remove from the shelves in Paola's study. Years ago, some months before the birth of their daughter, he had renounced claim to what had been his study so that their second child could have her own bedroom. Paola had offered his books sanctuary on four shelves. At the time, Brunetti had suspected this would not suffice, and eventually it had not: the time had come for The Cull. He was faced with the decision of what to eliminate from the shelves. The first shelf held books he knew he would read again; the second, at eye level, held books he wanted to read for the first time; the third, books he'd not finished but believed he would; and the bottom shelf held books he had known, sometimes even as he was buying them, that he would never read.

He decided to begin with the books at the bottom. He knelt on one knee and studied the spines. Halfway along, he saw the familiar face of Proust, and the face of Proust, and the face of Proust. Slipping his hands into the space before the first book and after the last, he said aloud, 'Now,' and extracted them in one block. He stood and carried them over to Paola's desk, tilted his hands, and set them down in a wobbly pile, then patted them into order. He stepped back and counted the faces of Proust: seven.

He went to the kitchen and returned with one of the paper bags the city distributed to hold paper for collection. He opened it and lowered the Prousts carefully inside, then returned to the shelf, carrying the bag. He set it beside him, knelt again, and glanced more carefully at the remaining books, making a series of visceral judgements, adding the books to the bag without bothering to give them the opportunity to plead for their lives from the temporary safety of Paola's desk. *Moby Dick*; *The Man of Feeling*; *I Promessi Sposi*, which he'd been forced to read as a student in *liceo* and had hated. It had survived this long because, until now, he'd lacked the courage to believe a 'classic' could be such a bore, but into the bag it went. He came to four volumes of D'Annunzio's plays and poetry and knew instantly that they were for the bag: was it because he was a bad writer or a bad person? To settle it, he opened one of the books of poetry at random and read the first line of the first poem his eye fell upon. *'Voglio un amore doloroso, lento …'*

Brunetti's hand, still holding the book, fell to his side. 'You want a love that's painful and slow, do you?' he asked the deceased poet. 'How about fast and painless?' He bent and picked up the sixteen centimetres of D'Annunzio and tucked them in beside Manzoni. 'If ever a marriage was made in heaven,' he said, looking down into the bag, content with his decision. The used book-store at Campo Santa Maria Nova would gladly have them all.

Brunetti studied the empty spaces on the shelf, wondering how he could fill them. Before an answer came, his phone rang.

He started to give his name, but a voice he recognized as Vianello's spoke over his, asking, 'Guido, can you meet me at Piazzale Roma?'

'It's Saturday, Lorenzo,' he told his friend and colleague. 'And it's raining and it's cold.'

'And it's important,' Vianello added.

'Tell me.'

Pausing only long enough to give a heavy sigh, Vianello said, 'I had a call from Fazio.' It took Brunetti a moment to recognize the name, a sergeant on the Treviso force and someone with whom both he and Vianello had worked. 'Alvise's been arrested.'

'Alvise?' Brunetti asked, unable to disguise his astonishment. Then, to be sure, he repeated, voice lower but no less shocked, 'Alvise?'

'Yes.'

'Where?'

'There. Treviso.'

What in God's name, Brunetti wondered, would Alvise be doing in Treviso? Indeed, what would anyone be doing there, especially on a day like this?

'What was he doing there?'

'He was at the protest.'

Brunetti paused a moment and searched his memory for any protest threatened for that weekend. Not the train drivers, not the remaining No-Vax, not the workers at Marghera – who seemed in a perpetual state of protest – and not medical professionals, who had protested two weeks before.

'Which one?'

'Gay pride,' Vianello said with absolute dispassion.

'Gay pride?' Raising his voice, Brunetti repeated, 'Alvise? We don't have anything to do with patrolling Treviso,' he reminded the Ispettore.

'He wasn't on patrol.'

'Then what was he doing there?'

'That's why we're going to Treviso. To find out.'

'What happened?'

Over the line came the sound of a vaporetto changing into reverse to slow for a station stop. A voice – not Vianello's – came over the line: 'Ca' Rezzonico.'

Brunetti was already walking towards the door, where he'd left his raincoat and umbrella that morning after coming home from having a coffee and picking up the newspapers.

Switching his phone to his left hand, he felt in the pocket of his raincoat for his house keys. 'All right. I'll meet you in front of the taxis,' he said. Then, before Vianello could disappear, Brunetti asked, 'What was he arrested for?'

'Resisting arrest.'

Brunetti could find no words.

'And violence to a public official,' Vianello added.

Brunetti had no trouble making the translation from police vocabulary to reality. 'Violence? Alvise?'

'Fazio wasn't sure what happened. He called me when they brought Alvise into the Questura. He asked me to come. And bring you,' Vianello said.

'All right. I'm leaving now.' Brunetti broke the connection.

Despite the rain and cold, Brunetti chose to walk: the vaporetti would be overheated and crowded in weather like this. The thought of the feral mug of warm, damp air in the passenger cabin only confirmed the wisdom of his choice.

As he made his way towards Piazzale Roma, he considered what Vianello had told him. Alvise? Alvise had been on the force for as long as Brunetti, but in that time, while Brunetti had increased in rank, Alvise – slow, polite, inept, thoughtless, well liked although generally considered a fool – had remained a simple officer. Even with all of his contradictory qualities, Alvise had still become the mascot, one could even say the beloved mascot, of most of the Questura. He had never fired his gun and had never had the sudden realization of who was responsible for a crime, but he had more than once put himself in danger to help a fellow officer. His hair had thinned a bit, the sides growing white; his face had aged, and he'd put on some weight. He never talked about himself, was interested in his colleagues, remembered the names of their spouses and children, was loyal and did his best. And now he'd been arrested in Treviso at the gay pride parade and had, it seemed, struck another officer.

Brunetti tried to recall ever having encountered Alvise beyond the Questura or his position as a policeman and found it impossible. Alvise, perhaps by virtue of his not being taken seriously by his colleagues, did not register fully with them as a person. Brunetti stopped involuntarily at the realization that he might not recognize Alvise if he saw him out of uniform. He turned his head and stared into a shop window for a moment, trying to recall what Alvise looked like: the best he could come up with was a roundish face, no moustache or beard, hair still mostly brown, eyes that contracted when he smiled, and a general inability to remain entirely still when standing. Beyond that, Alvise was pretty much a cartoon figure of a man in uniform, his hat always seeming one size too big for his head.

Brunetti muttered, 'It's like he doesn't really exist,' which led him to wonder how many of the other officers didn't really exist for him, and that led him to wonder if all of them had managed to separate their private lives from their professional lives. He turned from the shoes in the window and resumed walking, having calculated the time Vianello's boat would arrive.

He tried to recall incidents in which his colleague had been involved, and in all of them Alvise had managed to cause confusion: he'd gone to the wrong address to make an arrest, had left a briefcase full of witness statements on a bus. But he had also disarmed a man who was threatening his wife with a kitchen knife and had once prevented a fight in a restaurant when a client, seemingly displeased with his dinner, had thrown a plate of pasta at the waiter and turned over the table where he sat. Somehow, Alvise, at the next table, managed to calm the man down, spoke with him for a few minutes, then suggested that he apologize to the waiter and help him put the table upright again.

The man's mother, Alvise had told the owner, was in the hospital and not expected to live: the pasta had been so much like hers that it had broken him. The man's apology was both tearful and sincere. The next day, the story had filtered into the Questura. Alvise had said no more than that it had been a waste of very good pasta.

He saw Vianello, wearing corduroy slacks and a thick parka, waiting at the head of the line of taxis, and joined him. When he saw Brunetti, the Ispettore leaned forward and opened the back door of the cab, then went round and got in on the other side. Before Brunetti could say anything, the Ispettore gave the address of the Questura in Treviso and sat back.

'Well?' Brunetti asked.

Vianello leaned forward and slid the glass panel between them and the driver closed. He turned to Brunetti and, keeping his voice low, said, 'The parade was the usual thing: about two hundred people, holding signs and chanting slogans. Fazio said there was a lot of good feeling, even with the rain.'

'Where'd they begin?' Brunetti asked.

'In front of COIN. They had permission to go along Via Lazzari. There was supposed to be singing and maybe a few speeches, but they hadn't figured on the rain, so things got confused, and it was after eleven by the time they left COIN.'

'So?' Brunetti asked. Being late when you had two hundred people seemed hard to avoid.

'That's when some people began giving them trouble,' Vianello went on.

'What?' Brunetti asked. In this rain? On a Saturday morning?

'Fazio was there. He said there were about twenty of them. The usual: fat men with biblical texts printed on signs. No women. Name-calling, telling them they were damned.'

'They sound as crazy as the anti-abortion people.'

'Don't forget the No-Vax,' Vianello said.

Brunetti nodded and sighed, remembering one particularly unpleasant demonstration in front of the hospital. 'What happened?'

'Fazio was detailed to go along. In uniform. He said that one of the anti-marchers ...' Vianello paused to consider that word, shook his head, and went on, '... came running at the people in the parade, holding his sign stuck out in front of him horizontally, and deliberately ploughed into them. Three or four were knocked down.'

'Hurt?'

'Not really. Surprised more than anything.'

'What happened?'

'Fazio said the guy started waving his sign around, swinging it at people. So he ran towards him, but before he could get there, one of the people from the parade grabbed the sign, pulled it away from him and slammed it on the ground a couple of times. Broke it into pieces.'

'What did the other man do?'

'Fazio said he started screaming at the guy who'd taken his sign – the usual: "fucking faggots", "you're all sinners". But then Fazio had a radio call from his lieutenant, and when that finished, he looked around and saw that one of his men was putting handcuffs on the guy who'd trashed the sign.'

'Are you going to tell me this was Alvise?' Brunetti asked, unable to keep the surprise from his voice.

Vianello nodded.

'Did anyone see what happened?'

'Fazio managed to get the names and addresses of a few people who were there, but – you know how it is – no one saw anything.'

Brunetti knew how it was. Unless they filmed it on their phones and could boast about that, few people were willing to say they had witnessed a crime, reluctant to be caught up in the slow-grinding maw of the justice system.

The car slowed, and Brunetti glanced out of the window of the cab. They were in front of the Questura of Treviso.

Vianello paid and got out of the taxi; Brunetti followed him and, as he had the first time he was there, stood and gawked at the multistorey building and again tried to count the floors. As ever, he failed, defeated by the architect, who had granted more than one horizontal window to each floor. Brunetti gave up and followed Vianello into the building. As the Ispettore led him down corridors, no one asked them who they were or why they were there. Brunetti had no idea if this was lack of security or whether the two of them somehow looked like policemen and were thus left alone. Or perhaps, as many criminals had told him, it made no difference where you tried to go: so long as you looked like you knew where you were going, no one would interfere with you. He followed Vianello into the elevator, got out with him on the second floor, and stayed close behind him as the Ispettore turned right and then left, ending in front of an office with the name 'Danieli' on the door.

Vianello knocked, a male voice said something, and they went in. A short, thick man sat behind a desk. His hair was equally short and thick, dark, and cut close to his head. He was wearing a grey suit with a white shirt and a red and blue striped tie. He looked up and got to his feet: his eyes were a very pale blue and tilted faintly upwards at the outer corners. 'Ah, gentlemen, I'm glad you could come. I was told he'd called you.' He turned his attention to Brunetti, somehow scenting that he was of superior rank, and said, 'Danieli.'

Brunetti gave him their names and Vianello's rank. Instead of offering his hand to the men, Danieli waved it towards the chairs in front of his desk and waited until they were seated before he sat down again.

Brunetti was searching his memory for the name, which he had recognized, although he couldn't remember why.

'You're here about your man,' Danieli said, making it a statement and not a question, aimed at either one of them.

'Yes,' Brunetti said, 'Alvise.' Then, summoning his first name, added, 'Dario.'

A file lay open on Danieli's desk; he glanced at it before asking, 'How long has he been on the force in Venice?'

Brunetti turned to Vianello, who said, 'Decades.'

'What's your assessment of him?' Danieli asked, using the plural so either could answer.

Brunetti said, 'He's reliable, honest, deals well with people.'

Danieli looked at Vianello, who said, 'He's one of the most popular men on the force, has never had any disciplinary problems, and more than once has managed to defuse potentially violent situations.'

Brunetti nodded in agreement.

'Has his homosexuality ever caused any difficulty?'

Stunned, Brunetti leaned back in his chair, almost as if the word had given him a shove. He folded his hands and studied the map of Treviso on the far wall. Alvise? Finally he said, 'Not that I can think of, no.' That was certainly true. Then, hoping to divert the course of this conversation from wherever the other man was trying to direct it, he added, 'I like to think those times are over.'

'What times?' Danieli asked politely.

'The times we all lived through,' Brunetti said, 'when our gay friends had to lie and pretend, and – some of them – get married, even have families.' He shrugged, glanced at Vianello and then back to the other man, and asked, 'For what?'

'To keep their jobs, chiefly, I suppose,' Danieli answered. 'And what used to be called their respectability.'

Vianello interrupted here and asked, 'Excuse me, Signore, could you tell me why you asked about that?'

Danieli closed the file – which Brunetti noticed contained no more than a single page – and said, 'I've heard conflicting stories about what happened. Someone who was there said that your officer resisted my officer when he put the handcuffs on him.' Before Vianello could say anything, Danieli continued, 'Another person said that my officer was deliberately, and unnecessarily, rough in treating yours.'

'What has Officer Alvise said?' Brunetti asked.

Danieli tapped at the cover of the file with his forefinger. 'So far, he hasn't had the chance to say anything to anyone.'

'Meaning that he's sitting by himself in a cell, waiting for us to come and get him out?' Brunetti enquired.

Danieli, as Brunetti had intended, smiled at the question. 'Yes, something like that. He was put there when he was brought in. One of the men on the squad at the protest recognized him as being on the force in Venice.'

'I see,' Brunetti said.

'So I asked Fazio to call someone on the Venice force he knew – and trusted – and tell him that we had one of their men here and we'd like someone to come out and help us find a way to settle this.'

'Settle it among friends?' Brunetti asked.

'Of course,' Danieli answered without hesitation. 'The last thing any of us needs is the *Gazzettino* banging on about police brutality.' He looked past them, as though there were a projection of the first page of the *Gazzettino* flashing on the wall behind them. 'You'd think this was the Bronx, the way they go crazy anytime someone claims to have been injured while they were being detained.'

Brunetti noted that word, 'detained' rather than 'arrested'.

'It happens, doesn't it?' Vianello asked.

'Rarely,' Danieli answered in a flat voice. He glanced back and forth between them. 'I think you'd have to admit that.'

Brunetti nodded, followed by Vianello, who said, 'It's probably because Venice is such a small place – tiny gene pool – so it's always possible we'll be detaining the cousin of someone we know or our son's mathematics teacher.' Brunetti liked it that Vianello had repeated the word: 'detaining'.

'Notoriously violent, mathematics teachers,' Brunetti said to inject a lighter tone.

Danieli gave a small laugh and said, 'So, shall we try to settle this like colleagues?'

Brunetti, noting that 'friends' had been demoted to 'colleagues', paused a moment before asking, 'Can we speak to Alvise first?'

Danieli made no attempt to hide his surprise, but answered calmly. 'Certainly. I'll have him sent up.' He reached for the phone on his desk and punched in two numbers. While he waited for someone to answer, he waved his hand around the room and said, 'You can talk to him here.'

Before they could protest his generosity, he held up a hand and spoke into the phone. 'Gianluca, could you bring that man who was detained this morning up to my office? He's in one of the holding rooms on the ground floor. Two men are here to talk to him.' He paused a moment, then answered, 'Yes, at the protest march.' The other man said something; Danieli thanked him and hung up. Looking up at them, he said, 'Shouldn't be long.'

This was the moment, Brunetti knew, when the three of them should engage one another in talk about sports or any one of the conversational methods men used to fill up time. But they all lacked the will or simply had nothing to say.

Four minutes passed, which is a long time for people who are waiting for something to happen.

There was a crisp knock at the door. Danieli called out, *'Avanti,'* and the door opened.

A uniformed policeman entered and made a semi-salute towards Danieli, then stood aside to allow the man behind him to enter.

Alvise, hands at his sides, took a few steps into the room. Seeing Vianello, some of the tension disappeared from his face, only to return when he saw that Brunetti was there with him. He brought his feet together and snapped out a salute in Brunetti's direction, but did not speak.

It was Alvise, good old Alvise, dressed in jeans and a thick dark blue sweater that zipped up the front, a dark blue windbreaker over it, the sort worn on a boat or on a rainy day.

Out of uniform, he looked less like the Alvise they knew; smaller, somehow, but more clearly seen. Making him seem even less like himself was the dark red bruise that was gathering on his left cheek and the large bloodied bandage on his forehead that covered most, but not all, of what looked like a graze wound, as though his face had been dragged along a rough surface.

Without thinking, Brunetti stood and pulled another chair over towards them. 'Have a seat, Alvise,' he said.

Perhaps uncertain how to behave in the company of men who outranked him, Alvise did nothing but salute and stand rigid to attention.

Vianello slipped into Veneziano and said, 'Good God, Alvise, what happened to you?'

Still rigid, fingers apparently stuck to his forehead, Alvise took the opportunity to answer in dialect, and finally said, 'I fell down the stairs.'

2

Taking this as his cue, Danieli closed the folder on his desk and got to his feet. To Brunetti, he said, 'I'll leave you to speak to your officer, Commissario. When you're finished, I'll be in the first office on the left.' Leaving the file on his desk, Danieli let himself out of the room.

Alvise, still statue-straight and motionless, lowered his hand to his side.

Vianello stood and moved the third chair closer to Alvise. 'Sit down, Dario, and tell us what happened.'

As they watched, Alvise slowly unfroze and took a few steps towards the chair. He placed his hand on the back and walked around it, then sat. He looked at Vianello and then at Brunetti, and then closed his eyes, as if afraid they were going to begin yelling at him.

The officer finally turned his head towards Brunetti and said, 'I didn't really fall down the steps, Commissario.' His lips closed after he said that, part of him apparently reluctant to go on.

They waited, silent, and finally Alvise said, 'I don't want to get the guys here into trouble.'

'Forget what you want, Alvise,' Brunetti said in a voice he kept level, 'and tell us what happened.'

Alvise lifted his shoulders for a moment, lost interest in them, and let them fall. 'It doesn't really matter, Commissario. Besides, it was only one of them.'

'Which one?' Vianello asked.

'Petri,' Alvise answered. 'I've known him for a while.'

Vianello nodded, as though he also knew the man.

'He used to work in the city,' Alvise said, obviously meaning Venice, 'but he transferred to Treviso two or three years ago.'

'Did you ever work with him?' Brunetti asked.

'A few times, sir,' Alvise answered, unable to hide his reluctance to say more.

'And he didn't recognize you?' Brunetti asked, making it clear that this was not a question but a request for an explanation.

Alvise slipped his hands, palms down, under his thighs, as though he feared they would betray him with a gesture, and said, 'He decided not to recognize me, sir, so I think I don't want to recognize him.'

'And cause him trouble?' Vianello interrupted.

'And cause anyone trouble,' Alvise answered.

'Could you tell us a little more, Alvise?' Brunetti asked.

The officer's hand was halfway to his forehead before he realized they were seated and Brunetti was making a request, not giving an order. He changed its flight path and flew his open-handed fingers through his hair before landing them on the arm of his chair.

'He's ... ' Alvise began, but failed to find the next word. 'Umm ... some of the guys have had trouble with him.'

'But you never did?' Vianello asked.

'Not until today,' Alvise answered, looked at Vianello and then bowed his head as though he'd caught himself in a lie. 'Physical, that is.'

It took Brunetti a moment to work this out, and when he did, he asked, 'So you've had other trouble with him?'

Brunetti saw that this question had put Alvise on the cross: to say yes might lead to trouble, and to say no might be a lie.

'Verbal trouble?' Brunetti asked.

Alvise's face contracted as he worked out the meaning of Brunetti's question. When he did, he asked, 'You mean did he ever say things to me?'

'Yes,' Brunetti answered, quelling the impulse to congratulate Alvise for having understood the question.

'He was like that, sir,' Alvise said softly, almost as though he were offering a defence of Petri or, more likely, avoiding the question. Brunetti found Alvise's reticence interesting.

'What's that supposed to mean?' Vianello interrupted again.

'Well, he says things to people. And about people.'

'For instance?' Vianello asked, still sounding angry.

Alvise directed his attention to the cuffs of his sweater and carefully folded back first one, then the other. He suddenly looked up and met Vianello's eyes. 'You know Biozzi, don't you?'

Vianello and Brunetti exchanged a sudden glance. Who on the force didn't know Biozzi, or know about him? Or about his wife, murdered by the lover she'd taken six years after her divorce from Biozzi.

Both men sat quietly, waiting for Alvise to explain.

'He was in the squad room when he came back to work.'

Biting back the urge to pick Alvise up and shake him, Brunetti said, 'I'm not sure who these "he's" are, Alvise.' He glanced at Vianello, as if to ask if he'd been a bit confused as well. Vianello nodded in agreement.

'Petri was in the squad room,' Alvise clarified. 'And Biozzi came in.' He looked around; both his listeners nodded, understanding now. 'It must have been about three years ago.

'Petri was talking to someone – I don't remember who it was.' Alvise raised his hands in a cancelling gesture and started again. 'He must have seen Biozzi when he came in. His voice got louder and he said something like, "If nothing else, it's more direct than getting a divorce."'

Alvise paused and a look of disgust crossed his face, making Brunetti regret having shown his impatience.

'What happened?' Brunetti asked.

Alvise didn't answer.

'Well?' prodded Vianello.

Overcoming his reluctance to speak, Alvise said, 'I was reading the paper. So I stood up and grabbed it and walked over to Petri's table and slapped it down – hard – in front of him. Then I went over and put my arm around Renato's shoulders and said it was good to have him back.'

None of them said anything else for a long time, until Brunetti finally returned to what was important and asked, 'So when they brought you in, only Petri knew what had really happened?'

Alvise looked at him in surprise and nodded. 'Yes, Commissario, and all I wanted to do was get out of there before anyone learned I was a cop.' He shrugged and added, 'I didn't want any fuss, and I certainly didn't want to bother you and the Ispettore, sir.'

'So far, the only thing that bothers me is that they pushed you around at the demonstration.'

'It was only one of them, sir. I heard someone else tell him to stop it.'

'Are you sure it was Petri?' Vianello asked.

Alvise gave what in another man would have been a considered pause, then said, with audible reluctance, 'No, Ispettore. They were behind me.' With wide-eyed curiosity, Alvise asked, 'Does it make a difference?'

'Probably not,' Vianello answered. 'If we're going to get you out of here,' he began, and then slowed his speech and spoke every word slowly and carefully, 'then it has to have not happened.'

It took Alvise a moment to figure this out, but when he did, he said, 'That's best, isn't it?'

After giving it some thought, Brunetti said, 'For all of us, probably.'

'What about this?' Alvise asked, tapping the bandage, ignoring the bruise he couldn't see. 'How do I explain this?'

Vianello's response had the softness of restrained impatience. 'You already did, Alvise. You fell down the stairs.' Then, to prevent Alvise from pointing out that there were no stairs outside, Vianello said, 'When you got to the Questura.'

Both Brunetti and Vianello watched as Alvise digested this. 'Of course, sir. I remember now.' His smile showed them that he finally understood.

Brunetti stood and took two steps towards the door, then paused to look back at them. 'Are we agreed on this, Officer Alvise?'

'Oh, yes, sir,' Alvise answered. 'I just have to lie, and it will become the truth,' he said. Was this irony? Brunetti wanted to know. Or sarcasm? Or was Alvise simply being himself and telling the truth slant? Brunetti paused to give Alvise time to explain or elaborate, but the officer smiled at him and nodded, so Brunetti assumed they had an agreement.

He opened the door and went along to knock on the first door on the left. Danieli came over and answered it, saying, 'That was quick.'

'Alvise told us what happened,' Brunetti said casually. 'He remembers now that he was so upset when he was brought here that he missed his footing and tripped on the stairs.'

Danieli's smile was broad. 'That's exactly what I thought might have happened, Commissario. I'm very relieved to hear it confirmed by … '

'Alvise,' Brunetti supplied.

'Indeed,' Danieli agreed. 'Then let's do the paperwork and let you all get back to Venice.' The manner in which he said this made it clear how relieved he was to have the matter settled.

'I'm glad you're pleased with the result,' Brunetti said.

Hand already on the handle of the door, Danieli turned back to Brunetti and said, 'It's not often that things can be resolved so easily, Commissario.' Then, making no pretence of asking an idle question, he asked, 'Did he tell you who hit him?'

Rather than answer, Brunetti posed his own question: 'Why do you ask that?'

'Because I don't like bullies.'

Brunetti, who hated fewer things more, nodded and said, 'I think it's his business to decide to say who it was, not mine.'

Danieli nodded. 'I'd do the same thing if I were in your position.' He extended his hand and offered it to Brunetti. 'Filippo.'

'Guido,' Brunetti said, smiling, offering his own.

3

Danieli provided a car and driver to take them back to Venice; Brunetti, remembering that this was Saturday and they were not meant to be working, did not refuse. Before he left, Alvise's personal belongings were returned to him; the first thing he did when they were outside the Questura was walk a few metres into the piazza to make a call. Brunetti saw the moment the other person answered the phone: Alvise's face brightened as he turned away, leaving only his back for Brunetti to study. Brunetti was glad to see that it looked like quite a happy back.

Brunetti, Vianello, and Danieli waited in front of the eight orange towers of the Questura. Brunetti, as he had every time he'd been there, marvelled at the sheer size of the buildings. Venice had once had an empire to govern – though its leaders were canny enough never to call it that – and now they had a run-down palazzo and a few modern buildings to house their police. Treviso, never a great power, had eight multistorey towers that bore a close resemblance to nothing so much as filing cabinets with air slots.

The car came, and Brunetti was glad it was not a light blue police car but the sort of blue sedan used by politicians. He thanked Danieli and, once they were in the car, slid closed the glass panel that separated them from the driver. He could hear the light sound of the motor. Was this an electric car?

Seated in the back, they fumbled with their seat belts, Alvise more than the others. When they were secured in place, the driver moved off from the piazza in front of the towers and started towards Venice. Alvise turned minimally towards Brunetti and said, formally, 'Thank you for coming out to get me, Commissario,' and turning towards Vianello, added, 'You too, Lorenzo.' Then, to both of them, 'I'm sorry to ruin your Saturday.'

'I think the rain did a good enough job of that for us, Alvise,' Brunetti said.

Now was the time to do it, Brunetti knew. If he didn't ask him now …

But before he could think of how to phrase the question, Alvise cleared his throat, said 'Um' a few times, and then said, 'That was my companion I called.'

Neither Brunetti nor Vianello said a word.

'He's a carpenter,' Alvise said, then added, 'He's been trying to call me. He was worried.'

'That's understandable,' Brunetti said.

Alvise rested his palms on his thighs and raised and lowered his fingers a few times before adding, 'That's the first time I've said that to anyone.'

'Said what?' Vianello asked.

'"My companion".'

'How does it sound?'

'Sort of strange,' Alvise said, but quickly added, 'but nice. I like it. How it sounds. I like saying it.'

'If he's your companion, you should,' Brunetti confirmed.

'Why don't you try it again, using his name?' Vianello asked, poking Alvise in the side with his elbow. 'It might sound even better.'

'Are you joking?' Alvise asked nervously.

'It's too important for anyone to joke about, Dario.'

Alvise affirmed this with a quick series of nods and said, 'Cristiano. My companion.'

Quite naturally, Brunetti asked, 'How long have you known him?'

'Six years.'

Brunetti was stunned. Six years, and everyone at the Questura thought that Alvise lived on the Lido with his widowed mother.

'He came to the house when my mother needed someone to fix the double doors on a walnut cabinet that's been in the family for a long time,' Alvise said. 'He told her he'd have to come back with his truck to get it because there was a large crack in the back panel and he'd have to take it to his workshop.'

Brunetti was struck by the ease with which Alvise told his story. He always made a hash of his reports, verbal or written: there was no chronology, no description of anyone, no record of what they'd said. Alvise often went back and told contradictory stories.

Yet here he was, noting the kind of wood, that there were two doors, and explaining why the cabinet had to be taken to his companion's workshop. Did the fact that he was speaking of someone he loved make the story more important, easier to remember?

The car swerved a bit to the left. The motion must have surprised Alvise. He put one hand over his mouth, as if to stop the stream of words he'd just become aware of. 'Sorry,' he said, looking back and forth at the other two men and then looking at the back of the head of the driver, as if worried he might have heard it all.

Brunetti wondered if any of the other officers knew about Alvise and quickly realized there was no way he could try to find out. Nor, he had to admit, did it make the least bit of difference.

Alvise was happy: that's what mattered.

Suddenly, Alvise blurted out: 'He has to take care of his sister's kids on Saturday.' Some time passed before he added, 'That's why he couldn't come.'

The three men sat in silence for the rest of the ride to Piazzale Roma. The driver pulled up just after a departing bus and stopped. Vianello opened his door, and the three of them got out.

They stepped up on the pavement and formed a triangle. 'Will that be the end of it, Commissario?' Alvise asked Brunetti.

'I think so. Danieli seems reliable. After all, you tripped and fell.'

Vianello nodded his agreement.

'And if anyone asks what I was doing there, Signore?' Alvise asked Brunetti in a soft voice.

Brunetti was close to telling him that he could easily say he'd tried to help his colleagues from Treviso when things turned violent, but he'd seen a new part of Alvise and liked it, so he said, 'You have to decide that for yourself, Alvise.'

The officer nodded in a very stiff way, keeping his back straight so that to move his head he had to move his entire body forward and backward, as though he were consulting his entire body and not only his brain.

After some time, Alvise shrugged and gave a deep sigh. 'I think I'll have to tell the truth, Commissario,' he said. Again, his body made that strange motion. 'I was there because I think we should all be allowed to love the person we love.' He stopped moving and looked up at Brunetti, who was considerably taller than he. 'It's as simple as that, isn't it?'

'I wish,' Brunetti said.

Vianello said, 'I'm taking the boat. You coming, Dario?'

'Thanks, Lorenzo, but it's my turn to cook tonight, so I want to get the shopping done.' Alvise gave a wry smile and added, 'I didn't know I'd be so late getting back.'

'All right, then,' Brunetti said. 'I'll see you both on Monday.'

He watched Alvise's hand to see if it would move in its habitual, nervous desire to salute his superior. Instead, he took a step back, moving away from both of them, and pressed his hand to his heart. 'It feels so light. Like when I was a kid and came out of confession, knowing I'd been forgiven.'

'Except this time there's nothing to forgive,' Brunetti said.

Alvise lowered his hand, gave Vianello and Brunetti a smile such as they had never seen on his face, turned away very quickly, and started down the steps leading to the *imbarcadero* of the Number One going towards Lido.

4

The sun had returned to Venice with them, so Brunetti decided to walk home and take what advantage he could of what was left of a now pleasant day. He was presented with multiple choices: all he had to do was decide which church he wanted to see. If he went over the Tolentini Bridge, he could pass the Frari, or he could veer right and pass San Pantalon, and then quickly home.

He decided on the second because he had recently been at the Frari for a funeral so grim and boring that even Tiziano's *Assumption* had offered no consolation, no comfort. Instead, he'd had the distinct impression that the Virgin's ecstasy was the result of her joy at having been put in the Assumption fast lane. When and why had the liturgy become so tasteless and second-rate? The priests often showed no familiarity with the deceased; the family members who spoke to the congregation mouthed a list of clichés, as though they'd not known the person either. And the music – ugly enough to have driven him from at least two churches. This, the city of Gabrieli, Vivaldi, Marcello, where the mourners now got a recorded guitar strumming some sort of contemporary sludge that failed to keep them awake, let alone inspire the congregation to throw off their mortal coil and sing the deceased to their eternal rest. The only emotion to which the music led the congregation – at least as far as Brunetti could judge in the rare times he attended a Mass – was foot-shuffling embarrassment.

He sometimes wondered if he was the only person who noticed the abyss between the overwhelming visual glory of the churches and their aural horror. At least with an ugly painting he could close his eyes; with ugly music, it was not possible to close his ears.

On impulse, he cut left and walked to San Giacomo dell'Orio, where he'd not been for months. The interior was fortunate not to have any famous paintings – if one did not consider a scattering of Palma il Giovanes as famous – and thus presented a relaxing change from the churches with one or two masterpieces, the rest dismissed as 'products of his youth' or 'attributed to'. In those churches, Brunetti had often observed groups pausing in admiration of the 'good' paintings, while the others, sometimes of equal or superior beauty, wasted their sweetness on the desert air. Inside, Brunetti walked slowly from one painting to the next, puzzled by the collective habit of the persons depicted in religious art of hurling themselves to the ground, and equally confused by the inordinately large number of muscular, naked arms they then raised to the heavens.

When he emerged into the small *campo* in front of the church, Brunetti glanced at his watch and saw that it was almost four. Saturday had evaporated, and he was left with only the husk of the day and the quickly dissolving light. He pulled his phone from his pocket and dialled Paola's number. When she answered, Brunetti said, 'I'm in Campo San Giacomo dell'Orio.'

Before he could say anything else, Paola asked casually, 'How has your day been?' Calm, curious, no question about where he'd been all day.

'Interesting,' he said. 'I had to go to Treviso to get Alvise out of trouble.'

'Alvise? How'd he get into trouble?' she asked, but before he could answer, she added, 'I can imagine him making a mess or doing something stupid, but not causing trouble.'

'He's gay,' Brunetti said.

Paola didn't respond. At the Questura, it would be the scoop of the year, but Paola hadn't said anything. 'Did you hear me?' he asked.

'Yes. But you said he got into trouble. What was that about?'

'He was knocked down by someone who was protesting the gay pride parade in Treviso, so the police took him in.'

'And the person who knocked him down?'

'I don't know.'

'A middle-aged man wearing a cross around his neck, I'd assume,' Paola said with audible disdain.

'Something like that. Probably.'

'And you had to go to Treviso?'

'Yes. With Lorenzo.'

'Did Alvise come back with you?'

'Yes.'

After a moment's pause, Paola said, 'You did a good thing.'

Brunetti heard that with his heart. He realized that even after all these years, these decades with one another, he still valued Paola's approval above a host of other things, surely above the approval of anyone else.

'He talked a little bit.'

'About himself?' Paola asked.

'About his companion. Cristiano. He's a carpenter.'

'Did you and Lorenzo have to rough him up to get him to tell you?' she asked.

'You've promised me that you'd never repeat anything I've told you about how we work,' Brunetti said in his tough-guy cop voice.

'Why don't you come home and tell me about it?'

Half an hour later, he had done that, drunk a coffee, and changed into a pair of brown woollen trousers and a thick beige sweater, the clothes that had helped him survive last winter in a building that was more than five hundred years old. He sat on the sofa in the living room, Paola in a chair opposite him, listening.

'You never thought about it?' Paola asked when it seemed he was finished.

'About what?'

'That he might be gay?'

'Alvise?' he asked, and then repeated the name, as though that would be sufficient to prove to any listener the impossibility of the idea.

'He wasn't married, must be in his fifties by now, and was thought to be living with his mother in a house on the Lido,' Paola began, 'and it didn't occur to anyone that he might be gay?'

'No one ever even suggested it as a possibility,' Brunetti insisted. 'I never heard it mentioned.'

'Men,' Paola said in a tone that dismissed the lot of them.

'What do you mean, "men"?'

'That not one of you paid enough attention to him as a person to take a look at those facts and think about them.'

'That's absurd,' Brunetti said. 'No one would think that.'

Whatever Paola was going to say in response was cut off by the sound of a key in the lock of the front door. The caution with which the door closed whispered that it was Chiara.

Paola put her hand over her mouth and coughed to let her daughter know that someone else was home. A moment later, Chiara appeared in the doorway and came over to kiss them both.

'Chiara,' Paola said, 'may I ask you a question?'

As expected, Chiara turned and smiled and said, 'Can you ask me an answer?'

Paola ignored that and went ahead. 'What would you say about an unmarried man who lives with his mother on the Lido?'

Chiara stopped smiling. 'Is this a trick question?'

'No.'

'How old is he?' Chiara asked.

'Early fifties, I'd say,' Brunetti answered.

'Ever been married?' Chiara asked, sounding like a prosecuting magistrate in a B-movie.

'No,' Paola answered.

'He's gay,' Chiara said, turned, and continued down the corridor to her room.

'Well?' Paola asked.

'All right. But it's because we don't talk about those things.'

'Who's "we"?'

Brunetti let the question run around the room for a few seconds while he considered how to answer it. 'All right,' he finally said. 'Men.'

'You don't speculate on the sexual behaviour of your colleagues?'

'Well,' Brunetti said after a very long time, 'I suppose we might do it. To ourselves, that is, or to our best friends.'

There was a fierceness about his wife that Brunetti both admired and feared, and he heard it in her voice when she asked, 'Have you and Lorenzo ever raised the question when talking about a colleague?'

Brunetti thought back over some of the conversations – the idle ones – that he and Vianello had had over the years. 'Well, not really,' he finally said.

She raised her eyes to the ceiling and called, 'Take me now, oh Lord, before my husband tells me a lie.'

Brunetti laughed. 'All right,' he conceded, 'maybe we have shown ... curiosity about some. But it's more likely that we'd do it about people we're questioning.'

'Why is that?' Paola asked.

This time, Brunetti prepared his answer, hoping it would allow him to shift the subject away from his interest in his colleagues' private lives. 'Because it adds to what we know about them.'

'And what does this information add to what you know about a person?' Paola asked mildly.

Brunetti, no fan of television, did occasionally watch nature documentaries, and so he was familiar with the pose cobras took when they were preparing to attack. They somehow managed to raise their heads about thirty centimetres into the air and begin a graceful side-to-side motion that Brunetti always found quite hypnotizing. They flicked their tongues in and out, in and out, preparing to strike, while their intended prey froze and tried to figure out what to do.

Long familiarity with his wife's tactics had somehow transferred portions of the genetic code of the mongoose into Brunetti, suggesting to him the correct motions that would remove him safely from the target area.

'For one thing, it makes us sensitive to the fact that they might be at risk of blackmail.'

'I see,' she said. 'Anything else?'

'Well, since most people have a bad opinion of the police, I'd like to tell you that many of us feel a certain sympathy for them.'

'I see,' Paola said. As he watched, her tongue ceased to flicker and disappeared into her mouth, and she ceased her restless side-to-side motion, turning again into his wife, the treasure and joy of his life.

5

Chiara had decided, years before, that she didn't want to eat meat any more, and since then the family had gradually acquiesced to her preference. Pork had galloped off to the horizon first, followed after another year or so by a flock of tiny lambs. But there the migration had ended, the gate slammed shut by Brunetti and his son, Raffi, the carnivore half of the family: the chickens could stay, and the cows could roam back occasionally. Once a week, however, Chiara had complete sway, and the others now went along without protest. On the present evening, therefore, the menu was baked zucchini and red peppers stuffed with a mixture of quinoa, feta, spices, and what Raffi insisted upon referring to as the 'entrails' of the vegetables.

A package had been delivered that day from a friend of Brunetti's who had left the police five years before to move to Sardinia and take over his family's farm. The package contained four grapefruit-sized white cheeses made of the same pecorino, but aged differently: eight, twelve, sixteen, and twenty months.

In most households, the oldest would have been eaten first, to be followed by the others in chronological succession. The Brunettis, however, under the tutelage of Paola, were served all four at the same time. Paola had written the numbers 1 to 4 on the outside crusts, but only she knew to which period of ageing the numbers referred.

No comments could be made, no judgement passed, until all four cheeses had been tasted, after which individual choices could be defended. This time, after much retasting, and a change to a milder white wine for Brunetti and Paola, there was a unanimous vote in favour of the cheese that turned out to be sixteen months old.

'I like that it's so grainy,' Chiara started, rubbing her fingers together as though she were feeling the texture.

'The others were all too smooth,' Raffi agreed. 'Pecorino isn't supposed to be like that.'

'I voted for the taste: it was best,' Brunetti said, only to be hooted at by Chiara, who said, 'Well, that's certainly helpful and precise.'

Paola cut off a sliver of the victor, speared it with her fork, held it up and stared at it. 'I like the musty suggestion of fresh-picked rosemary, the undercurrent of thyme, augmented by the consistency of aged pomegranate.' She pulled the fork closer, the better to examine the cracks that had formed when she cut the piece of cheese free. 'And the texture, with its hint of fine-veined marble, the eye appeal of the outer casing that so easily falls from its shoulders at the lightest touch ...'

'Before you rave further, my dear, why don't you just eat it?' Brunetti suggested. He got up from his place, went and took a jar of honey from the cabinet, and brought it back to the table. 'Sandro said to try it with honey.'

Paola opened her mouth to continue, but Raffi held out his hand, fingers splayed wide, and asked, 'You've been reading those cooking magazines again, haven't you?'

Paola reached out, pulled the honey nearer, and said, 'No, it was the prose of a wine brochure that came in the mail today.' She looked around the table, then asked, 'I suppose you don't want to hear more?'

None of them graced her with an answer. They finished their last pieces of cheese, and Chiara went over to the counter to get the platters of grilled vegetables that she was serving in the absence of meat.

When the dinner was finished, Brunetti went into the living room and, after some time, Paola brought in coffee and, for each of them, a whisper of grappa. She set the coffee and the glasses on the low table and sat beside him on the sofa.

Brunetti handed Paola her coffee and took his own. 'I'm sorry I missed lunch at your parents',' he said. 'How are they?'

She sipped, sipped, finished the coffee and set the cup down before she said, 'My father was grumpy.'

Because his father-in-law was usually in good spirits, Brunetti asked, 'Why?'

'Oh, it's one of those Venetian things that can go back fifty years,' Paola said, making no attempt to disguise her exasperation.

'Tell me,' Brunetti said, reaching for his grappa.

'It's complicated.'

'If it goes back fifty years … ' Brunetti answered, and left it hanging.

She smiled. 'It's not really that long a time. But it's tangled up with old friendships and business deals and having gone to school together.'

'I beg your pardon,' Brunetti said.

She took her glass but made no move to drink from it; instead, she rolled it back and forth between her palms. 'He told me an old friend asked him if he knew if Palazzo Zaffo dei Leoni was for sale.' Before Brunetti could speak, she went on. 'Apparently this man – my father's friend – had heard a rumour that a chain of hotels has made an offer to buy it.'

'Just what we need, another hotel,' Brunetti said bitterly.

As if he had not spoken, Paola went on with studied patience. 'It's not for a hotel, Guido. He's asking for his son. He and his family have been living in Rome for years, but he's homesick and wants to come back to Venice and raise his kids here.'

'And he wants to raise them in this *palazzo*?' Brunetti asked, placing special emphasis on the last word, even though he had no idea where the *palazzo* was, and regretted his tone as soon as he heard it.

Paola paused for what seemed an inordinate amount of time before answering. 'My father's friend knows the owner, Renato Molin. He teaches at the university: medieval history. But there was trouble between them years ago, and they haven't spoken to one another for ages, so he can't ask Molin about it. He asked my father if he could think of a way to find out if the *palazzo* really is for sale – that is, without letting Molin know who's interested.' She paused a moment, then added, 'That's why I said it's a Venetian story.'

Brunetti set his empty glass on the tray. Paola drank hers and did the same. He leaned back and folded his arms, then turned to her and said, 'The story is about to become even more Venetian.'

'What?' she asked, puzzled.

Brunetti smiled and remained silent for some time, then said, 'I went to school with Gloria Forcolin.'

'Luigi's daughter?' she asked.

'Yes. She was a couple of years behind me.'

Paola's face lit up. 'Of course. Of course. She's Molin's second wife, married him about ten years ago.'

'Gloria and I meet on the street once in a while and we exchange news,' Brunetti said, although no Venetian needed to have this explained.

'The way one does,' Paola said.

'Yes, the way one does.'

Neither spoke for some time, and then Paola said, 'Molin inherited the *palazzo* years ago, maybe forty.' Before Brunetti could speak, she went on as memory brought it back to her, 'From an aunt, I believe.' She held up a hand to prevent Brunetti from speaking and continued. 'There was something about two branches of the family claiming the title, so the issue ended up in the Consulta Araldica,' she said, not having to explain to Brunetti that this was the entity that decided all questions of noble lineage.

'He seems,' Paola continued, 'not to have been satisfied with inheriting the *palazzo*: he wants the title, too, and carries on as though he already has it. His aunt's will was very clear, and he was the only living descendant on that side of the family. But he also wants the right to use the title.'

Brunetti waited, but Paola seemed to have run out of gossip.

He smiled. 'That's more or less the story I've heard.'

Out of nowhere, Paola said, 'I can't imagine he'll ever sell it.'

'Why?'

'I heard him talk about it once or twice.' In response to Brunetti's expression, she continued. 'Not to me, because he knows I'm not interested, but to new professors or to students. "*Palazzo*" has an intoxicating sound to a lot of people,' she added with the disdain common to those who have grown up in one.

Ignoring what she'd said, Brunetti explained, 'I think this is how to do it.'

'Do what?'

'Find out for your father if it's for sale. If anyone knows, it's got to be Gloria.'

6

While Brunetti continued with the cull of his books on Sunday, he was accompanied by memories of the Conte's generosity to him. He had no idea how much of the store of favours the Conte had accumulated during his lifetime had been spent on Brunetti's behalf. Over the years, his father-in-law had warned him, informed him, complimented him, and had often made the path ahead of him easier to tread because of his willingness to ask his friends for favours for his daughter's husband.

Brunetti had seldom been able to repay even a fraction of what had been so smoothly passed to him. Thanks to the Conte's friendships, Brunetti had met, questioned – even once arrested – men whose wealth and connections would ordinarily have kept them free from solicitations from a mere policeman like Guido Brunetti, son of a port worker, the urban equivalent of a peasant.

It was only recently that Brunetti had been able to accept that what the Conte had originally done with a certain reluctance, he now did with love. To be able to return even a minimum of his largesse would be a way to show his gratitude. And his love.

It would be easy enough to ask Gloria if her home was for sale, but first he wanted to have an idea of what it looked like. One of the books he'd spared was a coffee-table book of photos of Venetian gardens at the turn of the last century, but photos of Palazzo Zaffo dei Leoni were there none. He found another book, published in 1973, with a colour photo of the façade taken from what must have been the door to the *calle*. Big door, two large windows on either side of it and more windows going up to the roof, where the peculiar, mushroom-like Venetian chimneys were visible.

Many of the buildings of similar size had long since been broken up into smaller units and were now inhabited by separate families. He could think of no *palazzo* that size that was inhabited by only two people.

The building stood in what seemed a formal garden, the grass short and manicured. Set into it with razor-sharp precision were rectangular flower gardens exploding with flowers he recognized but could not name. They ran parallel to the sides of the building and disappeared at the edges of the photo.

He checked Google Earth and found a recent photo of the *palazzo* and garden taken from a helicopter or a drone. It showed the chimneys and the roof and, surrounding the building, what looked like an encroaching army of green-draped monsters. Moving closer to the computer screen, Brunetti saw that they were not monsters but untrimmed trees and hideously overgrown bushes or hedges, tightly embracing one another and spreading all the way to a low stone wall visible on the right. Beyond the wall spread another lawn as well trimmed as the one in the earlier photo had been.

Google showed how near the *palazzo* was to Campo Santi Apostoli, news that surprised Brunetti, who knew the zone but had no idea of the existence of a building of this size.

Curious, he pulled down his copy of *Calli, Campielli, e Canali* and saw that the *palazzo* was indeed within a minute of that *campo*; another larger building and the garden beside it were listed as '*Convento*'.

His curiosity was roused by this hidden *palazzo* and abandoned garden. Even the '*Convento*' was confusing, since there was another one just beside the Miracoli church. Had the religious orders retained so much property and land?

He recalled, then, a photographic exhibition of Venetian gardens viewed from above. He'd seen it more than twenty years ago, but he still remembered his astonishment at the sight of just how much open space there was in Venice, how much green, and how many trees.

Thinking about real estate, Brunetti lost all policeman and became only Venetian, interested in square metres and storage space, and how high the *acqua alta* came. And why the garden was so neglected.

Like most Venetians, he didn't have to be in search of an apartment, or have one he wanted to sell. For a Venetian, it was enough to know that someone had property to buy or sell, and he'd hurl himself into conversation as though he'd studied the market for years and kept a file of properties in a drawer of his desk at home.

And thus Brunetti decided that, the next morning, he'd try on his way to work to learn if Palazzo Zaffo dei Leoni was for sale or not. Although a *palazzo*, it was not on the Grand Canal – Brunetti knew this because he'd been made to memorize the names of all the *palazzi* on the Grand Canal when he was a student – but it might well be attractive enough, even without the Canal, for the displaced son of a Venetian, longing to come home.

7

When he left the apartment on Monday morning, Brunetti carried with him one of the bags of books he'd culled, planning to take them to the used book store in Campo Santa Maria Nova. It was too early for his friend Carlo to have opened, so he took the books into the bar next to the shop and swung them up onto the counter. The owner nodded when he saw Brunetti and smiled when he saw the bag of books. He took the bag and slid it under the counter, turned and made Brunetti a coffee without bothering to ask.

Brunetti picked up the *Gazzettino* and spread it open on the ice-cream freezer, on holiday for the winter. Hearing the hiss of the machine, he went back to the counter to get his coffee, took it back with him and continued reading the paper.

He drank the coffee in three sips and had started back towards the counter to pay when his former postman walked in and set some letters in front of the barman. He looked much the same, round-faced and blue-eyed, like he'd just stepped off a tourist poster for Alto Adige.

'Commissario,' Maurizio said with evident pleasure, recognizing him. 'How are you and how's your wife, and the kids?'

He set some envelopes on the counter and hoisted his bag higher on his shoulder. He put out his fist, which Brunetti happily bumped with his own.

'Fine, fine,' Brunetti said, all late letters and misdelivered bills washed from his memory. 'So you're in Cannaregio now?' he exclaimed, as though Maurizio had received a promotion. Then, instinctively, 'Can I offer you a coffee?'

'No, no, thanks. It's as though I'd drunk it, really, thank you.' He set his bag down on the newspaper, stood up straighter, and rolled his shoulder around a few times. 'New faces. It's a change.'

'It's been at least a year,' Brunetti said, then slapped his head and said, 'No, it's far more. Since before all this started.' Instead of defining 'this', he pulled his mask from his pocket and quickly stuffed it back.

'More than long enough,' the postman said. 'You're all fine? Kids still doing well in school?' As he spoke, he continued to roll his shoulder. When he seemed satisfied that he'd loosened it enough, he hoisted his bag up to the other shoulder and said, 'Are you on your way to work?'

'Yes,' Brunetti said, opening the door and holding it for the other man. When they were both outside in the tiny *campiello*, he said, 'Maurizio, you've had enough time to learn the area.'

The postman nodded but said nothing.

'Do you know the couple who live in that *palazzo* in the *calle* leading to the Coop – has a garden next to the nuns?'

It took Maurizio some time to find the right way to answer. Brunetti was, after all, a policeman, and it was always risky to let them know anything about anyone. But Brunetti had always given a good tip at Christmas, even after people stopped getting letters and began to pay their bills online.

'She gets the *Gazzettino* every day and tips at Christmas, the way you did,' Maurizio said with an easy smile. After a pause and erasing the smile, he added, 'Her husband has *Il Giornale* and

La Verità delivered.' The political message was clear: Maurizio, Brunetti recalled, could smell the scent of the Lega from the newspapers a person read and was probably willing to man the barricades against the forces of the Right in any way he could.

Brunetti nodded to show he had heard the words and understood the message.

'I've heard they want to sell the place,' he said. 'You know anything about that?' When Maurizio remained silent, Brunetti added, 'A friend of mine knows someone who's looking for something big. When I saw you just now, I remembered, so I thought I'd ask.'

The postbag had slipped lower on Maurizio's arm. He pulled it back into place and said, 'I've never even been inside the front door. If I have a *raccomandata* for them, she comes down and signs it, even gives me a tip. Nobody does that much any more.' The postman paused a moment, then added, 'The Prioress does, though. And an envelope at Christmas.'

'But to answer your question, Commissario, no, I've never heard anything about that. It's not likely she'd say anything about it to me, anyway.'

'Thanks, Maurizio,' Brunetti said, automatically placing his hand on the other man's arm, forgetting, as he always did, that these were the new times, and the old ones were gone.

He went over the Ponte San Canzian, leading to Campiello de la Cason, and, as always, touched the metal rings in the wall on the right, acting on the conviction that if they failed to bring the good luck legend said was summoned by the gesture, nor would they bring the bad.

He stopped in front of the new bar and glanced inside. The place had once been a *palestra*, though he had never seen any exercise equipment from the door; it had then been closed for years, only to be resurrected in its current manifestation, he recalled, soon before the *pandemia*. Metal grates were shut in front of the wooden door and paper cups and napkins stuffed between them. This was one of the symptoms the city had begun to show when a business was no longer terminal, but dead.

He turned right and took a few steps down the *calle*. The wall that surrounded the garden was more than three metres high, and the usual moronic graffiti writers had used it freely to demonstrate their inability to spell or to think. '*Capitalizmo = Furto*'. Well, perhaps capitalism *was* theft, but it was many other things as well, some far worse.

A few steps put him in front of a tall, dark wooden door. To the right, there was a single bell in the centre of a polished brass plate, the letters RBM engraved below. Carved under the letters was what he thought must be the crest of the Molin family: the usual lion, with flames issuing from behind him, although it might just as easily have been a pair of water wings.

Brunetti smiled when he saw the combination. One of the habits of the remaining nobility of Venice was to put only their initials – in capital letters – on or below their doorbells, never their surnames. Professore Molin might well have the trappings and suits of nobility, but his branch of the family had not yet been recognized by the Consulta Araldica, his surname might have been given, but hardly the coat of arms.

He backed away, the better to study the height of the wall; he braced one foot against the house behind him and tilted his head back. Indeed, at least three metres, perhaps closer to four. At any rate, it was a height that would prohibit entry by anyone but the most eager and talented climber.

He heard footsteps approaching from the left, which meant from the Coop or, farther, the entire area running down to Fondamenta Nuove. He glanced in the direction of the sound just as a tall, thin woman turned into the *calle* and, although she must have seen him, continued to approach at the same speed.

Brunetti put his hands behind him and pushed away from the wall, into the middle of the *calle*. He came down heavily on his left foot and made no attempt to correct his balance. Instead, he slung out both arms and took two staggering steps in the woman's direction before stamping down on his right foot, apparently to prevent his fall.

The woman had stopped herself less than a metre from him and raised a hand protectively. A few years younger than he, she had a long nose and soft eyes that diminished its effect. She lowered her hand slowly, keeping her eyes on him.

'*Scusi, Signora*,' Brunetti said. 'I pushed too hard and lost my balance.' He gave her a worried glance and said, 'I hope I didn't frighten you. Please forgive me.' That said, he stepped back from her until he was standing where he had been, back pressed against the wall but both feet on the ground.

'It's nothing, Signore,' she said.

Brunetti nodded but didn't speak. Perhaps to fill the gap, she said, 'It's strange how many people stop to see how high that wall is. You'd think it's the only wall in the city.'

She had spoken in Italian but Brunetti, to soothe any nervousness, slipped easily into the Veneziano revealed by the cadence of her speech. 'I've walked past this wall since I was a boy, but it's only today that I noticed how high it is.' That said, he continued, 'The old people are right: there's something new to discover every day.'

She smiled and answered in dialect. 'That's exactly what my grandfather told us all the time: "Go for a walk and see how many things you'll see that you never noticed before. You just have to look."'

Brunetti stepped away from the wall and began to brush at the back of his coat. He raised an arm and tried to use the other hand to wipe at the side and back. The woman, as he suspected she would, stepped to her left and looked at the side of his coat. He turned a bit more towards her and she said, 'It's fine.'

'Thank you, Signora. I don't want the people inside to think I'm a vagabond.' He lowered his arms to his side and pulled down both cuffs.

'Inside?' she asked, and then, failing to disguise her curiosity, 'Why is that?'

'A friend of mine called this morning to tell me that the owners have decided to sell it. Someone told him at a dinner last night.'

'You're Venetian,' she said, rather than asked, as if to suggest he should have a list of the houses that were to sell branded into his memory.

'Yes, raised in Castello, but I live in San Polo now. Near ex-Biancat,' he said, naming the florist who had gone out of business more than ten years before, one of the first canaries to die in the mine and a name bound to strike a chord in the mind of any Venetian.

'Do you know the *palazzo*?' she asked.

'No, not at all,' Brunetti said. 'This isn't a part of the city I know at all well.'

'Then why are you interested?'

'Another friend of mine works in London for an NGO,' Brunetti invented, 'something to do with alternative energy.' Stuffing his hands in his pockets, he went on. 'I never paid much attention, I suppose, but he said once that they're look-ing for a place in Venice where they can set up their office and asked me, if I ever heard of anything big ...' He paused after this, as though considering the meaning of the word. 'And my friend – the one here, not in London – said that this place is big.

'He didn't know anything else,' he went on, 'not even the name of the people who own it, but because it's about two minutes out of my way to work, he asked me if I'd ring the doorbell and see whether it's true.' Brunetti removed his hands from his pockets, raised one, and waved his fingers quickly in the air to the right of his head.

'It's a crazy idea, but he's a good friend, so I said I'd do it.' Sounding resigned and perhaps not best pleased to be doing this favour, Brunetti shrugged and smiled as he turned towards the door, saying, 'Things can happen.'

He raised his hand and rang the bell, and both of them heard it sounding off at a distance on the other side of the wall.

The woman smiled and said, 'Good luck with them.'

She turned away and Brunetti called after her, 'Will I have trouble?'

She turned back and said, 'No more than they please to give you.' Before he could ask, she continued, 'I've lived in Campiello de la Cason all my life, so I know a bit about them.'

'Ah,' Brunetti said. 'All I want to do is ask. It doesn't concern me.' That, at least, was certainly true, he realized.

She started to say something, paused to see that she had his attention, and said, 'There's a Sri Lankan servant of some kind who lives in the garden house: he might be able to tell you. But from what I've heard, it's not likely they'll want to sell.' Then she shrugged and added, 'If you can, speak to the woman.' She took a step to the right and continued on her way.

Brunetti had been so attentive that he had not heard the approaching footsteps behind the wall. He heard a sudden metallic noise, and then the door moved slowly away from him to reveal a thickset, dark-skinned man. He wore brown corduroy trousers, the white collar of a shirt rose from beneath a beige sweater, and on top he wore a heavy woollen tweed jacket.

His skin was entirely without a wrinkle, not around the eyes nor the mouth, making it difficult to judge his age. Fifty? Sixty? More? He was made of muscle, not fat, Brunetti observed, but there was no suggestion of menace in his stance or his expression.

'*Sì?*' the man enquired neutrally, leaving Brunetti with no idea whether he spoke Italian or, if so, how well.

'I'm sorry, Signore,' Brunetti answered, making no attempt to step closer. 'I'm afraid I have only a strange question to ask and then I'll be back on my way to work.' He looked at the man to see if he'd understood. When he nodded, Brunetti said, staying with the story he'd given the woman, 'I had a phone call this morning from a friend, telling me he'd been informed that this *palazzo* is for sale.'

He kept his own face motionless, perhaps a bit embarrassed, as he said this, then held up both his hands, empty palms turned towards the man. 'I'm not a real-estate agent, I don't have any interest myself in the *palazzo*. I'm merely doing a favour for a friend who asked me to see if I could find out.'

The man neither moved nor spoke, but he made no attempt to close the door. Brunetti was careful to remain where he was and not approach him, nor did he try to look past him at what lay behind. He tried a smile, making it small and nervous. 'I'm merely the messenger.'

The man nodded and his face softened, as if to suggest that he too had experience in doing things he was not involved with. He shifted his weight to the other foot and said, 'No, Signore. The *palazzo* is not for sale.' His Italian was correct, his pronunciation precise: there could be no misunderstanding what he said.

Brunetti nodded but made no motion to move away from the door.

'So now, if you don't mind, I'll go back to my work,' the man said, then, with another softening of his face and a very friendly nod, he closed the door.

Brunetti waited and listened to try to detect where the man went, but he heard nothing. After a full minute, he said aloud, 'And I'll be on my way to work as well,' and did just that.

8

Pleased with his success, Brunetti delighted in his walk. The sun was hidden behind clouds, but as he walked he gradually opened the buttons of his coat; by the time he reached the Questura, they were all undone and he felt faintly uncomfortable with the five layers he was wearing: T-shirt, shirt, sweater, jacket, and overcoat.

The guard at the door welcomed him with the good news about the sun, almost as if he were responsible for it. 'Sun all day, Commissario. Tomorrow too,' the man in uniform said, raising a hand in greeting.

'Good,' Brunetti replied, at a loss to think of anything more interesting.

He proceeded undisturbed to his office, hung up his coat, and went to his desk to turn on his computer to check the staffing assignments for this week. Somehow, an email came in response to his search, sent by Signorina Elettra. He opened it immediately.

When you look at the staffing schedule, you'll see that I will not be at the Questura for a few days. I've had an invitation from the organizers of a conference on spyware and other potential threats, to be held in Geneva. I will not, however, abandon you, Commissario. I shall keep an eye on your mail and any documents you consult (so long as the activity takes place on your computer). I wish you all a pleasant and successful week.

She had not told him. Geneva? 'How'd she manage that?' he asked himself out loud. She'd had 'an invitation'. To attend or to participate? She had not said. There was nothing complicated going on at the Questura just now, no crime that needed research, no nosing around in places where one was not permitted – or at least where the police were not permitted. She would learn, make contacts, return to Venice more fully prepared – he thought he could at least tell the truth to himself – to break into any office, site, organization or email account, to make no mention of government offices and, most recently, the Vatican, with renewed skill and delight. But still, she hadn't told him in advance. Nor had she said how long she'd be gone.

There was a second paragraph. *The flowers will be delivered, as is customary, on Tuesday morning. I've asked that they all be put in Dottor Patta's office to apologize for my absence.*

He looked down at his fingers, apparently fused to the keys of his computer. Gently, he pulled them up, one by one, decided to get on with it, and finally had a look at the staffing assignments for the week. He read the names of the officers who would be on duty and, more important to him, the pairings that had been made between them. Riverre and Alvise had been on patrol together all of last week, a wise assignment because they were good friends as well as good colleagues.

This week, however, Riverre was assigned to Murano, both morning and afternoon shifts, while Alvise would spend his days at the Commissariato at San Marco, which dealt almost exclusively with the lost: lost tourists or their lost children, lost wallets (usually stolen), lost passports, lost old people with lost minds, lost patience that had led to arguments or fights, lost backpacks that might as easily contain bombs as lunch, and lost time in spending an entire shift dealing with problems that would be better handled by social services than the police.

He then looked to see who would be assigned with Alvise and found what he did not want to find. His partner was Brandini, a devout member of a semi-laical organization called Peace and Reflection, currently under scrutiny by the not-very-high-resolution microscope of the Vatican. A jolly group of good old fellows, they let the women make the coffee while they brought the rigour of their male vision to the examination of women's proper place in society, the horror of abortion, and the vicious lies circulated by the Left to bring suspicion upon the pure intentions of the clergy in their dealings with unaccompanied children.

God prevent … Brunetti began to implore, before he remembered that nothing could prevent the news about Alvise from becoming a topic of conversation at the Questura. And Brandini, he feared, might be filled with virtuous revulsion at the thought of spending five days – even five minutes – in the company of a now known homosexual. The law could protect Alvise from overt actions or words, but nothing could protect him from the cool, manifest disgust of a colleague.

As if timed to distract him from these thoughts, Brunetti had a call on his office phone from an old friend who had recently been transferred from Trento to Brindisi. He'd called to tell Brunetti he'd gone into a bar that morning and found it filled with portrait photos of Mussolini, newspaper accounts of great World War II naval victories, and bottles of wine for sale with portraits of both Mussolini and Hitler on the labels.

'What did you do?' Brunetti asked.

'I was so shocked, I didn't know what to do. Or say. So I drank my coffee, paid for it, then thanked the barman and left.'

Neither of them spoke for some time, until finally Brunetti said, 'It's a different place, down there.'

When his friend said nothing, Brunetti wished him good luck and said goodbye.

Hearing a noise at the door, he looked up and saw Vianello standing there. 'Come in, Lorenzo, and close the door, would you?'

The Ispettore did as he was asked and walked to Brunetti's desk. He had no papers, no files, yet his face was tense and his usual easy smile was absent. Vianello sat and Brunetti raised his chin in an interrogative manner.

'Alvise and Brandini,' Vianello said. So it *was* police business, Brunetti realized. In a way.

'Alvise and Brandini, indeed,' he answered and waved Vianello to a chair.

'Is there anything we can do?' the Ispettore asked.

'I don't think so. I can't change the schedule, and we can't ask Brandini what his feelings about gays are, and we can't very well ask Alvise to be careful.'

'Careful?'

'I don't even know what I mean by that,' Brunetti admitted. 'Saying something: making a comment about one of the staff, giving an opinion about one of the female officers. I have no idea what might set Brandini off.' It took him only a second to add, 'And I don't even know if he would be set off.'

'He's a member of Peace and Reflection, isn't he?' Vianello asked. 'And he's got six kids.' Before Brunetti could speak, Vianello added, 'We have a family of them in our building. The wife's stopped Nadia a few times and asked if she'd like to come to one of their reunions.'

'"Reunions"?' Brunetti asked.

Vianello nodded. 'It's not a "meeting", and it's not a "prayer session". It's just a "reunion", as if it were the Boy Scouts or a chance to meet the teachers in your children's school.'

'And what does it turn out to be?' Brunetti asked.

Vianello shrugged and gave a half-guilty smile. 'I have no idea. Nadia's always very polite and says she's busy.' He rubbed his face with both hands, then said, 'I keep telling myself it's entirely innocent, and it probably is. But … '

'But what?'

It took Vianello a long time to think of what to say. 'I suppose it's not really Brandini. It's Alvise. I don't know how he'll behave if people change towards him.'

Brunetti stopped himself from saying, 'If he notices,' for he was sure that even Alvise, dull as he was, would notice, although he didn't understand why he knew that. Finally he said, 'No one does, Lorenzo, least of all Alvise.'

'Then why do I feel so protective about him?'

'You and I certainly do,' Brunetti answered. 'I think we have to be optimistic and pin our hopes on both of them.'

'Hoping what?' Vianello asked.

'That Brandini behaves the way he has in the past. He's never been reported to me as a troublemaker, and he seems to get on with people.' Turning his thoughts to Alvise, he said, 'And Alvise is … well, he's Alvise.'

Vianello nodded, shrugged, nodded again.

'With Patta's new system,' Brunetti said, 'they'll be at the Commissariato all day and report back here following the afternoon shift. With the number of people who end up in the Commissariato, there won't be much time for conversation.'

Both sat silent for a while, Brunetti considering the possible interchanges between the two officers.

'Alvise probably doesn't realize … ' Brunetti began.

'Anything,' Vianello finished for him.

Brunetti smiled, and the tension dissipated.

Brunetti thought about his instinctive suspicions of Brandini. 'I wonder if I'd respond like this if Chiara said her boyfriend was a, oh, I don't know, a member of the Flat Earth Society.'

'Guido, unless your family has known his for six generations, and you've put him through an eight-hour interrogation about his intentions, you're going to respond badly when Chiara starts talking about any boyfriend.' Before Brunetti could protest, Vianello added, 'It's what fathers do. It's in our genes to resist the arrival of a new male.'

'You make it sound like jealousy,' Brunetti said, sounding offended.

'Well, why shouldn't it be, at least in part? He comes and takes our place, doesn't he? She'll think his ideas are right, let him pay her way, want his arm to be around her, expect him to protect her.'

Because it was Vianello speaking, Brunetti listened; he even considered if there was truth in what his friend said, regardless of how the words surprised him.

Brunetti let some time pass before he said, 'We seem to have wandered away from Alvise and Brandini.'

Accepting the offer of a change in subject, Vianello said, 'I think the best thing to do is assume that two men who've worked well together for years will continue that way. We don't have to be so paternalistic.' He looked across at Brunetti to see how he responded to his use of that last word.

Brunetti nodded. Sooner or later, Chiara would find Prince Charming and bring him home. And then he'd see ...

'We're agreed on waiting to see what happens, then?' Vianello asked.

Brunetti nodded. 'Nothing else we can do.'

Hearing that, both of them decided it was a good time to go home for lunch.

9

Brunetti had been at his desk for an hour after lunch when he heard a noise from the door and looked up to see his colleague, Claudia Griffoni. 'Do you have a minute, Guido?' she asked, staying near the open door.

'Of course, Claudia. Come in, please.'

She stepped in and closed the door. She was wearing jeans and a dark blue jacket: double-breasted, stand-up collar, three narrow golden stripes on the cuffs. A Hussar could wear it on parade. No medals, although the cut and, when she got closer, cloth were such that it could easily support a few decorative diamonds on a neat diagonal across her chest – no one would find them out of place.

Either it was high fashion or it had been stolen from the daughter-in-law of some Eastern European dictator who had spent her youth watching old war movies. Brunetti knew that if he were to compliment it, she would look down, flick at it with the back of her fingers, and ask, 'You mean *this*?'

After she'd taken a seat, Brunetti asked, anyway, 'Where'd you get the jacket?' thinking that Chiara would run mad to have one like it.

'What? *This* thing?'

Griffoni never disappointed him.

'Yes.'

'It's something a cousin of mine picked up in a thrift store.'

'Where?'

'Tashkent, I think,' she said seriously. 'Anyway, someplace where there had been a recent change of government.'

'Then it wasn't Uzbekistan,' Brunetti said neutrally, adding, 'How may I help?'

She smiled at his graceful manner. 'It's more that I have something you might be interested in having.'

'And that is?'

'Information about Luigi Rubini. I've been told he's stirring to life again.' And the person who told her was no doubt one of her informers, Brunetti thought.

'Aha,' was all Brunetti permitted himself to say.

This led her to ask, 'Were you expecting this?'

'Sooner or later, yes.'

'Why?'

Brunetti spoke before he thought. 'Poor fool. He'll be back inside before he knows it.'

'Do you really mean that?'

'What, that he'll be inside?'

'No, that he's a "poor fool"?' she asked, emphasizing the last two words. After a moment's reflection, she added, 'Poor anything, for that matter.'

Brunetti's expression changed and he said, after some delay, 'I suppose I spoke without thinking.'

'That's why it's interesting,' Griffoni said.

'You mean my sympathy?'

It took Griffoni some time to find the answer, but finally she said, 'No, not the sympathy, but that it was so impulsive.'

'It's because I like him, Claudia.'

'It's the way we are,' she said, smiling in a kind of verbal shrug. Italians? Men? Humans? he wondered, but did not ask.

Silence spread and filled the room. A boat swerved in from the Canale di Santa Giustina and roared at illegal speed past the Questura, obliterating the conversation. When the noise of the boat had diminished, Brunetti said, 'Tell me what you've heard.'

Griffoni glanced down and wiped a speck of dust from her knee. So much time passed that Brunetti thought she would not answer. His attention turned to her hands, fine and thin, nails cut short. He was studying the blue veins that were visible on the left hand but not on the right when the room suddenly brightened, as though someone had moved lights in from other offices and turned them on all at once.

Griffoni pulled in a breath of air and turned towards the window. 'Oh my God, the sun's back.'

Brunetti's glance followed hers and looked out at a sky Tiepolo would have loved to paint: corpulent clouds, patches of sky as blue as the Virgin's robe. There lacked only an angel or two, trying out their wings among the safe landings provided by the clouds. Brunetti rejoiced in the sight and viewed the sky as a sign of glory, not as the arrival point of the breezes that blew straight across from Torino to Venezia, bringing with them the most polluted air in Europe.

10

They gave the light a few moments to change their mood before
returning to the discussion of Rubini.

'You've never met him,' Brunetti began, 'so you've had no time
to learn much about him.'

'Such as?'

Brunetti grinned at the question and answered without giving it much thought. 'That in some ways, he's a bit like us.'

Neutrally, she said, 'Presumably, you mean the police.'

Brunetti nodded. 'Like us, he's rigorous in protecting his
sources.'

'What does that mean?'

'That he's never named anyone who worked with him or who
helped him in any of his … dealings.'

'Am I supposed to see that as a virtue?' she asked, her voice
still neutral. 'You sound as if the fact that he never does the
actual stealing and never runs the risk of being caught in the act
somehow makes him a better class of criminal.' She paused to
give Brunetti a chance to comment, but he remained silent.

'You even say,' she continued, '"worked with him" and "helped him", as though he had a *pasticceria* in Castello somewhere, and these people were helping him make panettone.'

Adjusting to the seriousness of her tone, Brunetti asked, 'Have you read the files?'

'Yes. After my ... source mentioned him, I had a look.'

'And ... .'

'And on paper, in the transcripts of his interrogations, I'm not sure everyone would feel sympathy for him.' She held up her hand and added, 'He might be charming in person, but on paper he's pretty cold-blooded.'

Before Brunetti could ask, she went on. 'I read three transcripts of statements he's given over the years, and he never once seems to understand that some people place an aesthetic value – even an emotional value – on an object. To him, whether it's pottery, a necklace, a painting, or a piece of Murano glass, an object is never anything other than a receptacle for money. It's a place where money chooses to rest for a time. So a person who loses it ... ' Griffoni paused here and looked at Brunetti to be sure she had his full attention, then continued. 'And that's the word he always uses – "loses" – as though the painting fell out of a window or someone was careless and left her great-grandmother's first edition of *Pinocchio* on the bus.

'Or it might be because he repeatedly presents himself as someone who's surprised to see he's done something bad and promises never to do it again.' She let a few seconds pass and added, 'But he does, and he does, and he does.' Finally, losing control of her voice, she said, 'He chose the wrong profession and should have tried politics. He's a natural.'

Brunetti, having always had a bit of sympathy for Rubini, was surprised at Griffoni's wrath. Then, her voice a bit calmer, she asked, 'Have *you* read the transcripts?'

Brunetti remembered questioning Rubini twice. In both cases, he'd not subsequently read the transcripts, but had relied on the notes he'd taken at the time. 'I took notes,' he said.

Griffoni stretched out her legs and said, 'A few days ago I spoke to someone who used to work for him. He said Rubini was complaining about how slow work is.'

Puzzled, Brunetti asked, 'What does that mean when it's translated into the language you and I speak?'

'I think it means that – let me put it into the language of business – that, as a result of the general disruption caused by the *pandemia*, and what economists call a "contraction of liquidity", the market is drying up. Further, taste is changing, and so Rubini has fewer customers.'

Brunetti rubbed at the place on one side of his forehead where his hair was beginning to thin. It was hard to judge, but he thought he could see it in the mirror when he shaved.

'Does that translate to: "People don't want Old Masters any more, so there's no sense stealing them"?'

'More or less,' Griffoni admitted. 'It's also apparent that it's not only paintings that are suffering: it's bronze miniatures, and you can forget about porcelain or carved ivory.' She slipped a hand into the pocket of the jacket, pulled out a small notebook and paged through it.

When she found what she wanted, she read off a list: 'Venetian glass is too fragile. No one takes it unless they have the chance to go back and forth frequently from the place where they find it' – she emphasized the last verb – 'and get a lot of it, but it's generally high risk. Don't bother with silver any more. Books are good, but only if they're small, at least four hundred years old, and in perfect condition.' She turned a page. 'There's still a market for cameos, especially Roman ones.' Then, not that there was any need to explain, she added, 'Because they're so portable.' Brief pause. 'Gold and diamonds and other precious stones: they're the most popular at the moment, it seems.' She looked across at him and said, lapsing into a deep, broadcast-worthy voice, 'Market's always firm for gold and stones.' With that, she appeared to end her report.

'So those paintings on the walls in homes all over the city are safe?' Brunetti asked.

She shrugged, as if to suggest this problem did not much concern her, which might well have been true. 'If they're big enough, they are.' She replaced the notebook and crossed her legs. 'I believe these changes will force Rubini to adopt new business practices.'

'What do you mean, exactly?' Brunetti asked.

Propping her elbows on the arms of the chair, she sat back and intertwined her fingers across her stomach. 'The people who used to steal and sell paintings – or who sent other people to steal them – had to know what was worth taking off the wall or out of the frame, or they'd been told which painting to take, maybe even had a photo of it on their phones. If they'd been in the business for a long time, they knew how to treat the canvases to prevent damage. Or they were shown how.'

This had certainly been true in Brunetti's experience.

'So we were dealing with a person with a certain ...' Griffoni began, and then paused to seek the proper word. She found it: 'With a certain culture.'

'And the men working now?'

'The man I spoke to confessed to being nervous when he dealt with these new people, thought they were dangerous.'

Before Brunetti could comment or ask, she said, 'If you think about it, you have to know something in order to steal the right painting. You can't just grab them all and walk out of the house with six portraits under your arm.'

She paused a bit. 'But if you don't know what anything's worth, except in the broadest sense, then you just grab at what you can: jewellery, pieces with the stones that shine, the green stones, the red ones. Just stuff it in a bag and out the window with you.'

Brunetti broke in to say, 'You make them sound like barbarians.'

'Well, they are, aren't they? They don't care if they drop things, or step on them and crush them. If someone loved that object, it doesn't mean anything to them. So, yes, they're barbarians, vandals.'

'And the pros who steal only good paintings?' he asked and then, forgetting when to stop, added, 'Are the old-fashioned thieves better?' Both knew Rubini was an old-fashioned thief.

She failed to disguise her shock at the question. She looked away from him for what seemed to Brunetti like a long time, then returned her attention to him and said, 'Think about those thieves in Boston, I forget how many years ago – thirty? They were anything but barbarians. They had a shopping list. Nothing but the best: Vermeer and a pair of Rembrandts, some Degas drawings, and I forget the rest. They did almost no damage and were never caught. They restrained the guards, but made no attempt to frighten or hurt them.' She gave Brunetti some time to consider that before finishing: 'They were thieves, but they weren't barbarians.' Her opinion of the latter lay in the way she pronounced the word.

'In Boston,' Brunetti said, remembering having read about it, 'half a billion dollars evaporated, and no one has an idea how it happened.'

Her answer was some time in coming. 'I know someone in Napoli who works in art fraud and theft,' she began.

'Works for us?'

She shook her head and said, 'Interpol. The Gardner case is like the Holy Grail for them, even though it happened in America.' A longer pause, and then she continued. 'That robbery's always interested me: their choices were excellent, and they were careful not to damage anything else.'

'You make them sound like art dealers,' Brunetti observed.

'I suppose I do,' she admitted after some time. 'They knew the best, and they seem to have been well trained and careful.'

'What did your contact think about Rubini?'

She closed her eyes, as if in tired resignation, and said, 'He pretty much had the same opinion of him that you do, as if his playing by the rules excused what he did.'

Brunetti decided not to go near that one again and, instead, interrupted her to say, 'You make it sound as if I think Rubini's a Tiepolo cherub.'

'Oh, stop it, Guido,' she said, even though she was smiling.

'All right,' Brunetti agreed. 'If I promise no more jokes, will you listen to me for a minute about Rubini?'

She nodded and leaned forward, as if alerted by some change in his voice.

'Three days after he was sentenced this last time, for the robbery in Padova, I met his wife on the street.'

Griffoni had grown very quiet in her chair, unconsciously tense about what she felt might be coming.

Brunetti's voice was calm, utterly dispassionate. 'I said hello but couldn't think of anything else to say. I'd had nothing to do with the case because it was out of our jurisdiction, but I still … well, I worked for the other side.

'The two of us stood there – right in front of Mascari.' It had nothing to do with anything, but Brunetti added, 'Paola had asked me to go and get a bottle of Calvados for something she was cooking.'

He allowed time to wipe away the triviality of what he'd just said. 'And I finally said I was sorry about what had happened.' Without waiting for Griffoni to comment on that, he added, 'She told me that he'd pleaded guilty because they'd told him that unless he did, evidence would be presented at the trial showing both her fingerprints and their daughter's on the paintings, making them accomplices.' He paused to let Griffoni consider this, then added, 'It was easier that way. He pleaded guilty, got a short sentence, and there didn't have to be a trial.' He paused a moment. 'I wanted you to know why I think of him as a "poor devil", even though I know he's not.'

Griffoni sat silent for a long time until she finally said, 'Rubini told my contact he has some art deco jewellery and asked him if he might be interested.'

'Might he?' Brunetti asked.

'If Rubini gives him some photos to show his clients,' she explained.

'"Clients",' Brunetti repeated. 'I wonder if it's to make it sound less like theft,' he speculated.

She shrugged. 'From what he said of the new group Rubini is involved with now, I doubt they much care how it sounds. They're just thugs who steal what they're sent to steal.' Then, more thoughtfully, 'And they're more dangerous.'

'Why?' Brunetti asked.

'Because if someone found them when they were in the house, they wouldn't run away.' Smiling in concession, she added, 'From what you say, I suppose Rubini would.'

'Of course he would,' Brunetti said, 'And these others? What do you think they'd do?'

She considered this for a long time before saying, 'Whatever they had to do to keep what they were stealing.'

Brunetti agreed. He never could understand why people, almost always men, attempted to resist or overpower thieves. Many were thugs, and thugs were accustomed to violence: Griffoni was right about that.

As was often the case, their conversation had wandered away from what had started it.

Griffoni seemed to have reached the same conclusion.

'Is there anything we can do about Rubini?' she asked.

'He's a free man, Claudia,' Brunetti answered. 'There's no way we can stop him.'

'Even if he starts selling stolen jewellery,' she said, not as a question but as a statement of fact.

Brunetti pushed himself to his feet. Silence stole into the room, in train with her handmaiden, Embarrassment.

'Let's go downstairs and pick up Vianello and go have a coffee.'

11

The Ispettore was pleased to see them, and even more pleased at the idea of going down to the bar at the bridge to have a coffee. As they walked along the *riva*, Brunetti asked Vianello if he'd heard anything from Alvise, or even from Brandini, that suggested how things were going at the Commissariato at San Marco. Unspoken, of course, was the question of how things were going between them.

Hearing his question, Griffoni, who had been walking on the right side, closest to the buildings, changed places to walk between the two men, the better to hear what Vianello, who was walking near the water, had to say.

'Very little,' Vianello finally answered. 'The only trouble they've reported – real trouble – was a fight between a tourist and his girlfriend this morning.'

'What happened?' Griffoni asked, at the same instant that Brunetti asked, 'Who told you?'

'Brandini,' Vianello said, and Brunetti wondered how such a thing might have come about. Brandini had called Vianello?

Musing on this, Brunetti missed the first part of what Vianello said next.

' ... blamed his girlfriend for talking to him when he was looking at the map on his phone to see where they were.' Griffoni had opened her mouth to ask for clarification when Vianello added, 'A woman with a baby bumped into them, and he didn't notice for a minute or two that she'd taken his wallet.'

'Which he probably had sticking out of the back pocket of his jeans,' Griffoni said.

Discussing this, the three of them entered the bar and stood at the counter. The Senegalese barman came towards them, dressed in jeans and a dark blue sweater, having recently abandoned his white robe. Along with the long white robe, his nickname, Bambola, had also disappeared, replaced by his given name, Bamba. He asked what he could bring them.

'Three coffees,' Griffoni said from force of habit and suggested they sit to drink them at the far booth, which was empty. Bamba nodded and said he'd bring the coffees in a minute.

When they were seated, Brunetti asked Vianello, 'What happened to the two tourists?'

'Brandini told me the man kept yelling at his girlfriend or wife or whatever she was, saying it was all her fault.'

Hearing this, Griffoni put her hand across her open mouth and patted it, as though she were fighting back yawns.

Vianello ignored her. 'There was another tourist sitting by the door, filling out his *denuncia* for the same crime, only he'd had the sense to leave his passport and credit card in his hotel, so all he lost was some money.'

Bamba arrived at this moment and set the three small cups in front of them, placing beside each a glass of water.

Ripping open one of the small envelopes of sugar, Griffoni asked, 'Then what happened?'

Vianello swirled his sugar around, then all but tossed the coffee into his mouth. He set the cup back on the saucer, saying, 'No surprises here for any of us. He kept yelling at the girl to shut up, and finally grabbed her by the arm and started to shake her.'

Brunetti had finished his coffee, and his cup stopped in mid-air as he waited for the rest of the story. Like every good storyteller, Vianello had introduced a third character – the other tourist – and had then abandoned him by going back to the major action.

'The other tourist looked up from where he was sitting and said something in English to the one who was yelling at his girl-friend. So he pushed her away, grabbed the guy who'd spoken to him, and pulled him up from the chair. Then he made a fist, like he was going to hit him.

'Brandini said he didn't have any choice. He put his arms around him, picked him up and held him until he stopped shouting. It didn't take him very long to stop kicking, and then Brandini set him down. The guy must have realized a police station wasn't the best place to attack someone.'

'Attack two people,' Griffoni said, then asked, 'Where was Alvise when all this was going on?'

'I asked him that,' Vianello said. 'Seems one of the men in the Piazza found a lost kid and brought him in. The boy was scared and said he had to go to the bathroom, so Alvise showed him where it was. By the time he came back with the boy, it was all over.'

'Praise the Lord,' Griffoni said with exaggerated zeal, then asked, 'Is it too early to think they might get through this week without … '

None of the three managed to find the right term, so they let the subject die and shifted their concern to the 'baby gangs' that continued to roam the city at night. At first, they'd broken into stores closed by Covid, but the gangs of boys, some of them as young as twelve, no longer found much amusement in looting and vandalism and so had turned to more entertaining forms of violence. Like most predators, they preferred small prey, so their ideal targets were young women or, failing that, boys their own age, so long as there were fewer of them. Or, even better, they were alone.

The week before, there had been a particularly upsetting incident when two gangs had met a bit after midnight, entirely by chance, in Campo San Simeon Grando, a small *campo* not far from the station, but on the other side of the Canal Grande. There were no witnesses, only people whose houses faced on the *campo* and who had heard the first shouts and then the mounting noise. By the time they got to their windows, most of the boys had fled, leaving a twelve-year-old lying on the pavement, his right arm at a strange angle and his left cheek-bone shattered by a blow from a metal rod his assailant had dropped in panic at the first cries from the people at their windows.

The number of boys involved varied from witness to witness: four, six, more. They seemed to be fighting anyone they saw: the groups were wild and chaotic, and then they were gone, leaving behind only the broken boy on the ground.

'What did his parents say?' Brunetti asked, assuming that the boy would have been taken to the hospital, the parents called – in that always dreaded night-time call – and asked to come.

'I don't know,' Vianello answered, sounding tired. 'Some variant on, "We can't control him any more".'

After a long pause, it was obvious to them all that their willingness to abandon the subject was no less equal for being unspoken.

'I had an email from the Vice-Questore this morning,' Brunetti tossed into their silence. 'He wants to see me this afternoon. At four.'

'Did he say why?' asked Griffoni.

Brunetti shrugged. 'When I read his email, I wished I'd had one of those Roman augurs in the next office.'

Griffoni broke in to say, 'That would be useful for everyone. So long as we guaranteed the augur a fresh supply of chickens, he could go out into the garden and slaughter one every morning, then read the auspices and announce what the Vice-Questore wanted to talk about, and why. That way, we could prepare ourselves psychologically for whatever it was he wanted to tell us.'

Brunetti was about to say something when he was interrupted by an impatient Vianello, who asked, 'And what would Signorina Elettra charge his chickens as? "Office expenses"?'

Laughing, they got to their feet. Brunetti went to the bar, paid for the coffees, and followed them to the Questura, listening to their laughter all the way back, thinking that being a policeman was not a bad thing.

He was prompt for his meeting with Patta, had even changed after lunch into an old dark grey suit he'd never much liked in order not to offer a hint of sartorial competition to the Vice-Questore. He arrived at the small office of the Vice-Questore's Cerberus, Signorina Elettra Zorzi, at three minutes to four, hoping to have a moment with her to suggest the hiring of an augur, but then he remembered that she was away. He knocked twice, heard the *'Avanti,'* and opened the door, a more official expression already tightening his face, as though it reflected a mind convinced of the importance of their meeting.

'Buondì, Vice-Questore,' Brunetti said in a serious voice.

Patta raised his eyes from the piece of paper on his desk and nodded Brunetti to one of the chairs in front of him. When Brunetti was seated, Patta said, 'I'd like to talk to you about the incident in Treviso.'

Patta today wore a suit so dark that it could be either blue or black: Brunetti wouldn't know until he had a chance to look at his superior's shoes. Black and the suit was too; brown and the suit would be blue.

'Gladly, Dottore,' Brunetti answered, then studied Patta's tie to find a clue, but it was a dull burgundy and so could go easily with either colour. Brunetti thought of bending down to retie a shoe, but he wasn't sure of getting a glance at Patta's feet.

Then an inner voice spoke to him, telling him it didn't matter in the least: what mattered was that Patta's suit was better than the one Brunetti was wearing. So long as that was self-evident, their meeting had a chance of an amiable resolution. Should Brunetti mistakenly reveal a burgundy silk lining, razor-sharp pleats on the legs, a jacket length that managed to make him appear taller, then he would be well advised to remember a non-existent medical appointment or an incoming phone call from the president of Fiat, even a call from his own father-in-law. He could then leave, go up to his office, throw his jacket against the wall a few times and return to Patta's office to continue their conversation.

As it was, Patta's eyes passed over Brunetti without taking notice of anything other than his face before he said, 'How much do you know about it?'

Brunetti had to consider carefully how to answer this question: he could not say that he had gone out to Treviso to help get Alvise released; even worse, he could not say that Vianello had gone with him. Nor could he suggest that it was Alvise's right to do what he wanted with his private life.

'Certainly less than you do, Dottore. I'm sure of that.' Before Patta could respond, Brunetti added, 'I did read the report, but when I saw that there had been no arrests, I put it aside.' It was the best Brunetti could come up with, and he hoped it would suffice to satisfy Patta.

Patta was immediately alert. 'Tell me what you've heard about the demonstration. I was told it became violent.'

Brunetti put a sceptical expression on his face and said, 'Not as much as it might have.'

'What does that mean?'

'One of our men was there – he was just leaving COIN when the trouble started. He saw how few uniformed officers were present, so he went over to the person in charge to show his warrant card and offer to help, but before he got there, one of the protesters attacked him with a hunk of wood and knocked him down. By the time he could stand, there was chaos, and all he could do was try to defend himself. In the end, one of the men from Treviso grabbed him and put him in the back of a car and had him taken to the Questura.'

'One of *my* men?' Patta demanded, as though Brunetti had had something to do with it.

'*Sì, Signore.*'

Patta suddenly went very still. He stared at Brunetti, as if he were getting ready to weigh him or accuse him of something. 'Who was it?' he asked.

'Officer Alvise, Signore.' Then, certain that all uniformed officers were as identical to Patta as pieces in a game of checkers, he continued: 'He's been on the force for decades. I've worked with him often and have always found him an excellent officer.'

'Complaints?'

Brunetti had anticipated this question, so he made use of the surprised expression he'd prepared and said, 'Never.' He permitted himself an easy smile. 'I spoke to a friend there, Danieli – a good man – and we pretty much sorted it out between us. He apologized for his men and said ...' Brunetti paused so as to prepare the Vice-Questore for the importance of what was about to be said, '... that he owes us a favour for this, especially in these times when people are so ready to criticize the police for even the smallest error.'

Patta relaxed against the back of his chair. After some time, he said, "'Owes us a favour",' in a tone that, had Patta been capable of thoughtfulness, would have been thoughtful. As it was, it made clear the pleasure the Vice-Questore took in having another police officer in his debt.

Brunetti sat quietly, waiting to see what Patta would do or say. As the silence continued, Brunetti thought of his resolution to, as it were, play by the rules and said, 'I wanted to ask your advice, Dottore.'

Perhaps because it was Brunetti saying such a thing, Patta gave him a suspicious look and asked, warily, 'Yes? What about?'

'In the last few days, both Dottoressa Griffoni and I have heard the name Luigi Rubini mentioned.' He stopped to give Patta a chance to say he recognized the name, or not. Not, it seemed, so Brunetti went on. 'He's worked in art theft for years, but always as a middleman: he must have a list of clients who don't much care about the provenance of the objects – chiefly paintings – that he sells them. And the people who have them – have them to sell, that is – seem to know him and trust him.'

'I've heard about him,' Patta said.

'You know he's been out of jail for a year?'

Patta seemed startled at first, but then nodded.

'Both of us have been told that he might be getting ready to go back into business.'

Patta held up his hand and opened his mouth, as if to speak, but then lowered his hand and remained silent. If this was evidence that he would respect the privacy of Brunetti's and Griffoni's sources, all the better.

'It's nothing more than a whisper, sir,' Brunetti said. Then, in a show of deference, he asked, 'Do you think there's any chance we could persuade a magistrate to authorize access to his phone?'

'Do you mean access to the numbers that have called him and that he's called, or do you want to record those calls?'

'No, sir, it's really nothing more than whispers, so I think it would be enough to ask for only the numbers that have called him and he's called.' Brunetti, as ever, had to judge exactly how much to ask of Patta to strike the perfect balance: the request had to provide some important information at the same time it appeared innocuous. If the phone numbers somehow led to an arrest, it was sure to have been Patta's request for the numbers that had initiated the trail to discovery. If they led nowhere, then it was yet another one of Brunetti's unsuccessful efforts. Brunetti cared little which it turned out to be, so long as he could study the phone numbers.

After keeping Brunetti waiting for the answer for some time, Patta said, 'Do whatever you decide is better,' then returned his attention to the papers on his desk. 'I'll verify it if the magistrate you ask agrees.'

'Thank you, sir,' Brunetti said, eager to escape with Patta's agreement still sounding in his memory.

12

After he left Patta's office, Brunetti went down to see if he could find Alvise and get a clearer sense of how things were going. As it turned out, both he and Brandini were in the squad room, though both had already changed from their uniforms and, as a result, looked younger and almost entirely harmless. They stood, each with his arms folded across his chest, leaning back against two desks, seemingly in the middle of an animated conversation.

As he got nearer to them, Brunetti heard Alvise say, 'He doesn't know much about cooking, or food, or eating, so I might just as well stop at a supermarket on my way home and get a roasted chicken, boil a few potatoes, and put them on the table.' Then, his annoyance sounding through, Alvise added, 'He doesn't care at all what he eats.'

Brandini – Brunetti noticed only now how tall and broad he was – had apparently been stunned to open-mouthed astonishment by what Alvise had just said. He shook his head in consternation. 'Incredible,' he said, his voice softened by shock.

'On the weekend, I do what my mother always did,' Alvise continued. 'Fix a special Sunday lunch so that all anyone wants to do afterwards is sit in the living room, watch an old movie on television, and have a nap. To help digestion.' Turning to Brunetti, the officer said, 'We did that every Sunday I lived at home. Didn't you, Commissario?'

'Pretty much the same thing, yes, Alvise,' Brunetti said, though his family had never had a television and only occasionally enough food for a big Sunday lunch. But he still remembered Sunday afternoon naps, always taken in a chair in the living room, though usually with a book fallen open on his lap. Brunetti turned to the other officer and asked, 'What about you, Brandini?'

'Same as Alvise's family, sir.' Then, smiling at the memory, he added, 'It was the only time during the week I felt I'd had enough to eat.'

'That's terrible,' Alvise burst out spontaneously. 'Kids should have enough to eat. Always. Hunger's terrible.'

Although it was considered unwise to venture into personal discussions with the enlisted officers, Brunetti was struck by the passion with which Alvise spoke. 'Was that how it was in your family?' he asked.

Alvise's habitual smile burst across his face. 'Oh, no, Signore. Nothing of the sort. My father was a butcher, so we always had—'

'Where?' Brandini broke in before Alvise could say more.

'On Via Garibaldi: halfway down on the left, between the greengrocer and the barber.'

'*Maria Vergine*,' Brandini exclaimed. 'My mother always went there.' Brunetti saw him look over at Alvise, as though he were seeing him for the first time. 'She said he always had good meat.' Brunetti watched as something tapped at and then entered Brandini's memory. The officer leaned forward and touched Alvise's arm to get his attention.

'She told me – my mother – that he always put an extra piece of meat – a steak, or a sausage, or a couple of chicken legs – into the packages of the women with three kids or more.'

Alvise lowered his head and looked at his feet; his face grew red.

'Did he really?' Brandini asked. Silence. 'Really?'

Head still bent towards the floor, Alvise could be heard to say, 'He made me promise.'

'Who?' Brandini asked.

'My father.' Pause. 'He's retired now.'

'Promise what?'

'Never to tell.'

'Tell what?'

'That he did that.'

'With the extra meat?'

This time Alvise did no more than nod his assent.

'But why?'

Alvise finally looked up, as though he had been trapped into confessing. 'Because he thought the women would be embarrassed if he knew how poor they were,' he said, and let his head sink down again.

Brandini stood motionless and silent, and Brunetti was put in mind of something he'd read in the Bible, at about the same time Alvise's father was perhaps giving the other man's mother a few extra chicken legs, or a sausage with thyme and garlic, or perhaps even a steak: as had Lot's wife, so too had Brandini been turned into a pillar of salt.

Brunetti stepped forward and slapped Alvise on the shoulder. 'It's too early for all this talk about food. I can't leave for another hour, and now all I'm going to do is sit in my office and wonder what we're going to have for dinner tonight.' He looked at his watch and said, 'Your shift's over, so go on home, you lucky devils.'

Brandini emerged from his trance. Alvise shoved himself away from the desk and turned towards the door. 'See you tomorrow, Commissario,' he said, giving Brunetti a half-wave, half-salute. Brandini followed without speaking to Brunetti, his face not yet decided on how to react to what he had just heard from Alvise.

To make time pass quickly, Brunetti went back to his office to do what he never ceased admonishing his children not to do: sniff around on the Web. He thought he'd see what he could find about Professore Renato Molin, whom he remembered having met at some university dinner, years ago. Surely he must have published something during his years teaching at the university.

Paola's membership number and pin for JSTOR gained him access to most of the academic journals published in Europe and America, and he began searching for anything written by Renato Molin, professor of medieval Italian history at Cà Foscari.

It took Brunetti some time to compile the list, a total of seventeen articles, written over the span of twenty-three years. One discussed the contested election of an eleventh-century doge. Another discussed the sack of Zara, on the Dalmatian coast, in 1202. Others explained various sieges here and there. One article made the prostitutes of Venice sound dull. More than half discussed the vicissitudes of the Molin family. Skimming the titles and first paragraphs of these, Brunetti saw that, with almost Aristotelian precision, the Molins had followed the philosopher's pattern for tragedy: there was the rise to high estate during the tempestuous seventeenth century, the peak of success with Francesco Molin serving as doge for almost a decade, and then the swift decline from that point to finish as a family divided in two, racked by discord as both sides claimed the title and the wealth.

Brunetti decided to read one article about the loss of the family's
noble status and one about the siege and fall of Zara. Both articles were much documented and flatly written, as though Molin
thought he could win his argument by the weight of his foot-
notes and the solemnity of his style. The siege – the sack and
pillage of a city of fellow Catholics – was a tedious list of numbers: of men in arms, of transport ships, of silver marks paid and
received, of horses, and of just about anything that could be
counted. The tumult, the climbing of the walls, the hacking and
smashing of stones and bones, the looting and madness: they
passed almost undescribed, as though the author had worn
himself out with all those numbers and was asking the readers
to fill in the missing actions – the plundering and pillaging, win-
ning, losing, and dying – by themselves as they read. In short,
the sack of Zara was boring.

Curious now about the writer, Brunetti remained in Paola's
account and accessed the university library, hoping to learn if
the ham-fisted prose style of Professore Molin had been with
him in his earliest publications or if his years as an academic had
passed it on to him, like head lice.

Before Brunetti could begin to access that material, he glanced
at his watch and saw that he had already spent more than an
hour in the company of Professore Molin's prose. That was, in a
word, enough. It was time to leave these dates and phrases, broken truces, and burning cities behind and return to his wife and
his children, glad that this, and not conquest, was the centre of
his life.

13

Late the next morning, Brunetti was at his desk to talk to a colleague at the Questura in Genova who was asking for information about a Venetian arrested the previous year for stalking who had avoided a criminal charge only by explaining that he was being transferred from Venice to Genova. Because the woman who had made the complaint lived and worked in Venice, it was decided to allow him to transfer to the other city, so long as he reported to the local police there once a month and did not return to Venice without informing the police.

Brunetti's colleague in Genova called to report that, although he was indeed working for the same company, the man had never presented himself to the police in Genova. The police officer went on to say that he had been trying to contact the man for more than a month, but he did not answer phone calls or emails, and the Commissario had called to ask Brunetti if he knew this individual.

'I questioned him,' Brunetti said. 'Twice.' He was about to say that he thought the man was both a liar and dangerous when he considered that he did not know the man who was calling and thus had no idea of how discreet he needed to be. One never knew the future of a phone call, when or how it might be turned against either of the persons involved in the conversation.

Brunetti remembered having distrusted the man he questioned – distrusted and, truth be told, disliked. He acted as though the woman he'd followed and phoned and written to should have been complimented by his attentions, not to mention his persistence. Instead, he insisted, she had overreacted to what was no more than a manly expression of admiration and, yes, he would admit, interest.

At no time during the hour they spent together did Brunetti detect any remorse for having disturbed, even frightened, the woman. He remembered the man asking him, 'Well, shouldn't she have seen it as a compliment? I'm well educated, polite, have a good job and a lot of interesting friends.' He not only failed to mention to Brunetti that he also had a wife and two children, but he went on to say that the woman shouldn't have made such a big thing out of it. 'Calling the police!' the man had exclaimed, as though she'd set fire to his home.

Brunetti, who had had similar conversations with other men – rapists and stalkers and killers – remained impassive and took notes, knowing that he might be asked afterwards what he thought of the man.

Brunetti had found him arrogant, dishonest, deluded as to his own charm and intelligence. Brunetti was unsettled by the way the man spoke of the woman he insisted he respected and admired, despite having nothing good at all to say about her and instead speaking of her arrogance and lack of sympathy for him. He appeared to believe, Brunetti was aware at the time, that she had an obligation to repay him for his interest.

By the end of their talk, Brunetti had been convinced that the man posed a threat to this woman's safety and thought that a transfer to Genova would not suffice to rid him of his various beliefs regarding all women. Brunetti saw how utterly justified the man found his opinions to be and how strongly he believed in his rights over this woman.

It was Brunetti's responsibility, as the officer who had conducted the interview, to write a summary and opinion about what he'd been told and had observed during their time together. Brunetti, who knew there was no chance at all that the judges would send this man to prison, had advised, very strongly, that he be assigned to a psychiatric social worker and made to speak to that person at least once a week. Furthermore, he'd suggested the man be given a bracelet to show his location at all times of the day or night so that the police could check he was staying more than two hundred metres from the woman or her place of work or home. At first, Brunetti had baulked at writing that the man was 'dangerous' and had thought of adding 'potentially' before it. But then he recalled the way the man had spoken of the woman and submitted the document with an unadorned 'dangerous' in place.

Even as he made these recommendations, Brunetti had known they would be ignored. The man had proof from his employer that he was being transferred to Genova, so why go to the expense of paying attention to his movements? He was one of the top managers of the company and, it had been stated from the beginning, married with two children.

And now, after a year, someone was going to the trouble of following up on his sentence. From the beginning of the call, the other man's voice displayed concern and a certain measure of dislike for the behaviour of the missing man. But even that was not enough to strip Brunetti of the protective layer of caution he had managed to wrap around himself in his many years of police work.

'I'm sorry I can't be of more help to you,' Brunetti said. 'So long as he doesn't come back here unannounced, there should be no trouble.'

"'Should be"; the man in Genova repeated, thanked Brunetti for speaking with him, and hung up.

The conversation lingered in Brunetti's mind, troubling him. What good was done by all this dancing around reality and renaming of facts to make them seem less serious than they were? The man in Genova was dangerous: either he'd come back and bother the woman in Venice, or he'd find someone else in Genova and project all of his feelings on her until such time as she complained about him to the authorities or he decided that she had to be forced somehow to recognize his desires.

His time as a policeman had shown Brunetti that when violence was done to a woman, she too often wondered if she had done something to provoke it. Show violence to a man, and he'd give violence right back.

Finding himself with the phrase "recognize his desires" stuck in his mind drove Brunetti to his feet. The woman shouldn't "recognize" anything about her stalker except that he was dangerous and should be … And here Brunetti stopped, realizing that he was unable to finish that sentence. He carried that realization down the stairs and out of the Questura, hoping that, like a bad smell, it would evaporate as he walked home for lunch.

Brunetti spent the afternoon writing personnel assessments of members of the uniformed branch, a task he put off, every year, from month to month. This year, he had been asked to comment on the performances of three new recruits as well as Brandini and Foa, the pilot.

The recruits' performances were all adequate, although one was perhaps too much taken with the authority given to him by his uniform. Brunetti, who had spoken to this young man, Garofolo, a few times, was of a mind to believe that his inflated sense of self would disappear with time and so wrote only: 'Gives promise that he will become a fine officer.' He spent the next quarter of an hour writing similar nothings for the other recruits, both of whom seemed to Brunetti to be intelligent young people who had a sincere interest in being of help to society in some way.

He paused when he got to Brandini, set his file aside, and took Foa's. He looked at the screen, raised his fingers over the keys of the computer and was startled, after a moment's inattention, to discover that he had written 'Montisi' instead of 'Foa'. He yanked his hands away but could not stop himself from recalling the other pilot. How long since he had been killed? Ten years? More?

'Such a good man,' Brunetti said and, deciding to let that serve as his epitaph, cancelled the name – not without pain – and replaced it with 'Foa'. It was easy to praise the pilot. He had the *laguna* in his veins, as did most of the real boatmen in the city, although Brunetti found a more elegant way to write this on the evaluation report.

And now Brandini. Brunetti read through the various comments that had been filed in his record and found a certain restraint, perhaps coolness, in them. All were positive, everyone talked of his 'professionalism', but it didn't sound as though anyone was eager to be assigned to go on patrol with him. Brunetti ignored this and, in his own assessment, mentioned Brandini's obvious – Brunetti was torn between 'apparent' and 'obvious' and chose the latter – concern for people in distress. He gave as an example his handling of the incident at the Commissariato, which could easily have grown violent had Brandini not had the wisdom to intervene. Brunetti added a line, stressing Brandini's skill as a negotiator.

Soon after he'd finished, Griffoni came to his office and asked him if he wanted to go down to the bar on the corner and have a hot chocolate.

'Just like in American crime books,' Brunetti answered with a smile. 'The two hard-nosed detectives go down to the bar and have hot chocolate and talk about whether or not they should have whipped cream on top.'

'Good thing I've got my gun with me,' Griffoni said seriously, patting her hip, where there was no sign of a gun. 'No one's going to stop me from having whipped cream.'

While they were drinking the hot chocolate, Brunetti told Griffoni about the way Brandini had reacted when he'd learned about Alvise's father's generosity. 'He looked like he'd been hit in the face by a door,' Brunetti explained.

She nodded. 'I suppose it's strange to him that a homosexual could have had decent parents, or still have them, if I understand what Alvise's said all these years – that he and Cristiano go there for lunch almost every Sunday.'

'Do you know him?'

'Who? Cristiano?' she asked.

Brunetti nodded.

'Yes,' she said, taking another small sip of the chocolate. 'He's done ... some work for me.'

'That's right. Alvise said he's a carpenter.'

'A very good one,' she said. 'If you ever need a ... '

'How many are left in the city?' Brunetti asked, not as if he thought she'd know, but merely to state the obvious in another way: all the artisans were closing or retiring or dying. He heard his own grumpy voice and recognized the same old lament about the dying out of the old ways, the distortions caused by tourism, the impossibility of finding decent coffee, bread, shoe-makers, buttons, persimmons – who knew what else?

'But at least Bamba still makes the best hot chocolate in the city,' he said, intentionally moving away from lamentations and gloom to drinking the last of his chocolate. It wasn't a proper *aperitivo*, both of them knew, but at least it would ward off hunger for another two hours.

Brunetti was standing at the door to the terrace, looking out across the city, thinking it was time to go to bed, when his phone rang. He had left it in the pocket of his jacket and, for a moment, he told himself not to answer because he was at home and had had dinner, and whoever it was could call him in normal office hours. After six rings, it stopped, and he was immediately certain he'd lost an important call and regretted his bullheadedness.

As he turned back towards the living room, Paola appeared with his *telefonino* in her hand. She said, 'It's Vianello. He's using his bad news voice.' Her own voice was without irony. She'd taken many calls from Vianello and knew when the news was bad. She passed the phone to Brunetti and went back to her study.

'Tell me,' Brunetti said.

'We've just had a call from a man who says he thinks he saw a body in the water.'

'Where?'

'Just at the beginning of Giacinto Gallina. Near the underpasses.'

Brunetti made a noise that signified he understood and asked, 'Who's gone?'

'No one yet. I just got the call.'

'Where are you?'

'At home. But Foa's on the way. Shall I stop and get you?'

Brunetti glanced at his watch. It was almost eleven. 'Yes. It's probably faster to come up the Canal and pick me up.'

Vianello grunted in agreement, then said, 'I'll be at the end of your *calle* in fifteen minutes.' Brunetti thought the Ispettore was finished, but Vianello asked, 'Should I call the Carabinieri over at the Gesuiti?'

Brunetti heard the wail of Foa's siren over Vianello's voice and said, 'I'll call them.' Then, because he didn't want the pathologist to agree to come because he had asked him, Brunetti said, 'Would you call Rizzardi?'

'Of course,' Vianello answered and broke the connection.

Brunetti immediately dialled 112, gave his name and rank, and reported what Vianello had told him, saying that they'd be at Ponte Panada in about fifteen to twenty minutes.

He went down to Paola's study and told her what Vianello had said.

'I thought it would be something like that,' she said. 'I hope it turns out to be a false alarm.'

Brunetti nodded in agreement.

'Wear that vest, Guido. It's cold.' She had given him a Skier's vest a month ago, easily big enough for him and weighing less than a pair of sunglasses, or so it seemed to him.

'I don't want Chiara to know I own such a thing,' he said. 'She'll know immediately what bird it came from.'

'She wouldn't like it, would she?' Paola asked.

'We could make her sleep on the terrace some night so she'd know what it is to be cold.'

'She'd probably call the police and have us arrested,' Paola ventured.

'I hadn't thought of that,' Brunetti answered and returned to their room to find a heavier sweater.

He was back in a few minutes, wearing a dark duffel coat, with a thick woollen scarf around his neck.

'The vest?' she asked.

Brunetti pulled down the collar of the jacket and showed her the dark blue of the vest.

'Good.'

'Don't wait up,' he said.

'You always say that.'

'And you always wait up.'

'All right. Tonight I'll go to bed at two if you're not here.'

'I'm glad you told me to wear the vest,' he said, came over and kissed the top of her head, then went to the door and left the apartment.

*

As he stood on the embankment, looking across at Palazzo Farsetti, Brunetti thought how much he liked this moment of being a policeman. Out late in an empty city, he was able to move around as he pleased and as fast as he could. No one to stop him, no one to ask him where he was going. And the opaque black water in front of him, almost flat, and in these days of reduced tourism, almost always motionless after a certain hour.

He studied the buildings on the other side, then turned to look at the Rialto, lit from beneath, arching above the blackness. Who would believe this? Who could believe this?

Off to his right, he heard the launch, no siren – what was the need? The Canal was empty as far as he could see, down to the turn at the university. No boats, no floating birds, no sign of human activity.

The launch, its searchlight glaring ahead of it, swept around the curve and seemed to pick up speed as its course straightened out. Fleet as a bird, slim and slick, it came at him, Foa familiar with every landing. The lights came straight at him, and then suddenly the engine shifted into reverse. Momentum tried to do its best but failed; the boat slowed and then slid to a stop at his feet.

Brunetti grabbed Vianello's outstretched hand and stepped aboard, then down into the open cabin. Foa nodded, but said nothing, pulled them out into the centre of the Canal and continued, picking up speed with every moment. 'Rizzardi's on his way,' Vianello said by way of greeting. 'Just in case.'

After that, neither of them spoke. There was no crime yet; only when they had one could they talk about it. They could not comment on the beauty they passed, for there was nothing new to say. They watched, slipping, all of them, into the strange state of habitual wonderment. All of what passed before them was normal.

There were no people on the bridge as they sped under it. Brunetti noticed that there were even more buildings, on both sides of the Canal, draped in the long shrouds of protective plastic coverings that obscured what went on within. He knew the progression: the metal-tube scaffolding went up – four, five, six floors. The roof donned a rectangular plastic helmet. The white drapes unrolled, covering everything, roof to pavement. As if the buildings had been eviscerated, the ramps of stairs from floor to floor were now on the outside. Conjured up by the magician's apprentice, elevators appeared at various places on the façades and sides.

Men climbed up and down all day, or rode the elevators accompanied by head-high packets of insulation panels, or tons of roof tiles. Enormous cranes nested on the waters of the Grand Canal, their beaks slowly lifting beams, window frames, bathroom tiles of various dimensions and colours, to set them on the roof or at various points behind the white plastic veils.

It is said that birds must find and eat from a quarter to a half of their own weight every day. How much did these cranes select? How many tons to keep them moving all day long, remorseless in their desire to make it all authentic and respectful and acceptable to the new rulers? Old, yes; but make it convenient too. Could you find us a nice Tiepolo, and we'd like a big room to use as a study. Yes, with books. And don't forget the pizza oven: the kids want one. And the entertainment centre.

The launch turned to the right and started to slow, pulling Brunetti free from thinking about one of the many family stories that had developed in the last years. A cousin of his worked in Mestre as what he called 'a thing pimp', persuading wealthy foreigners who moved to Venice what to choose and what to buy and where to place it. Some years before, he'd taken Brunetti to see two homes he'd planned, and Brunetti had been surprised and cheered to find them both beautiful. 'I do it for the house,' his cousin had protested. 'It knows what it wants, even if they don't. I can't let them make it ugly.'

The Carabinieri had got there before the police, but it couldn't have been by much: their pilot was still tying a rope to a metal ring on the embankment on the left side of the canal; when he finished and stood, Brunetti was struck by how tall he was, at least a head taller than anyone else who was there. Two other Carabinieri stood farther along the embankment. They stood still, staring down at the water of the canal. Between them stood a man in a dark overcoat who was pointing in the direction of the new arrivals, although at the water, not the men. Vianello and Brunetti walked over to say hello to the Carabinieri. Brunetti and Vianello both knew the lieutenant, Filini, who introduced them to Massimo De Mori, the officer with him, and then to Paolo Comisso, the man who had seen what might have been a body in the water.

'It was at least a half an hour ago,' Comisso said, pushing back the sleeve of his coat and looking at his watch. 'I was on my way home.' He pointed down the embankment, which ended in a doorway that served as a dead end. 'I think I saw a hand in the water.' He shook his head a few times, either still in shock or to help clear it of the memory. 'Just there,' he said, pointing to the water in front of him.

Leaving Vianello to talk to Comisso, Brunetti walked to the edge of the water and ran his eyes over the area in front of them, then to the left, and then to the right. He saw a paper cup floating past and, calling to Foa, waved to him to come.

The pilot walked over quickly, and Brunetti, pointing to the cup, asked him to estimate how far something underwater would have drifted in half an hour.

Foa walked to the cup and put his wallet down level with it. He looked at his watch for two minutes and then went to stand beside the cup's new position: it was a barely noticeable two centimetres farther along the canal, carried by a lazy tide.

He went to pick up his wallet, walked over to Brunetti, and said, 'My guess – and this depends on size and buoyancy – is that it couldn't have drifted even a metre.'

'Thanks, Foa,' Brunetti said and clapped him on the shoulder. Then, turning to the lieutenant and the others, he said, 'You heard him.'

They advanced in a slow line, eyes on the water, Vianello at the head. Foa and the other pilot arrived, both carrying flashlights. They moved to the middle of the group and stood half a metre apart, thus creating a single oval of slow-moving illumination.

The minutes moved as slowly as they did. A few people walked up and down the bridge: all of them were very careful not to stop and stare. Foa pointed to the left, saying, 'There's something up there, parallel with the stanchion.'

The others followed the line his finger indicated and stared at the patch of water below the stanchion. Brunetti saw only the flashlights and the glow from the street light. Vianello, from up ahead, said, '*Niente.*'

Lieutenant Filini turned to the tall man beside him and said, 'Get the boathook.' The pilot returned quickly, the long pole in his right hand. In the other, he still held the flashlight, which he handed to the lieutenant. Holding it before him, Filini moved closer to the water.

The lieutenant bent over, raised his left hand to his forehead to block the light from the street light above him. Crablike, he slid his foot to the left, then dragged the other to join it, keeping the flashlight on the surface of the water.

And then it was there: a hand, in the middle of the canal, and suddenly all of them saw it.

'*Oddio,*' someone whispered.

Filini turned to the pilot and said, 'Do you think you can reach it?'

'Yes, sir.' It was only then that Brunetti realized the pilot's greater height would be an advantage in what he was being asked to do. The pilot walked to the edge of the embankment, held the hook out before him, took it in both hands, and leaned forward to extend it towards what they'd all seen. He extended the pole as far as he could, then turned to his superior and said, 'Could you hold on to my jacket, Lieutenant?'

Filini moved behind him and grabbed the belt of his jacket.

The pilot nodded his thanks, moved two short steps to the left, leaned forward again, and lowered the hook into the water. He grunted once, twice, then holding the rod steady, took a small step backwards, then another, and then he and Filini moved back in step with one another until they all froze at the sight of what was floating towards them.

Brunetti noticed that the Carabinieri pilot shifted the boathook to his left hand and made the sign of the cross, then took the hook in both hands again and started pulling it gently towards them, advancing his grip slowly, hand length by hand length.

Vianello and De Mori went to the edge of the embankment and got down on their knees, one on either side of the long handle of the boathook. 'All right,' Vianello said, holding a hand up in the air.

The pilot with the hook stopped pulling and held it still. Vianello and Di Mori spoke to one another softly, then Vianello got to his feet. He looked up and down the embankment and saw a short flight of stairs going down into the water. He took the pole from the pilot and walked slowly towards the stairs, guiding whatever was caught at the end along with him. De Mori stood up and followed.

Brunetti, approaching the stairs, saw that the first two steps were free of water, though each had a thick coat of seaweed growing on them, glittering wetly in the light. Reaching the stairs, Vianello returned the pole to the pilot and walked down the first two steps, then stuck his hand out towards Brunetti, who went to stand on the dry pavement next to the steps and took it.

Lieutenant Filini did the same on the other side of the stairs and waited while De Mori went very gingerly down the slippery steps.

The man with the pole stepped farther back, guiding what was floating towards the centre of the staircase. When it was within hand's reach, Vianello and De Mori leaned forward. Instinctively, Brunetti knelt on the pavement to help extend Vianello's reach; Filini did the same.

That done, both of the men on the steps leaned out and down, and plunged their hands into the water, grabbing at what they could see.

Brunetti felt Vianello's grip tighten and leaned forward himself to grab his friend's wrist with his other hand.

Hesitantly, Vianello put a foot backwards on the higher step, waited for De Mori to do the same, then said, 'Now,' and stepped back onto the higher stair. De Mori was a second late, and Vianello was yanked forward. Brunetti grabbed harder and succeeded in pulling him upright. When he was steady on his feet, Vianello said, 'Again,' and this time the other man moved in perfect synchrony with him. And once again: this time they stepped up onto the embankment, dragging with them a human figure, a man, his clothes melded to his body by the water of the canal.

Vianello and De Mori pulled the body fully out of the water; Brunetti and Filini took his feet and the four of them carried the dead man farther away from the canal and set him, stomach down, on the pavement.

Standing near the dead man's feet, Brunetti could see only that he had dark hair: his hands were trapped under his body.

Brunetti pulled out his phone and called the Questura. He identified himself and told the officer who took the call to contact the crime-scene crew and tell them to come to the Ponte Panada, where a dead man had been found in the water. No, he didn't know. No one had looked at the body yet, but Rizzardi was on his way.

As if being named were enough to conjure him up, at that moment the chief pathologist, Ettore Rizzardi, appeared at the top of Ponte Panada, saw the group of men, and started down towards them.

He carried his small leather bag and wore the dark overcoat he had worn for many winters. When he reached them, Rizzardi shook hands with Brunetti and nodded to the others, all of whom seemed to know him.

He walked over to the dead man and paused a moment, standing next to him. Over the years, Brunetti had observed that the doctor, a non-believer, always paused for as long as a prayer would take before bending down over the dead person, as if to ask their acceptance of him as the one to pronounce them dead and thus free them from the rules and rigours of this life.

Rizzardi looked at the lieutenant and asked, 'Could you ask your men to turn him over for me, please?'

Although the dead man was thickly built and wearing a water-sodden woollen overcoat, this was quickly done. Rizzardi knelt down and paused, then brushed the thick dark hair back from the victim's face.

Something in the thickness of the body and the length of his hair might have alerted Brunetti, because the sight of the face of the Sri Lankan who'd answered the door to Palazzo Zaffo dei Leoni did not come as a complete shock to him. Still, he pulled in a gasp of air, walked over to the kneeling Rizzardi and placed a hand on his shoulder.

'I know him,' Brunetti said.

'Who is he?'

'I don't know.'

14

Brunetti leaned forward to take a closer look at the dead man's face. There was no error: this was the man who had answered the door to the garden, who had told him the *palazzo* was not for sale, and who had told him in excellent Italian – complete, Brunetti recalled now, with the Veneto cadence of someone who had been in the region for some time. The face was relaxed in death: as Brunetti watched, Rizzardi placed his index and middle fingers on the man's face and held his eyes closed for some time. When he took his hand away, the eyes remained closed.

'How do you know him?' Rizzardi asked.

'I spoke to him on Monday.'

'About what?' Rizzardi asked in confusion, then added, 'If I might ask, that is.' He reached across the man's chest and worked at the soaked cloth to unbutton his coat.

'He lives on the grounds of a *palazzo* near Campiello de la Cason. Someone I know said he thought it was for sale, so I knocked on the door and asked.'

'What did he say?' Rizzardi was now working at the third button.

'That it wasn't for sale.'

'That's all?'

'That's all he said to me. Then he closed the door in my face.' Realizing how this must sound, Brunetti quickly added, 'Very politely.'

A silence ensued, then Rizzardi said, 'Guido, this is going to be very unpleasant.'

'What is?'

'His body.'

'What? How do you know that?' Brunetti asked, completely confused.

'I saw his hands,' Rizzardi explained, then started to say something else, but stopped himself.

Brunetti looked at the one that was visible, palm up, and saw the red flesh exposed in two long lines, running across it.

'What … ?'

'Defence wounds.'

Brunetti was reluctant to ask and so said nothing.

Rizzardi continued. 'His clothing, under the coat, is stained.'

'Blood?'

Rizzardi nodded.

Brunetti made a noise deep in his chest.

Rizzardi, still kneeling, reached to unbutton the jacket and the shirt, then peeled them both back.

The sight of the body was shocking with its gaping, red-rimmed puncture wounds. A bloody segment of what looked like grey tubing was slipping its way out of a wound at the bottom of the dead man's stomach, staining his white shirt to flamingo pink. There were more wounds, but Brunetti turned his eyes away from those strange holes.

'*Oddio,*' Brunetti sighed. And then, 'He seemed a very gentle man.'

'Buddhists often are,' Rizzardi said.

'How do you know he's a Buddhist?'

Rizzardi pushed aside the collar of the dead man's shirt to reveal a simple gold chain with a small flat metal figure of the Buddha.

Rizzardi got to his feet and put his hand on Brunetti's arm. 'You don't have to stay to look at this, Guido.'

'I know. Thanks, Ettore, but I don't want him to be alone.'

'He's dead, Guido,' the doctor said, but not unkindly.

'I know that. But I think Buddhists believe the spirit stays near the dead person for a time. I'd like his spirit not to be alone.' Brunetti gave a nervous shrug, embarrassed to hear himself talking like this. Luckily, they both heard the approach of another boat. The crime-scene crew had arrived.

Brunetti went over to the boat and asked if they had a blanket. He took it and carried it back to cover the dead man.

'Excuse me, Signore,' Brunetti heard a man's voice say from behind him. He turned and found himself facing the man who had seen the body in the water and called the Questura. He was shorter than Brunetti, shorter still because of the way he hunched his shoulders as if in perpetual humility. 'If you're in charge, are you the person who can give me permission to go home?' Comisso asked, diffident in the face of authority.

'I'm sorry to have forgotten,' Brunetti said. 'If you'll give me your number, you can go.' He took out his notebook and wrote down the man's name and then his phone number.

Timidly, Comisso asked, 'Could I say something, Signore?'

'Of course.'

'I, er, I live around here.' He pointed in the direction of the bridge. 'Down there, in Calle della Testa.'

'And the number?' Brunetti asked, writing down the address. 'I don't think we'll need you to do more than come to the Questura tomorrow and make a statement.'

'I understand that, Signore,' Comisso said. 'But it's something I thought. More like that.'

'And what did you think, Signor Comisso?'

'Well,' the man went on, nervous or shy and very uncomfortable, 'I watch a lot of television. The crime series.' He looked away, as if he'd told a shop owner he was buying things from the competition.

'Ah, do you?' Brunetti asked.

'Yes, and that's why I thought about where this could have happened.'

'Really?' Brunetti said. 'And where is that?'

Comisso took Brunetti's arm and pulled him over to the edge of the canal. Pointing to the other side, he said, 'See that small courtyard over there?' Brunetti saw a very small, cement-covered space with three steps leading down to the canal. 'Most of the houses there are empty,' he said, leaving it to Brunetti to imagine the rest. 'You can get to it from the *calle* over there.'

Brunetti looked across the water and noticed the shuttered windows.

'The *calle* cuts off to the left, but it's a dead end,' Comisso began, but, hearing the word he'd just said, slapped his hand over his mouth and whispered, 'I didn't mean that, Signore.'

'Of course not,' Brunetti said easily.

Comisso suddenly looked nervous, so Brunetti asked, 'What else, Signor Comisso?'

'It would be better than here, I think,' he said with a certain insistence.

'For what?'

'For killing someone.'

Brunetti fought down his astonishment and asked, 'Why is that, do you think?'

'As I said, it ends in the water, and no one lives in the houses there any more. So no one has any reason to go there. And there's no light.' Comisso tried to smile, but he was too nervous to manage it.

'I see, Signor Comisso. I'll have the men check.' Comisso gave a small smile this time and bowed his head, prompting Brunetti to add, 'Thank you for being such a good citizen.'

'Oh, thank you for saying that, Signore. I try.' He nodded and walked away, down towards his home, and Brunetti went back to talk to the crime squad to suggest where they could begin their search for the scene of the crime. He told Vianello about the small courtyard, said he'd go with the crew, and asked the Ispettore to stay at the canal until the ambulance arrived and then go back to the hospital with the body.

As it turned out, Signor Comisso was right. The two white-suited technicians set up powerful lamps at the entrance to the courtyard, which was littered with the detritus of city life: faded newspapers, sweet wrappers, a single sock, and small piles of plaster crumbled at the base of the walls on all sides. They ran the beams back and forth on the sandy, junk-strewn paving, up and down the walls. After each sweep, they moved the lights forward a metre and repeated the process. The third time they switched on the lights, one of them said, 'There.' Brunetti, following close behind them, looked where he pointed and saw a splash of red at the bottom of the wall. Above it, there was a red mark on the flaking plaster.

The second technician went back to a black bag he'd carried from their launch. Opening it, he pulled out a camera and tripod and set them up between the two lamps.

Brunetti had moved out of the courtyard to let them work, but as soon as the camera was set up, he went back in and continued to watch. Flash and flash and flash. Turn the camera to the right and flash, to the left and flash. Move the camera forward and repeat, and then repeat and then repeat until scores of photos had been taken of red splotches on the ground and on the wall, of footprints left in the piles of fallen plaster and flecks of cement that lined both sides of the courtyard, and of a long smear of red that led across the sand and filth to the three steps leading down to the water. Red was visible on the top one. The water had already covered the others and had drunk any trace of colour that might have been visible on the lower steps.

Brunetti was vaguely aware of the sound of a boat passing by, then another, and then he saw a single rower in a gondola slide by, leaving no trace that he could hear or see on the water. By the time Brunetti thought of looking at his watch, it was after one: he decided to hope that Paola had lost patience and gone to sleep and chose not to phone to tell her he didn't know when he'd be home. Why bother: she knew that already, didn't she?

While they were still taking photographs, Rizzardi called to Brunetti from the entrance to the courtyard, saying he was leaving. He'd scheduled the autopsy for ten, he added, said goodnight, and backed away into the semi-darkness of the larger *calle*.

Some time later, the boat from the hospital arrived. Brunetti went back to the place where the body lay. The attendants were just stepping down into the boat, careful with the large black bag into which they'd placed the body.

Behind him, Vianello said, 'I'm here,' and Brunetti immediately felt calmer about consigning the body to their care. He gave Vianello a hand to steady him as he stepped down into the boat, then moved back from the edge as one of the attendants unmoored the boat and it slowly pulled away. Remembering,

Brunetti called after Vianello, 'Check what he's got on him. See if there's any identification.'

Vianello raised his arm in acknowledgement, and the boat moved towards, and then disappeared under, Ponte Panada.

The Carabinieri drifted back to their boat except for Filini, who came over to Brunetti. Nodding to indicate the courtyard, he asked, 'Anything?'

'Blood. Along the ground and down the steps.'

'Those guys any good?' the lieutenant asked with another tilt.

'Very.'

Filini nodded.

Brunetti considered for an instant why Filini would ask such a question and asked, 'Trouble?'

Filini raised his eyebrows and shook his head. 'You wouldn't believe it.'

'Tell me.'

Filini gave him a direct glance and Brunetti answered, 'I'm a tomb. What happened?'

'Bad accident last week. Usual thing: guy tried to pass on a curve and drove into another car coming on the other side of the road. Killed the people in the other car.' He paused, then added, 'He walked away.'

Knowing this was only a small part of the story, Brunetti waited, asking nothing.

'Married people, in their fifties.' Brunetti still said nothing. So Filini said, 'My guys forgot to do an alcohol test, and the people in the hospital thought they had. No one noticed until the next afternoon.'

He took a step back from Brunetti. 'So I'm nervous now about the technical people.'

Brunetti nodded in agreement, though he was struck by the futility of that: the married couple were still both dead anyway.

Filini looked at his watch. 'Can I offer you a ride home?'

'That's kind of you, Gianluca, but it's too far out of your way. Let your guys go back to sleep.'

Happy with Brunetti's answer, the lieutenant nodded, then said, 'I saw an American gangster movie last week. One of the good guys had to go home late, late at night, and the other one said, "Get home safe".' He paused, but Brunetti could only smile, not give him the laugh the other man clearly anticipated.

So Filini laughed out loud himself, clapped Brunetti on the shoulder and turned back to his boat. Halfway there, he turned and waved back to Brunetti, then called across to him, speaking in American, 'Get home safe.' He turned and laughed his way back to his boat.

It was almost three when Brunetti got home. He found Paola asleep in bed, switched off her reading lamp, marked the page in the book lying open on her stomach, then closed it and set it aside. It would have been nice if she'd still been awake so that he could tell someone about his sense that the dead man's spirit wanted to be kept company for a time while it adjusted to the new world in which it found itself. As it was, Rizzardi was probably the best person to whom he could have tried to explain this, perhaps Vianello: he didn't know the others well enough.

Certainly not Filini, he thought, looking at himself in the mirror, especially after his remark about the American film. God, people were strange. We never knew them, not really.

He slipped back the covers, although well he knew that he could have begun hammering at the walls and drilling holes and Paola would have continued to sleep the sleep of the just and innocent. He smiled at that and fell asleep, still smiling.

15

He woke at nine-thirty, alone in bed. He tuned himself in to the sounds of the family but heard nothing. Chiara was not scrambling through papers, looking for her Latin homework, nor was Raffi searching for his football spikes. And Paola was no longer roaming back and forth between her study and the kitchen for another cup of Japanese tea.

He turned over and prepared to return to sleep – he could always claim that he was busy trying to discover the identity of the dead man – when he remembered Rizzardi saying the autopsy was planned for ten. Twenty minutes later, whimpering at his coffee-less state, Brunetti left the building and took refuge in Rizzardini for a brioche and a life-saving *caffè*.

Somewhat restored, he started towards Rialto, ignoring the smell of the fresh – he had his doubts – fried fish and the sight of the equally repellent ice creams that bordered him on both sides of the narrow *calle*. How could people not realize that fish was not to be eaten for breakfast and ice cream only in temperatures in excess of 27 degrees?

He took the *traghetto* from the fish market across to Santa Sofia and turned right in the direction of the hospital. More gelato on the right and then straight ahead, meat on the left now, not fish. By the time he reached the hospital five minutes later, he'd passed used books, two pharmacies, a hardware store, six bars and a fully automatic laundry with washers and dryers. He went into the hospital, nodded to the man at the desk, and proceeded uninterrupted towards the back and the *obitorio*.

He had not been there in some time but still remembered the way, turning without conscious awareness into the correct corridors and crossing the open garden. He reached the *obitorio* and took a seat outside the double doors, in no way eager to enter. He paged through that day's *Gazzettino* which someone had left behind, even though he knew it was far too soon for the death to be mentioned. He returned to the front page and read the usual stories: young people dead in their cars, an investigation by the Guardia di Finanza of a company that recycled plastics, an injunction against the restoration of a famous museum in the city, apparently being conducted without the bother of obtaining authorization from the Superintendent of Fine Arts.

He was just turning the page when the door to the inner room opened automatically and Rizzardi emerged, still dressed in his protective white plastic gown.

'Ah, Guido,' he said. 'I'm sorry that we always meet for dreadful things. Sometime we should meet for a coffee or a drink.'

'And talk about the weather?' Brunetti said. 'It would be wonderful, at least to talk of something other than … '

'Exactly,' Rizzardi said. 'Come and I'll tell you what I've found.'

Brunetti got to his feet and abandoned the paper on his chair.

Brunetti could never adequately prepare himself for this, had given up even trying to. On a metal table in the centre of a very cold room, there lay a human figure – dead body, corpse, cadaver – that – Brunetti asked himself when the body was no longer a 'who' but a 'that' – had been the victim of violence. The body was covered with a sheet, having been examined by a person who had the right to poke into its most intimate places and secrets to discover diseases the dead person might not have known he'd had or perhaps passed on to others.

The doctor had no interest in the motives or thoughts or any reflections that might have affected the deceased's behaviour: the doctor knew only what was revealed by the tests or the scalpel, and the only person who had a right to that knowledge was the person in charge of the investigation.

Rizzardi went over to the sink, as he had done almost every time Brunetti had come here to talk to him. He dropped his gloves into a metal container beside the sink, then untied the gown and put it on top of the gloves. He turned on the water, adjusted the temperature, and washed his hands carefully, soaping them twice and drying them thoroughly.

He turned to Brunetti. 'There's no sense in your having to see him, Guido. There's an old scar on his head, where he was hit with something, not cut, and he has deep cuts on both hands. In fact, he's missing a part of one finger.' After a pause, the pathologist added, 'I didn't want to tell you last night.'

This was a surprise to Brunetti, one that drove his memory back to the time he had spent in the courtyard. He tried to remember what he'd seen on the ground. If it had been there, the technicians would have found it. And photographed it. He couldn't bring himself to ask Rizzardi to say any more about it.

'All he could do to defend himself was hold up his hands. But that wasn't enough.'

Brunetti nodded.

'Once he couldn't protect himself any more, the person who killed him – and I'd say this was a right-handed person – stabbed him in the back, piercing a lung, then twice in the chest and once in the lower abdomen.'

'Why wasn't there even more blood?' Brunetti asked, remembering what he'd seen the night before.

'His clothing soaked up a lot of it,' Rizzardi said. 'And he went into the water almost immediately after he was stabbed.' That said, Rizzardi walked to a metal locker and took out his jacket. He put it on and pulled out his dark overcoat, the same one he had been wearing the previous night, the same one he had worn for years, and folded it over his arm.

'How do you know that?' Brunetti asked, trying to remember what signs of disturbance there had been on the sand and earth in the courtyard.

'Because he drowned,' Rizzardi said. Before Brunetti could comment or ask questions, the pathologist went on: 'He would have died anyway: the killer punctured a lung and nicked an artery. Those things would have killed him; falling into the water just made it faster.'

Brunetti nodded again, then asked, 'Aside from being right-handed, can you tell anything else about the killer?'

'Not very tall, perhaps a metre seventy, seventy-five.'

'Could it have been a woman, do you think?'

Rizzardi was obviously surprised by the question. 'It's usually men who use knives, and this was probably a hunting knife of some kind: smooth-bladed, about eleven centimetres long. It's the force of it that makes me think it was a man. On the wound to the chest, the flesh is faintly bruised above and below the point of entry. But it had to go through his overcoat, so there was a lot of force behind it.'

Brunetti studied his shoes but found no other questions there. 'Anything else?' he asked.

'Not really. The victim was in good health; I'd guess he was in his early fifties, didn't smoke, and if he drank, he did so moderately, but I'd guess he didn't drink at all. No signs of serious disease. Heart looks fine.'

Brunetti nodded a few times, then said, 'So we're looking for an average-size, right-handed man who seems to have become agitated when he was stabbing another man to death.'

Rizzardi had the grace to smile, and said, 'I couldn't have expressed it better myself.'

'You have time for a coffee?' Brunetti asked.

'I'd like to, I really would. But I've got to sit in on an interview.'

'Who?'

'My successor,' Rizzardi said, and Brunetti saw what delight he took in surprising him with what he'd said.

'Successor,' Brunetti repeated neutrally.

'Yes. I'm due to retire next year.'

'What will you do?'

'Alessandra and I have a place in the Salento that we've been restoring for the last few years.'

'You're going to move to Puglia?' Brunetti asked, as though Rizzardi had said he was moving to the Bronx.

'To the Salento, Guido,' Rizzardi corrected him. 'And for three or four months of the year.'

'To do what?'

'To be retired people and go swimming and out on our boat.'

'That's all?'

'Well, we might get a dog and go for long walks and lie around the rest of the day and read.'

Brunetti stopped himself from saying more. He looked across to the centre of the room and saw the sheeted figure. And thought about the other sheeted figures, the hundreds of sheeted figures.

'Good,' Brunetti said, walked over to Rizzardi and pulled him close in a bear hug, then pushed himself away and turned towards the door. The South would be good for Rizzardi, he realized, even if all it did was remove him from this terrible cold he worked in.

He turned at the door and asked, 'Are we invited to visit?'

'Yes. You and Paola can walk the dog,' Rizzardi said and turned to close the locker.

When Brunetti arrived at the Questura, the officer at the door told him the Vice-Questore wanted to see him. He handed his coat to the officer and went directly upstairs, knocked on the door, and went into Signorina Elettra's empty office.

'Get in here, Brunetti,' Patta shouted from inside his own, by way of a greeting. When he entered, Brunetti saw that Patta was at his desk, no papers in front of him, perhaps a good sign, for it indicated that he was disposed to listen to what he was told and might at least delay any accusations. Brunetti nodded and, without being told to do so, took a seat in front of Patta's desk.

'As I'm sure you've been informed, Vice-Questore,' Brunetti began, 'a man was murdered last night.'

'I know. Over near the Miracoli,' Patta said. 'What have you learned?'

'Very little, Dottore. I was there when they found him last night.'

'Ah!' Patta exclaimed. 'I thought it happened this morning,' he went on, as though he'd discovered Brunetti attempting to mislead him.

'Excuse me, Signore. A bit after midnight.'

'In the water, I was told.'

'Yes, sir, near the Miracoli, as you said,' Brunetti affirmed.

'Stabbed?'

'Yes, Vice-Questore. Multiple times.'

'Who is he?' Patta demanded, quite as if he believed Brunetti knew and didn't want to admit it.

'That's not clear yet, sir,' Brunetti began, complimenting himself on the grace of his own words, hinting as they did that the man would be identified in due course, and it was merely a question of time.

'A foreigner, wasn't he?' Patta demanded.

'Dark-skinned, certainly.'

'But not an American,' Patta said, sounding like he was praying, perhaps to the Statue of Liberty, that they be spared the murder of an American tourist.

Delightful as it would be to leave Patta with this fearful possibility for some hours, Brunetti was unwilling to take the risk of misleading him. Better – although probably useless – to be the one who brought the good news. 'No, Vice-Questore, I think he belongs to the Asian community.'

'You mean African, don't you?' Patta asked, happy to have heard Brunetti make such a basic error.

'No, sir, the South Asian population: Pakistani, Sri Lankan, Bangladeshi, Indian.'

Although the term might have been new to Patta, he lost no time in adjusting himself to it. 'Of course, of course, *those* Asians.' Changing course, he asked again, 'What have you learned?'

'Precious little, Dottore. The only thing certain is that he was not a tourist,' Brunetti began, taking the opportunity to shift about in his chair so as not to be a witness to Patta's sigh of relief. 'I haven't had time to go through his possessions. I was on my way down to the lab to ask about them.'

Brunetti crossed his legs and said, 'I haven't filed a report yet. Since you're here, sir, I thought I'd take this opportunity to report to you directly.'

Never one to lose a good opportunity, Patta shoved back his sleeve and said, 'Of course I'm here. It's after eleven. Where do you think I'd be, Brunetti, down at that bar, having a coffee with you and your friends?'

Brunetti smiled and made a noise that turned Patta's question into one of his clever remarks.

Silence fell between them, and after a moment, Brunetti risked getting to his feet. He pushed his empty chair closer to Patta's desk and said, 'I'll go speak to the technicians and see what they've found, shall I?'

'Yes,' Patta said, apparently pleased that someone else was doing something. 'Keep me informed, Brunetti,' he said with a disinterested voice, and slid a thick file closer.

That settled, Brunetti went to the laboratory at the back of the ground floor, Bocchese's den, where alembics and retorts were still to be found and mysteries deciphered and made plain. Bocchese was at his desk, along with the detritus of days, if not years. Papers, reports, surveys, drawings lay across his desk like leaves in October. There was no order, no plan, only apparent chaos, anti-design, mess. Yet Bocchese, by some system he nursed in his bosom and revealed to no one, could find in that clutter, with the accuracy of a heron spearing a fish, any paper requested of him.

'Hello, Guido,' the chief technician said, then asked, 'You here about the man who was found last night?' At Brunetti's nod, Bocchese turned and pointed to a table further back in the lab. 'Everything's in that plastic bag, and what we know is already in the report next to it. You can have a look. There are gloves: please wear them.'

'Thank you,' Brunetti said.

Bocchese pushed himself back from his desk, stood, and stretched his arms over his head.

Brunetti pointed to two masked technicians at a high counter, bent over a number of small glass vials.

'What's that?' Brunetti asked.

'The samples they took last night to see that it's his blood on the ground.' Saying that, Bocchese waved a hand towards the other table and sat again. Brunetti went to the long table and put on the plastic gloves, then pulled over the transparent plastic bag. The chain and Buddha were inside. He unzipped the bag and poured the contents out onto the desk. The Buddha fell face up. I'm sorry you couldn't protect him, Brunetti told the figure, but not aloud.

There was a still-damp zippered wallet containing thirty-three euros and seventeen cents. There were two crumpled paper tissues, a plastic pocket comb, and a small horse chestnut, its shine not at all affected by its time in the water. A second transparent zip envelope held a small cylindrical piece of what appeared to be ivory, shaped like a short segment of smooth, uncooked penne. The laboratory tag taped to the bag read, 'Found in watch pocket'. Brunetti looked at the object again, rolled it around in his palm for a few moments, until he realized it was a partially decomposed piece of bone: perhaps from a finger, perhaps from a toe. He placed his hand, palm up, on the table and studied the piece of bone, then picked it up with his right hand and walked back to Bocchese.

16

'Who's your expert on bones?' Brunetti asked the head technician.

With no hesitation, Bocchese called out to the men working at the back of the room: 'Rodella, could you come over here for a minute?'

A short officer with glasses who couldn't have been more than twenty turned from the group, said something to them, and walked over to Bocchese. He had an amiable face and clear blue eyes, slightly magnified by his lenses.

Brunetti got to his feet as the young man approached.

'You know Commissario Brunetti, don't you?' Bocchese asked.

'Yes, sir.'

'Good. He'd like to talk to you.'

The young man was obviously surprised; Brunetti watched him run through the things he'd done recently that might be misunderstood or misinterpreted.

'But … ' the young officer began.

Brunetti smiled at the much younger man and said, 'Don't worry, Officer. I only want to ask for your help.' He paused and let the effect of that word sink into the conversation. 'Lieutenant Bocchese tells me you're the bone expert.'

For a second, Rodella's face went blank, but then he must have repeated Brunetti's remark to himself, and he started to smile.

'Oh, that's not true, sir. I'm not an expert. I don't have the right equipment here to be really good.' As if he'd just said something that sounded very much like a complaint, Rodella quickly added, 'But they have those instruments in Mestre, and I can use them if I need to.'

'What sort of equipment?'

'A much better microscope, to start with,' he said with what sounded to Brunetti like real longing. 'That's basic.'

'What does it do?' Brunetti asked, although he had a pretty clear idea.

Rodella looked across at Bocchese, apparently asking if he could answer this man's questions.

Bocchese nodded and Rodella, with a nervous look at his superior, said, 'Well, sir, it lets you see finer structures more clearly.' His pause was awkward, but then he added, 'It's essential for ballistic examinations.'

Brunetti nodded, but said nothing. The pause expanded until the young man, in the face of Brunetti's continued silence, said, as though appealing to Holy Writ, 'You see it all the time on television, sir.'

When Brunetti still did not respond, Rodella said, 'Really, sir. You do.'

'Yes, I've been told that,' Brunetti said amiably.

'Did you want to know about the bone that was in the man's pocket, sir?' Rodella asked, like a salesman afraid that a client might leave without buying something.

'Yes.'

'It's a bone from a digit, Commissario. There's no question about that. I'd guess a finger, rather than a toe. I checked it online and looked in my pathology and anatomy books.'

Brunetti smiled, remembering when he was new to the job. 'Thank you, Officer. I'll put that in my report.'

'Thank you, sir,' said Rodella, and then, perhaps unable to think of anything else to do, saluted.

'Thanks again, Officer,' Brunetti said, and placed the fragment of bone on the table among the other things. Rodella went back to join the men at the table at the far end of the room.

Turning to Bocchese, Brunetti said, 'It's been some time since I've seen someone so enthusiastic about what he does.'

'Yes, he's a good boy,' Bocchese agreed. 'Bright, always stays until a job's finished, gets on with the others and – to give him even more credit – never lets them see how much smarter he is than they are.' Then, more reflexively, Bocchese added, 'I hope we can keep him.'

'Competition?'

'Mestre. There's a private laboratory there that wants him.' Seeing Brunetti's surprise, Bocchese explained: 'They've interviewed him twice.'

'Did he tell you that?'

'Yes.'

'Why?'

'Because he thought it would be dishonest not to tell me.'

After a moment's reflection, Brunetti said, 'I see.'

'But he wants to be a policeman. Ever since he was a kid, he's wanted to be a cop.' Then, recalling them to why they were talking, Bocchese asked, pointing to the transparent bag, 'You finished with this?'

Brunetti held up his phone and asked, 'Can I take a picture of the bone?'

'Yes.'

When that was done and the remnant was back in the envelope, Bocchese touched it through the plastic and asked, 'Why all the fuss about that?'

'Because it was in his watch pocket,' Brunetti said.

'What do you think that means?' the technician asked.

'I haven't the faintest idea.'

'But you want a photo?'

'Yes.'

'Why?'

'Because it has to mean something.'

Bocchese gave this a good deal of thought, reached down and touched the tube of bone, said he was going back to work, and left Brunetti to his own devices.

Brunetti decided that Griffoni would be the best person to discuss this with. She liked ambiguity and saw patterns or surprises where he did not.

Brunetti went upstairs and found the door to her miniature office closed, a sure sign that she was not there. He knocked anyway and was relieved to hear her call *'Avanti'* from within; he pressed down on the handle and pushed at the door. It did not move. He exerted more pressure, but no matter how hard he pushed down and forward, he could not open the door.

He heard a noise from inside, removed his hand, and took a step backwards. He saw the handle move down, and then the door opened outwards, towards him, revealing Griffoni, who saluted him crisply, then laughed out loud. For some reason, she was wearing her uniform, something she seldom did: he could see signs that a tailor of some skill had had his way with both the jacket and the skirt and that the flat-soled shoes were from Fratelli Rosetti and not Government Issue.

'Mamma mia,' Brunetti said. 'What did you do?'

Choosing to believe his question referred to her office and not her choice of clothing, she stepped to the side to reveal the room behind her. His first thought was that she'd discarded her desk, or someone had stolen it. But then he saw the back of her chair, protruding from a frameless doorway in the wall on the right side of the room. There'd been a locked door in a wooden frame, which she'd always believed led to a storeroom. But nay: it had led to an empty closet, large enough to hold her desk, which she had somehow angled into the empty space, leaving a gap of about three centimetres on each side.

'How did this happen?' he asked, making no attempt to disguise his delight.

'I asked Vianello to use his set of burglar's tools to open the closet door so I could finally see what was inside,' she explained, her pride evident.

'No one's supposed to know he has them,' Brunetti answered automatically.

'It's probably worse that he knows how to use them,' she replied.

Deciding to avoid further discussion, Brunetti took a step into the room and, not bothering to ask permission, pulled the door closed behind him, took the single unobstructed step to her chair and pulled it back and to the side, then leaned in to examine the space.

A lamp stood on the desk, in front of it a laptop. An extension cord led from the single socket in the room into the closet. There were bookshelves on the back wall: Griffoni would have to lean forward over the desk to place anything on them. Her bag was there. And her pistol.

'Very nice,' Brunetti said. 'Be careful you don't get lost.'

Griffoni nodded, then pulled the second chair back against the wall and sat, waving to Brunetti to use hers.

He turned it to face her and sat, then shifted the chair until the back touched the desk, giving him more room for his legs. 'What did you do with the door, and the frame?' he asked.

'After Riverre and Alvise took it off the hinges and removed the frame,' she began, not bothering to explain how this had come to pass, 'I asked them to carry it all out and prop it against the wall at the end of the corridor.' She paused a moment, then added, 'It's walnut, original to the building, seventeenth century.' When Brunetti said nothing, she pointed to the repainted wall where the frame had once been, saying, 'The frame's walnut, too: we scraped away some of the paint to see.'

He hadn't noticed a door in the corridor, nor any pieces of the frame stacked upright next to it. Brunetti, years ago, had bought six antique walnut doors to replace those in the apartment Paola and he had bought after their marriage. He said, 'If they are, they're probably valuable.'

'I know.'

'What will you do?'

Griffoni shrugged.

'Someone might steal it all if you leave it here in the building,' he warned, making a vague gesture towards the corridor.

'This is the Questura, Guido. And we're the police.'

'That doesn't mean someone won't recognize a door like that.' After giving it further thought, Brunetti added, 'Be hard to carry it downstairs and out to a boat, though.' When she merely shrugged again, he asked, 'Wouldn't it?'

'I told Foa and Vianello it was nothing important and asked them to help me get rid of it.'

'Rid of it?'

'To put it in the storeroom in my building until I could call Veritas and have the special garbage service come and take it all away.' She paused a moment or two and added, 'That's what I told them.'

'Did they believe you?' Brunetti, who knew her well, asked.

'I suppose so,' she answered, eyes on the empty door frame.

The conversation had become an enormously long carnival slide, leading Brunetti he knew not where. He could stop now and not learn more than he had just been told. That way, he'd not be a willing accessory, not be involved in the disappearance of government property.

'Is it still there?' he asked, taking his place in the child-sized seat just as she pushed it off.

She was surprised by the question and failed to hide it. 'I'm afraid not,' she said, not a trace of fear in her voice.

Now was the time. The tiny car he was riding in had slowed down as it entered a wide curve, and he could jump out, land on his feet, and walk quietly away, hands in his pockets, whistling an innocuous tune. Or he could remain where he was for the full ride.

'Where is it?'

'At Cristiano's,' she answered. 'I told you: he's a carpenter, in Dorsoduro, the one down the street from the framer.'

'Ah, Cristiano,' Brunetti said, nodding. 'Cristiano. What's it doing there?'

'He's stripping off six layers of paint, replacing the hinges with ones more suitable to its epoch, and then bringing the door and its frame to my apartment.' She smiled. 'It might take months. But there's no hurry.'

Brunetti paused a moment, then said mildly, 'No, there isn't.' Finally jumping free of the careening car, he asked, 'You've heard about the murder?'

'Yes.' Griffoni crossed her legs and sat up straighter in her chair. 'I've read the Carabinieri's report.'

Before she could ask, Brunetti said, 'I haven't had time to write mine yet.'

'Tell me.'

Brunetti told her first about Vianello's call, the scenes at the canal and in the courtyard, and then about what had been found by both Rizzardi and the technical squad. Finished with this, he backtracked to tell her about his brief contact with the murdered man, and ended by saying, 'That's all.'

She'd been taking notes as he spoke but flipped her notebook closed and asked, 'Now what?' When he failed to answer, Griffoni added, 'This is Venice, so shall I assume you know at least one of the people involved?'

Brunetti laughed. 'I went to school with the wife of the couple who own the place where he lived.' Remembering his conversation with Maurizio, Brunetti added, 'And I learned that the prioress in the convent beside them is generous.'

'And is she also going to turn out to be your long-lost cousin?'

'It's more likely she'll turn out to be a Filippina,' Brunetti answered. 'They seem to be the only ones who become nuns these days.'

Giving a sudden tremor, Griffoni had just enough breath to whisper, 'Better one of them than one of us.'

17

Brunetti decided to go and have a look at Palazzo Zaffo dei Leoni. He'd called the Questura on the way to the hospital that morning, ordering two uniformed officers to be sent there to cordon off the garden house in which the dead man was said to have been living. He had made it particularly clear that the officers were to stay inside the wall and see that no one other than the owners entered the property. He also asked that the crime-scene team be sent back to the *palazzo* as soon as possible.

Before he left the Questura, he asked for the phone number of one of the men stationed there and called him when he was nearing the *palazzo*. 'Pattaro, it's Commissario Brunetti. I'm just coming down the bridge from San Canzian. Could you open the door for me?'

'*Sì, Signore.*'

He made the same turns and found himself in front of the same tall wooden door. This time, it was opened quickly and by a man in police uniform whom he recognized. Another officer stood on the steps to the front door of the *palazzo*. Brunetti stepped in but remained near the entrance to the *calle*.

'Thanks, Pattaro,' he said. 'Anyone here?'

'A woman let us in. She said she was the owner. I saw a man with a cane going up the steps, but he didn't say anything to us.'

'How long have you been here?' Brunetti asked.

'Since half past nine, Commissario,' the other one answered. 'We had to wake them up.'

'What did you tell her?'

'That the man who lived here was dead.' He paused after saying this, as if eager to be questioned.

'How did she react?'

'It was strange, Commissario. She didn't say anything for a long time, just put her hand on her heart, and then she turned round and went back into the *palazzo*.'

Brunetti thanked him and told him he could rejoin his colleague while he had a look around the garden.

He walked to the right of the *palazzo*, where the most beautiful of the photos in the garden book had been taken. The photos, however, had not captured the current reality: Google had, although even its all-seeing eye could not have prepared Brunetti for what he encountered. A rectangle of wild grasses running the width of the property had been incompetently scythed, leaving behind a dead field of holes and tufts of beige, withered grass. About a metre from the side of the *palazzo*, the withered grass ran smack into a wall of overgrown plants that looked more jungle than garden to Brunetti, and faintly threatening. Nature imposes limits of height upon plants; in this case the various bushes and brambles had long since reached their highest point, only to collapse upon themselves or tilt to the sides and begin to work on the conquest of the lateral dimension, sending shoots out horizontally, seemingly in search of prey. A single path, no more than the sort of low trail left by feral animals, disturbed the clumps of grass and then disappeared under this maze of unfriendly, thorny plants.

Because of the shadows cast by the *palazzo* and the walls surrounding it, the ground was moist; drops of liquid still rested on the layers of dead leaves that refused to give up their grasp on the trunks. To the right of these enormous blotches of plants, Brunetti saw the beginnings of a stone wall, almost a metre high, that disappeared into the foliage, heading towards what must be the back of the property. On the other side of the wall, Brunetti saw a still-green lawn made for the playing of croquet or the enjoyment of champagne-graced picnics, for there began, Google Maps had told him, the garden of the sisters of the Order of Saint Benedict of Nursia, and there began the realm of order and routine and beauty. Although perhaps not of champagne-graced picnics.

On the left side of the *palazzo*, the evidence of abandonment and neglect was even stronger than on the right. The same plants, or their deformed progeny, stood in a pathless mass, the invisible earth smothered with matted decomposition, and all of it untouched, perhaps for years, even longer. While the garden on the right looked out of control, the one on the left looked dangerous.

Brunetti returned to the officers, who were still standing near the front door. Seeing Pattaro, he asked, 'Did you cordon off the garden house?'

'Yes, sir,' he said, his partner nodding in agreement.

'Did you go inside?'

'No, sir. We did what the regulations say: tape on the windows and outer doors. It was the first thing we did after I spoke to her.'

'Did she give you the keys?' he asked Pattaro.

'Yes, sir,' he said, reaching into the side pocket of his jacket.

He handed them to Brunetti, who said, 'It's close enough to the end of your shift. You can go back to the Questura if you like. I'll stay here until the crime-scene guys arrive. I'd like to walk around a little.'

'Thank you, Signore,' they both said, raising their hands as high as their chests by way of thanks.

When they were gone, Brunetti walked round to the right of the *palazzo* and saw the faint signs of an overgrown footpath leading towards the back of the property, where Google had told Brunetti that Rio dei Santi Apostoli ran, and where the water gate in the back wall of the garden must be. He followed the path for ten metres and came upon a small, one-storeyed brick house raised on a stone foundation about a metre high. The grass around it was shorter, but still well above his ankles.

Five steps led up to the door. As he'd been told, large X's of red-and-white tape had been drawn across the windows and doors, declaring the house a 'Crime Scene'. Brunetti walked back down the steps and around to the side. He looked through an X'd window and saw a single bed, a wardrobe, white walls, a wooden floor, and a chair at the foot of the bed. On a small table next to the bed, he saw a reading lamp and two books, neatly closed.

There was a small, windowless back door, X'd with the same tape.

He walked completely around the modest house, ever conscious of the menacing plants that loomed near it and, in some cases, above it. He peered in all of the windows and saw no sign of disorder, nor of violence. The kitchen table was entirely clear, as was the counter next to the sink. There was what appeared to be a living room with a bookcase and, against one wall, a desk holding a middle-aged laptop. There was also a very comfortable-looking easy chair with a floor lamp standing beside it. Should either of his children ever decide to run away from home, he thought, he would surely ask the person who lived in this house to replace whichever of them had chosen to leave.

Returning to the front, Brunetti went up the steps, pulling the keys from the pocket of his overcoat. Detaching the two strips of tape, he left them hanging from the frame. He took a package containing a pair of transparent plastic gloves, ripped it open, and put them on.

The second key worked, and the door opened without Brunetti having to find a way not to touch the handle. He entered directly into the living room. He stood and glanced around, careful to touch nothing, then passed slowly to the bedroom. He looked at the wardrobe – old, cedar, lovely – but did not open it. The single bed had a linen bedspread, neatly tucked under the pillow. He stood quietly in the room, asking it what sort of room it was and what kind of man had slept in it. The room remained silent, still; perhaps that was the answer.

While the other rooms were painted white, the living room was a very light green. It was not vulgar springtime, nor exhausted autumn, merely the sort of colour Nature would wear, not to the party, but around the house, something comfortable that could risk being splashed or soiled. He stood, but before the room could tell him anything, he heard a doorbell. After a moment, he realized it was a bell ringing in the *palazzo*, announcing someone on the other side of the wall.

He left the door to the house ajar and hurried down the path to the front of the *palazzo* and the door to the street. It was the crime squad, two men this time and without equipment or lights. Brunetti took them to the garden house and paused outside the door, explaining that the crime had not taken place here and asking them to look for anything out of place or anything that looked as though it was meant to be hidden.

He pushed open the door and followed them into the house, surprised by how much he already felt at home: perhaps because of the green.

The men divided up the rooms between them: one taking the bathroom and kitchen, the other the bedroom. That left Brunetti the living room. He walked over to the chair and sat in it and was immediately reminded of a fairy tale both children had been mad about when they were little, for this chair, too, was not too hard and not too soft, but just right.

The men were very quiet about their work: there could have been mice in the house, but surely not three men. A table to the left of the door supported a small wooden statue of the Buddha and a glass, half-filled with water, in front of him. A few wild flowers stood in the water, their heads bowed in acknowledgement of his sanctity. Three flat stones, sea-smooth, lay to the left of the Buddha, to the right, a pink seashell. Brunetti, struck by the serenity of the arrangement, pulled out his phone and took a picture of the altar, then turned it randomly around the room to record the tranquillity and quiet beauty of the dead man's home.

Brunetti went over and stood in front of the bookcase, wondering if the charm and individuality of the man who lived in this house would be repeated in his books. They, he quickly discovered, were divided into three languages: Italian, English, and what he took to be the round-lettered language of Sri Lanka. The titles of the books were so heterogeneous that he took three pictures of them to show how they lived happily segregated by language and then a fourth to show how easily they lived in peace together.

He pulled out one of the Sinhalese books and saw a very benevolent Buddha on the cover, and on the next, and on the next: not the same Buddha, but the same benevolence. He replaced them and took a step to the left and into English. He pulled down *Colonialism in Sri Lanka* and read a paragraph here and there; then he looked at *The Story of Ceylon*, its battered state leading him to check the date of publication, which was in the late fifties; *The Prabhakaran Saga* stood next to something called *The Broken Palmyra*. Brunetti read enough to see that they both dealt with the disastrous Tamil rebellion.

He closed them and put them on top of the others, then returned them all to the shelf.

The Italian books were divided into crime novels written in Italian, some translated from other languages, and books dealing with terrorism. There was a thick scrapbook with pamphlets and newspaper articles, most dating from about forty years ago. One was printed by an organization called End the Occupation of Italy and named, located, and provided detailed maps and photos of the American military bases in Italy. A small poster among the other documents stated, in red, that only armed violence could change the plight of workers. He replaced the scrapbook on the shelf and picked up one of the books, *A True History of Our Times*.

He read the introduction, which railed against the 'continuing oppression of our motherland' by the 'forces of international fascism' that were 'wearing the usual mask of the liberator who, to remain in power, gives stockings and chocolates to the women and children'.

Almost charmed by the rhetoric, Brunetti continued to read of 'the drugging of the masses with television', and the warning that readers must 'resist the temptation of consumerism and selfishness'. Brunetti glanced through two more, surprised to find in both the exhortation to extreme, even deadly, violence, then put the books back on the shelf, curious about how or why a Sri Lankan Buddhist would have these particular texts on his shelves.

Brunetti stepped away from the bookcase. He no longer believed, no longer even hoped, that the secret paper Revealing All would be stuck inside a book, so he went over to the computer. On the wall, just where the eyes of the person using the computer would fall, was a framed photo of a plump, dark-skinned woman in early middle age with soft eyes and streaks of white in her pulled-back hair. On either side of her stood, as if called to attention, two young men, as dark as she was and perhaps in their early twenties. They looked uncomfortable in navy blue jackets and ties, while the woman was fully at ease in a bold red blouse with long sleeves, a yellow shawl across her left shoulder. She smiled and was made lovely by it.

The keyboard was a revelation: single European letters on the top left of each key, and two Sinhalese letters, one on top of the other, on the right. Just as God was rumoured to have given dominion over animals to man, so too did this exchange rate requiring two letters in Sinhalese to equal one in English convey another form of dominion to the people of ABC.

The old laptop was closed, and Brunetti made no attempt to open it, even to turn it on. More out of a sense of obligation than anything else, he went into the kitchen, where the taller of the two officers was standing on a chair to search the top of the cupboards.

'You find any paper or plastic bags?' Brunetti asked.

'Below the sink, sir. Very neat and orderly, whoever lives here.'

Brunetti thanked him and said nothing about his use of the wrong tense. He found a paper shopping bag under the sink and took it back to the other room. He slipped a finger under the computer and then slid it into the bag. Taking it back to the kitchen, he told the man, who had moved the chair to the cabinets on the other side of the sink, 'Take this back when you go and see if anyone can get into it.'

'Just leave it there on the table, sir. We'll see Bocchese gets it.'

Brunetti thanked him and went back to the living room. He put himself in front of a window and allowed whatever it was that was gnawing at him to continue to do so. When had he ever seen a garden so ugly? The words 'garden' and 'ugly' were an oxymoron and should never stand together. How could they endure the sight of it? How could they live with those horrors so near them? Never being sure what might crawl out from under those bushes. Coming home at night and stepping on something that moved; hearing a rustling noise in front of them.

Suddenly the man from the kitchen was back, holding a plastic box in his hands, the sort of thing Paola used for leftovers, about the size of a cigar box.

'Look at this, sir,' the man said, holding it out to Brunetti. The top was a cheerful blue, the body transparent. Even before he opened it, Brunetti saw the money, the red and the blue of ten- and twenty-euro notes, and saw there would be no great amount inside.

He set the box on the table and pulled off the cover. There were a few ten-euro notes on top of the pile, and, at a glance, Brunetti guessed there might be a few hundred euros, no more than that.

He saw a flash of red beneath the euro notes and fingered them aside, revealing the corner of a stiff piece of burgundy cardboard.

He removed the banknotes to expose 'PASSPORT' and, below that, 'DEMOCRATIC SOCIALIST REPUBLIC OF SRI LANKA'. Had the circumstances been different, Brunetti might well have asked himself, 'Interesting political trio, isn't it?' but in the aftermath of violent death, the thought did not approach his mind.

He opened the passport and saw the dead man, alive now, not smiling. Brunetti looked away. Inesh Kavinda, born in Colombo, fifty-two years ago. The stamps showed that he had travelled back to Sri Lanka six years earlier and stayed four weeks, and again the previous year for the same amount of time.

'Where was it?' he asked the officer, remembering that his name was Donati.

'Above the stove, sir. There's supposed to be a fan in there, but someone took it out. The filter is so dirty you can't see through it, so you'd never know the fan's not there.'

Brunetti nodded approvingly. He was always pleased when people had hidey-holes in their homes. He wondered why so many of them were in the kitchen.

'What should I do with it, sir?'

'Take it back when you're ready to go and give it to Bocchese, along with the computer. Then stay there while he counts the money and you watch, then both of you write the total on separate pieces of paper, sign them, and put it all in the box, which goes into Bocchese's safe.'

He saw the expression on the man's face and said, 'Donati, it's to protect you and Bocchese. This way, there's no question about how much money was in it when it got to the Questura.'

Donati smiled and said, 'Of course, Commissario.' After a pause, he said, 'I'd never steal anything from a dead man anyway.'

'How'd you know he was dead?' Brunetti asked casually.

'Someone at the Questura told me, sir.'

Brunetti nodded. It had been some time since there'd been a murder in the city, at least one where the criminal didn't put down the weapon and call the police.

Brunetti shoved the plastic box to the centre of the table and went back to the bookcase. Something had set off a strange noise in his memory when he looked at the books, and he let his mind float towards them, and then away.

He looked at the titles on the bindings and concluded that it made sense for books about the history of Sri Lanka to be there. If he excluded from consideration those, then he was left with crime novels – which he dismissed – and books discussing the strange resurgence of terrorism in Italy in the eighties. It was a bit like being asked to find where the cat was hiding in the drawing of a tree.

He remembered that sometime during the years considered in the books in front of him, his father had emerged from the long sadness that his life had become after he learned of the reappearance of the Red Brigades. His family, accustomed to his passionate commitment to the Left, was astonished to hear him condemn the attacks against civilians as 'murders' and those who committed them as 'assassins'.

When questioned, Brunetti's father had said he knew the type, had known them all his life: children of the rich who wanted attention. 'Just wait,' he'd said one night after dinner, his rage gone, leaving behind only disgust. 'Just wait. In forty years, they'll all be lawyers and bankers and professors and will be voting Christian Democrat.' His father didn't know that the Christian Democrats would experience political rapture in the nineties and cease to exist; as for the rest of what he'd said, Brunetti thought he had been right.

But what interest would a Sri Lankan have in any of this?

18

'Excuse me,' a woman's voice, more than a bit peremptory, said from behind him.

He turned and saw Gloria Forcolin standing inside the door. 'Are you the pol—' she began to ask, but seeing Brunetti there, she furrowed her brows and said, 'Guido? What are you doing here?' Then, as memory struck her, she said, 'Your father-in-law's birthday?'

He smiled, pleased that she remembered, although the dinner had been at least four years ago.

'And you were wearing a lilac-coloured dress and a pair of shoes that made Paola sick with envy,' Brunetti answered, relieved that old friendship provided a buffer for this meeting.

She was an attractive woman, short and slender, with delicate, lovely hands that he remembered, and curly dark hair she wore as short as a boy's. He recalled, for some reason, that she knew a great deal about volcanoes, but he couldn't remember why that was.

He nodded. 'I'm sorry we meet again like this,' he said.

'I've known forever that you were in the police,' she said, 'but I didn't … I suppose I never gave any thought to what it is you actually did.'

She had used '*tu*', and Brunetti stuck with it, saying, 'You've probably never had the police in your house. Most people don't.'

She looked at the floor, then out the window, and asked. 'Is it true about Inesh?'

'Yes. I'm afraid it is.'

She shook her head a few times and waved the possibility away with her hand. 'Was it a robbery?' she asked, then quickly denied the possibility by saying, 'But that's impossible. He didn't have anything.' As if to give him proof, she waved the same hand around the room again, to the books and to the absence of almost anything else. 'Everything he earned, he sent back to his family.'

'They're in Sri Lanka?' Brunetti asked.

'Yes. His wife and two sons,' she said. Then, as though it made his death somehow matter more, she added, 'She's a teacher. The boys are at university.'

'Had he been here long?'

'I really don't know,' she said after some time. Then, looking back in the direction of the *palazzo*, she said, 'But he must have. He spoke good Italian when we met.'

'How was that?'

She turned to look at him then, obviously confused: it was evident that she did not understand why he would be asking this question. 'Why do you want to know?'

Had Brunetti had the least suspicion that she was somehow involved in the man's murder, his answer would have been both sharp and sarcastic, but as it was, he believed that she had yet to accept that the man was dead and not just absent. In this case, the best response was to remain silent and let her understand why it was necessary.

Statue-still, she continued to look at him, her face tight with confusion. He saw it hit her, heard the intake of breath and the muttered '*Oddio*' and then a noise that was not a word.

Brunetti accepted opera as a source of entertainment, but he was not really a fan, however many times he'd trailed along, obedient to Paola's enthusiasm. He remembered now how he had seen a singer whose character, given devastating news, tried to begin her aria but managed only three glorious, astonished, bewildered 'Ah's' before she found her voice and choked out, '*Addio, Roma*' and began to sing of failure and loss and desolation.

'Is it true that he was murdered?' she whispered.

'Yes, I'm sorry to tell you, it is.'

'I don't see how that can be possible,' she said and then suddenly cast her eyes around the room. 'Guido, can you help me?' she asked, taking a staggering step towards him.

He grabbed her forearms and held her upright, so that she was almost suspended from them. Slowly, matching his steps to the small ones she could manage, he guided her to the chair against the wall and kept his hands on her arms until she was seated. Her face had suddenly gone white, and she was forced to lean her head back against the wall.

Brunetti turned away from her and went to stand by the window, looking out at the horrid garden. Again, he was struck by the incongruity. He did not understand why the dead man would have the books he did, nor did he understand how he could live in such a tasteful, however sparse, environment and endure looking at something as ugly as this garden, menacing and untamed on all sides of the house.

'Why is the garden the way it is?' Brunetti asked, speaking without turning to her.

'What?' she asked, not as though the question puzzled her but as if she had not heard it.

'Why is the garden so ugly?' Brunetti turned to her to get her attention. He waved his hand around the room. 'This room is beautiful. It's simple, and everything in it is beautiful. And the other rooms as well. So why is the garden so hideous? In the years he's been here, he could have done something, cleared away something, planted something.'

She started to speak, stopped and considered it for a moment, then said, 'It wasn't his responsibility.'

Brunetti stopped himself from sounding impatient and waited until calm had returned to him, when he said, 'I don't think it matters what his responsibility was. There's no questioning his good taste, at least in this house. How could he … ' Brunetti was going to finish that sentence with '… live with that garden all around him?' but found the word 'live' a risky choice and so changed it to '… bear to look at that garden?'

'He told me he needed a place to live. It never occurred to me that he'd have any interest in the garden.'

'Didn't you?' Brunetti asked, removing all suggestion of criticism from his voice.

'No, not really.'

'And your husband?' He tried to make his voice light, merely curious.

'Even less. I think he once said something to Inesh, telling him not to bother with the garden.'

'Has it always been like this?'

'No. Renato's aunt had two permanent gardeners, but they died ages ago, about the time she did, and Renato never replaced them.' She raised a hand, as if to signify the way time changes things.

'And it became like this?' Brunetti asked, waving his arm at the invading foliage.

'From the time I've known Renato, it's been pretty much the way it is now.' She paused and gave him a long, confused look. 'Why are you so concerned about it?'

Brunetti paused, weighing up how much he could say to her, then answered, 'It's to keep you distracted until you've accepted his death, and then we can begin to talk about him.'

'Inesh?' she asked.

'Yes.'

She pulled her head away from the wall and sat up straighter in the chair, but made no move to leave it. 'He was a very good man, Guido,' she said, and then asked, 'We can continue with first names, can't we?'

'If you don't mind,' Brunetti answered.

'It might be easier. I've never had a conversation like this.'

'Few people do, I suppose,' he told her.

She nodded at that and said, 'Thank God.'

'What can you tell me about him?' Brunetti asked, going to sit in the easy chair with the reading light. He took out his notebook and pen and found the beginning of a blank page.

'I found him at my door.'

Surprised, Brunetti could think of nothing to say.

'One evening when I came home, I found him lying in the street. He'd managed to prop himself up against the wall. He held up a hand when he saw me coming and said, *"Aiutami, Signora."* I knelt down beside him and asked what had happened. He said he'd been attacked by two men. One knocked him down, and when he tried to get up, the other one kicked him in the side of his head. They took the money in the pockets of his jacket.'

'What did you do?' Brunetti asked dispassionately.

'I took him inside the garden and down here,' she said, waving her hand around the room. 'It was very different then. No one had lived in here for years.'

'And then?' Brunetti asked, turning a page.

'I called a friend, a doctor, who came and put stitches in his cheek and head, then gave him something for the pain and told him that he was to ask me to call him if his vision was cloudy in the morning.'

Intentionally, Brunetti did not ask the doctor's name. It hardly mattered. Instead, he asked, 'And then?'

'And then I got him a blanket from the bedroom and told him he could sleep on the old sofa that was in here and we'd talk in the morning.' Before Brunetti could ask for details, she said, 'The place was a mess, but the water was still working, so he could at least have something to drink.'

'Do you remember when this happened?'

She thought about this for a while and finally said, 'About eight years ago, in the late summer sometime.'

'Has he been here since then?'

'Yes.'

'Why did you let him stay?' Brunetti asked.

'He was a very polite, kind man – I could see that – and he'd been attacked and robbed. He spoke Italian quite well, and, as I told you, he seemed an honest, decent man. I ... we decided to treat him ... kindly, I suppose you could say.' Pressing her hands together, she said, 'We did the right thing.' He noticed she had chosen to remain in the plural.

'You say this house has been transformed? Has he done much work for you?'

'Just look around and you'll see what he's done. Believe me, it was a ruin: animals were living inside. He put in new windows, a new roof.'

'By himself?'

'Yes.' Then, after a second, 'Sort of.'

Brunetti considered these things for a few moments and asked, 'Do you, or did he, have any idea of why he was attacked?'

'He said he was robbed by two men who spoke very bad Italian. Luckily, he had left his passport with the friend where he was staying.'

'Why was he attacked?'

'Who knows? He hardly looked like a rich person, or a tourist. What troubled him was that he had two hundred euros in his wallet which he was going to send to his family. That's why he resisted them. He told me he knew he shouldn't have done it.'

'Did you believe him?'

She gave him a sharp glance and said, 'He was bleeding into a towel when he said it. Of course I believed him.'

'Why did you let him stay here so long?'

Her response came with no hesitation of any sort. 'Because he was a poor devil, without a home, without a visa to stay here, and with little chance of having either.' She paused after saying this and looked at Brunetti to see his response.

'It's what one does,' Brunetti said.

This time, her pause was even longer before she said, 'Even though it's illegal?'

Brunetti, his eyes on his notebook, turned a page, then turned back noisily as if to check something, and turned it again. He looked across at her and asked politely, 'Excuse me, Gloria. Did you say something?'

She closed her eyes for a moment, then said, 'The first thing he did was clean all the junk out of this place and contact the garbage men to take it away, even an old wardrobe that was falling apart. It was impressive that he knew how to do that, how to contact them and what to say. Then he washed everything, and when the walls were dry, he painted it all.

'Later, before autumn came, he said he'd put in new windows and a new roof if we'd pay for the materials and for a man to help him.'

'What did you do?'

'We gave him the money.'

'And?'

'And in a week and a half, they put in windows and a new roof.'

'Did you have to get permission to do it?'

That stopped her. He watched her consider lying to him and then decide to tell the truth. 'No. The materials came when it was still dark. They both worked twelve hours a day, and they had it done in about ten days, as I told you.'

Brunetti's father had often said he'd always have work because he was willing to take less money than other workers. As he grew older, Brunetti was often reminded how wise his parents had been.

'Anything else?' he asked.

'When they were done, he gave me a receipt with all the expenses listed and the number of hours his assistant had worked.' She looked at Brunetti as she said this and shook her head in amazement. 'And he gave me back the money he hadn't spent.'

'What did you do?'

'I refused to take it, of course,' she said brusquely, a criticism of his failure to understand even this little.

Brunetti turned another page and asked, 'Did he have friends in Venice?'

'Yes. Sri Lankans. They came here occasionally, perhaps once a month. He always asked if it would be all right for him to have some friends visit him.'

'Do you know anything about his life?'

'Almost nothing. He lived here in this house, did pretty much whatever we asked him to do in the *palazzo*.'

'Was he paid for that?'

'Yes. As time passed and he became more helpful – and more necessary – I insisted we pay him something every month.'

Brunetti found it interesting that she did not say how much they paid him, and he did not ask. 'In what way had he become necessary?'

'My husband ... ' she began, and then seemed to forget what they were talking about.

Brunetti said nothing and kept his head bent over his notebook.

'He's never been interested in practical work.' She stopped and gave Brunetti a questioning glance. 'I don't know what else to call it. So Inesh took over the care of our house and this one.'

Brunetti nodded; it certainly made sense.

'Then, two years ago, my husband had a stroke. A mild one, thank God. It took his left leg and weakened it, left it permanently unreliable.'

'Nothing else?' Brunetti asked.

'No, nothing – the doctors assured us of that. His mind wasn't affected at all.'

'Thank God for that at least,' Brunetti said, meaning it. 'How old is he?'

'The age when things like this happen to a person.'

'Is he still teaching?'

'Yes. That's why I mentioned Inesh. He accompanies him to the university, or to the library, three times a week and goes back to get him in the afternoon.' When she saw Brunetti's expression, she explained: 'He also needs Inesh's help to move about the city: getting on and off the vaporetto, crossing bridges.' That said, she put a hand to her forehead and said, 'My God, how long do people keep using the present tense?'

Because it sounded like a real question, Brunetti said, 'It differs. But it happens.'

Leaving her hand in place, she said, 'He was such a kind man.'

'Did you know him well?'

'No, not really. He told me the names of his wife and sons, but he never talked about them unless I asked.'

'What did he tell you?'

'As I've already told you, his wife is a teacher, and the sons are at university.'

'Did he ever talk about his life here?'

'Here?'

'In Italy. In Venice.'

'No,' she said with a small shake of her head. 'And it didn't seem right for me to ask him, to seem to pry.'

Brunetti turned to a fresh page and asked, 'Did he ever introduce any of his friends to you?'

'Only the man who helped him with the roof. He seemed to be a friend.'

'Do you know his name?'

'I think it might have been Anvith or Anvis; something like that.'

'Is that a first name or a surname?'

'I think first,' she said. 'Wait a minute – it might be on that receipt he gave me for the roof.' Pushing herself forward in the chair, she asked, 'Would you like me to see if I can find it?'

'Yes, I would,' Brunetti said, realizing that this was the first piece of information he'd obtained that might be of use.

She pushed herself to her feet, held up a hand to him, and left. He saw that she was heading towards the *palazzo*. Brunetti stood and went back to the bookcase, still unsatisfied and discontented that he could not find a reason why the material on Italian terrorism should be there. He pulled out the scrapbook with the pamphlets and posters and took it back to the chair with him. He opened it and leafed through, reading a sentence here, a paragraph there. How dated the language was, he realized, as though the familiar dreams of youth were being expressed in a foreign language or an outdated code. 'Suffering of the working class', 'imperialist greed', 'oppression', 'tyranny', 'exploitation', 'middle class', 'abuse'.

He closed the scrapbook and replaced it on the shelf. He noticed, tagged to the corner, 'Libreria dei Miracoli'. Of course, the shop in Campo Santa Maria Nova.

He heard the door open and looked up; she had a half-sheet of paper in her hand. 'I found it. But there's just the first name, "Anvith". Here, look,' she said, handing the paper to him. Before Brunetti could ask, she said, 'Inesh refused to take anything for his work. He said he'd agreed to take care of the house for us, and this was part of that agreement.' Her hand with the paper fell to her side. 'He wouldn't hear of it,' she said softly.

Indeed, Anvith had been paid 840 euros for ten days' work, twelve hours a day. Brunetti's calculation was instant: seven euros. For an hour's work. Brunetti had no idea what Paola paid their cleaning lady, but he knew that only the desperate would work for that little.

If you had no work and no permission to stay in the country, you would work for that, perhaps even consider it an honest amount. After all, you didn't have to pay into the system and see part of it taken away in taxes, to be returned on some far-off day when you received your pension, or had some paid back when you went to the hospital and made an appointment for a CAT scan that they'd give you in eight months, unless, of course, you'd like to pay as a private patient, in which case you could have it on Thursday afternoon.

He clapped mental hands in front of his face and told himself to stop thinking like that. As his parents had both known, ever since the world was the world, the big lived well and the small did not.

He gave her back the paper and stopped himself from asking who had decided what they would be paid for their work. Instead, he went back to the window, opened it and looked at the frame, closed it, opened it, and closed it again. He turned to her and said, 'They did a good job.'

She shrugged. 'My father's a builder, and that's what he said.' Then, laughing, she added, 'But he also said he would have done it for less.'

While her mood was still positive, Brunetti said, 'I'd like to speak to your husband.'

Her smile faded. 'Why?'

'From what you told me, it sounds as if the two of them spent a good deal of time together.' She tilted her head up, preparing to speak, but he kept on. 'It would take them a long time to get to the university or to the library and back. So I assume they talked a fair bit.'

'I don't know,' she said. 'Renato's never said anything about it to me. That is, he never mentioned any subject they talked about.'

'I'd still like to speak with him, get a better idea of Inesh and what he was like,' Brunetti said in his most amiable voice.

She looked quickly at her watch and said, 'This really isn't a good time for Renato. He usually lies down for a few hours about now.'

Brunetti said nothing. 'Perhaps another day?' he suggested, as though speaking of the inconsequential.

'Yes, that sounds better,' she said, unable to disguise her relief.

'Then I'll thank you for your patience and say again I'm sorry to meet in such circumstances.'

She walked over to the door with him and held it after he opened it. Neither suggested another meeting, and Brunetti started on his way to Campo Santa Maria Nova.

19

Luckily, Brunetti had anticipated being delayed and had called Paola while she was still at the university to explain that he could not be home for lunch. She reminded him that the children were at their grandparents' for lunch, so the two of them could eat whenever he arrived. She'd just 'throw something together'.

All pressure of time removed by her remark, he decided to stop in the bookstore in Campo Santa Maria Nova. When he entered the *campo*, he saw the proprietor at the door of his shop, wearing his ski cap, although the day hardly warranted it. Carlo recognized him and nodded in his direction, then, as if remembering something, he quickly retreated into his shop. A moment later, he emerged holding a book in the air and waving it at Brunetti, all but shouting across the *campo*, 'I've got your Pausanias for you, Dottore.' Although the bookseller was not a big man, his voice filled the *campo* and caused heads to turn.

Had Pausanias been a hunted criminal, Brunetti could not have been happier to learn that he had been found. In truth, Pausanias was a second-century Greek geographer, references to whom Brunetti had been reading for decades. He had, over the years, collected most of the Nibby translation except for volume III, containing books 7, 8, and 9, and had held off beginning to read it until he was sure to have the entire work, and this Carlo had finally found for him.

Carlo pushed the book into Brunetti's hands and stood back to watch his joy, his own face lit up by the delight known to those who love books. Brunetti opened it and found the title page: *Descrizione della Grecia Volume Tre*. This was surely it. He turned the page, read the words there, and stared across at Carlo. 'It's a stolen book,' he said in surprise.

'What?' Carlo said, his face falling in shock.

'Look,' Brunetti said, passing the open book to him. He watched Carlo's face as he read the page following the title page: 'New York Public Library. Astor, Lenox and Tilden Foundation'.

'*Oddio*,' Carlo said, and then, with angry contempt, 'They stole it from a library.'

Brunetti took the book back and paged through it slowly to give Carlo a moment to get over his indignation. When sufficient time had passed, Brunetti looked up, all jokes gone. 'I wanted to speak to you about something else.' Inesh was a reader who had much-read books on his shelf: if anyone in the neighbourhood knew him, it would be the person who had sold him those books.

Carlo responded to the tone as well as to the words and asked, 'The dead man?'

'Yes.'

'Inesh,' the book dealer said, as if he had to make it clear.

'You knew him?'

'Yes.'

'Could you tell me about him?'

Carlo looked off to the people seated on the benches facing his shop, but none of them seemed ready to help him answer this question. 'There's not much I can say, Commissario. He bought books from me for years.' Carlo gave a small snort of laughter. 'You could almost say his Italian came from what he found here.'

'The crime novels?'

Carlo's surprise was easily read. 'How do you know that?'

'He still has quite a few of them,' Brunetti explained, leaving it to Carlo to understand where he had seen them and realizing too late that he'd used the present tense.

'He'd come in every few months and give me back the ones he'd read and take the same number of new ones,' Carlo continued. 'It didn't matter which ones they were – he just wanted to learn the words and the grammar.' He glanced again at the people on the benches and then added, 'I eventually turned it into a lending library for him: I'd let him pay me fifty cents a book, no matter how long he kept them. He'd bring them all back at the same time, take twenty more, give me ten euros, and then come back when he'd read those.' His face softened, and he looked up at Brunetti. 'Each time, his Italian sounded easier to me, more fluent.'

Carlo's face tightened, humour disappeared. 'It's horrible.'

Brunetti knew that neighbourhoods are small, and in a city where everyone pretty much knows everyone, everyone in a neighbourhood also knows something about everyone. 'Yes, it is.'

Brunetti paused, but Carlo, not at all to Brunetti's surprise, displayed no lurid curiosity about the other man's death. He did no more than close his eyes and give the most minimal shake of his head. Very softly, he said, 'He lived a good life. I hope he rises to an even better one.'

'That sounds very Buddhist,' Brunetti said.

Carlo was obviously surprised by the remark. 'I went to school with the sisters until I was twelve, Signore. They taught me to wish that for those who die.'

'Of course,' Brunetti said, recalling that the sisters who had taught him for his first years had faced life with a considerably narrower vision.

Brunetti thought again of the books on Inesh's shelf and said, 'I've seen his books and can't make any sense of them.'

'Nobody's books make sense,' Carlo said in a soft voice. 'Unless they don't read much. Then they just stuff the shelves with classics and think they can fool people.'

Brunetti nodded, having often seen examples of this.

'Real readers read lots of books about different things,' Carlo said. Then, tapping Brunetti's shoulder, 'You, for example.'

'Thank you,' Brunetti answered, instinctively taking this as a compliment. 'What did he read?'

Carlo smiled at the question. 'As I told you, the crime books were to improve his Italian. The only time he commented further was to say that he couldn't understand why people would want to read them.' He gave a sudden grin and a snort of surprise. 'He told me he'd tried Westerns, but they were worse.'

How nice, Brunetti thought, that Carlo would remember this. Making no mention of that, he asked, 'And the books about terrorism? And the pamphlets and news clippings in the scrapbook?'

Confusion passed across Carlo's face and he said, 'I don't know anything about news clippings.' He thought for a moment and then added, 'The scrapbook came from the father of a friend of mine; well, from my friend. His father died a few years ago, and my friend found that in his papers: things his father had read and liked, and I suspect a few he had written himself. My friend offered it all to me, and I bought it to do him a favour, really, without bothering to look at it. Inesh bought it in the last few months as well as the books.'

'The struggle against capitalism, that sort of thing?' Brunetti asked, then smiled and added, 'I think that was the fashion some years ago,' recalling his own political enthusiasms during his first years at university.

'If you were a bank director, it probably wasn't,' Carlo said dryly.

It took Brunetti some time to process this, after which he said, 'I wonder what's worse, discovering that your father was a terrorist, or could have been, or finding that your father had another wife and family in Palermo?'

'I'm not sure there's much difference,' Carlo said, 'but I've always lived in the North.'

Brunetti smiled and returned to the topic of the papers in the scrapbook. 'I haven't read any of them yet, only glanced at them. Do you have any idea why Inesh was interested in them?'

'I asked him the same thing,' Carlo said. 'He told me he was curious about how people who have as much freedom as we do and who have such wealth could think like that and want to destroy it all.' He looked away and then back at Brunetti. 'May I say something that might be stupid, Commissario?'

'Of course,' Brunetti said, though he doubted that would happen. He'd seen the books Carlo chose to read in the back room that served as his office.

'I think it was because he was a Buddhist,' the book dealer said. 'We talked about religion now and again, and he really did believe it: do no evil, behave well, and seek enlightenment.' He paused here. 'So maybe he was trying to understand the opposite side. Or something like that.'

'That's your conclusion?' Brunetti asked.

'Yes.'

'Doesn't sound at all stupid to me.' He paid for his book, which Carlo placed carefully in a paper bag.

Brunetti had already started to leave when Carlo called his name.

'Yes?' Brunetti asked, stopping and turning.

'The last time I saw him, I asked him, almost as a joke, if he was any nearer to understanding evil.'

'And what did he say?'

'It took him a long time to answer, but finally he said he had discovered it much closer to him than he thought possible but that it still made no sense to him.'

'Did you ask him what he meant?' Brunetti asked, never patient with what he lumped together as Eastern Thinking.

'No. But he mentioned that the pamphlets kept him awake at night.'

'Odd thing to say,' Brunetti told him, then thanked him for finding the book, and started home for lunch.

Paola, it turned out, had thrown together fusilli with yellow peppers and peas, followed by grilled *rombo* smothered in mixed vegetables, filling Brunetti with great relief at having so easily avoided another working lunch of *tramezzini*. Instead, he ate a large helping of pasta, most of the vegetables, and left Paola the larger portion of *rombo*, a fish she adored.

During lunch, he told her about the murder of Inesh and his own conversations with Gloria and Carlo.

'What sort of man did he sound like when you spoke to him on Monday?' Paola asked while mopping up the olive oil puddled on her salad plate.

'No one special,' Brunetti said. 'I asked a question, and he gave a polite response.'

'Yet this is the same man who told Carlo that he had discovered ... what did you say? ... "Evil closer to home"?' She abandoned the bread in the centre of her plate and turned to Brunetti to say, 'I'm afraid his reading sounds more than a bit melodramatic to me, Guido,' then returned her attention to the bread.

Thinking aloud, Brunetti said, 'It could be his response to the subjects he was reading about: the slaughter of the Tamils, all those crime novels, even the trash in those pamphlets.' Hearing himself say this, Brunetti understood more clearly what had made him uncomfortable about the books he'd seen on the shelves: they were morally at odds with the man described to him by Gloria Forcolin and Carlo, as well as with the faint sense Brunetti had had of him in their very brief meeting.

After a short pause, he went on. 'I can't understand why he'd have those books and papers in his home, the same place where there was a small altar to the Buddha with tiny fresh flowers.' When Paola didn't answer, Brunetti added, 'It doesn't make sense at all.' Another thought occurred to him and he said, 'And the Benedictine sisters are just on the other side of a low wall, working in their garden, growing flowers, praying.' And then it came back to him, the essence of the rule of Saint Benedict. He said it aloud: *'Ora et labora.'*

He reached over and touched Paola's arm to get her attention. 'That's what's wrong. "Pray and work".'

'I beg your pardon, Guido. You've lost me entirely.'

'That's the sort of thing his bookcase should have held, or the Buddhist equivalent of it. All right, all right, we can exclude the crime books: he wanted to learn Italian. And maybe the histories of Sri Lanka. But the pamphlets are distilled madness.'

'You didn't think that when I met you,' she said.

Caught off guard and knowing that her airtight memory would recall every word he'd said in praise of political protest when they were at university, he defended himself by saying, 'I listened to people and talked to them: you know that. But you also know I was never persuaded, however interested I might have been. Violence frightened me, even then.'

He watched her checking the memory files until she finally said, 'Yes, that's true. I remember you had an argument with Ugo Satta. If I recall, he kept saying that workers had the right to destroy factories.'

Brunetti was so astonished that he could only say, 'Ugo Satta,' and then again, 'Ugo Satta.' The sound of the name set him off into clouds of laughter.

'What's so funny?'

It took Brunetti a moment to stop laughing, but when he started to talk, he was overcome by another fit of laughter. Finally he said, 'He's teaching business law at Bocconi,' and went off into another fit of laughter. 'My father was right.'

Conversation was impossible after that, for when Paola tried to remind him of their student days, which seemed to shine in her mind with perfect clarity, Brunetti would start to laugh. Finally he pointed to his watch, put on his coat, and left the house to go back to the Questura.

On the way there, he tried to recall some of the students he'd admired – he confessed this, but only to himself – when he was fresh at the university. It has not just been Ugo Satta, but also Umbaldo Nucci and Gabriele Cifoni. And where were these two now, the stars of his class? They'd fallen off the screen of his interest decades ago. He thought he'd heard that Cifoni had moved to someplace odd, or with an odd language: Hungary or Finland. To run a mine? It came in a flash: it was Canada, and it was a nickel mine. And Nucci? When Brunetti had last heard of him, Nucci had been appointed director of a multinational that was the largest importer of meat from Eastern Europe.

And so the firebrands of social equality and universal justice had moved on to a different world. As had he, as had he, Brunetti reminded himself. Just as his father, that disillusioned idealist, had predicted.

Brunetti found Rizzardi's and Bocchese's reports in his computer, copies having also been sent to Griffoni and Vianello. He started with the crime-scene report, sighing with relief when he read that the missing part of Inesh's finger had been found and returned, and his body was again intact.

Looking up at a sound from the door, he saw both Griffoni and Vianello standing there and waved them in; Griffoni turned to close the door, while Vianello pulled a second chair in front of Brunetti's desk. Vianello, who seemed strangely nervous or excited, stood behind the chair but did not sit.

'What is it, Lorenzo?' he asked.

'She's back,' he said, smiling with what looked like relief.

It took Brunetti a moment to realize what he meant. 'Signorina Elettra?'

'Yes,' Griffoni chimed in. 'We just saw her in the hallway.'

'But it's been such a short time,' Brunetti said, then asked, 'Why did she come back so soon?'

Griffoni rubbed at her eyebrow. 'She said she got bored. It was all so easy.'

'An international meeting about spyware?' Brunetti asked.

'That's what she told me.'

'God help us all,' Vianello whispered.

After a long pause, Brunetti, realizing this was not the moment for reflections upon Signorina Elettra's capabilities, asked, 'Did you have time to read the reports?'

They both nodded.

'Good,' he said. 'As it happens, I met the dead man only a day before he was killed,' he said to Vianello, and then explained why he had bothered to go past the *palazzo* and ring the bell.

'How did he seem?' Vianello asked.

'Busy, I'd say. He answered my question, said good day, and closed the door.'

'Not much else he could do,' said Vianello, then asked, 'You have any idea what it's worth?' proving that he was Venetian.

'Millions, I suppose,' Brunetti answered. 'I haven't been inside the *palazzo*, but someone told me it was more than a thousand square metres. And there's a lot of land on both sides, but it's all grown out of control. Whoever buys it will have to dig the whole thing up and replant it.'

Griffoni looked from one to the other, as if trying to assess whether this latest discussion of Venetian real estate had ended. At a nod from Brunetti, she said, 'I read Rizzardi's report. It's terrible.' She stopped, incapable of saying more.

'The hands?' asked Vianello. Brunetti's hands clenched.

She nodded, choosing to say nothing about the finger, for which Brunetti gave silent thanks.

Neither of the men spoke for some time. Eventually, Griffoni asked Brunetti, 'What did you learn about him?'

'Sri Lankan. In his fifties. Married, two adult sons. Worked for the owners of the *palazzo*. Spoke good Italian, was not known to the authorities ...'

'Does that mean he was never arrested?' Vianello asked.

'Yes, but it also means he had no *permesso di soggiorno* or work permit, no anything.'

'He was here how long?' Griffoni enquired, pausing over her notebook.

'He started living with them about eight years ago, but he already spoke adequate Italian.'

'You mean living in the *palazzo*?' Griffoni asked.

'No,' Brunetti answered. 'He lived in a small house in the garden. Apparently, he pretty much rebuilt it while he was living there.'

'Was he told to do that?' Vianello asked.

'No, I think he wanted to live in a better place, and it was certainly to the advantage of the owner to have it made more liveable,' Brunetti said.

'Was he working anywhere?' Vianello asked.

'I don't know, but certainly not recently.' Seeing their expressions, he continued. 'The man who owns the *palazzo* had a stroke two years ago, and he needed someone to help him move around in the city. Before that, there might have been other jobs – I don't know.' He paused before adding, 'She said she paid him.'

'How was it that he was living here, in Venice, or in Italy?' Griffoni said.

'Is that a real question, Claudia?' Brunetti asked.

She smiled. 'I suppose not. He was just one of scores of thousands.'

'At least,' Vianello agreed. Then he said, going back to practical things, 'So we have to find out about anyone who might have known him.'

'And get his phone records,' said Griffoni. 'Was one found with him?'

'No,' Brunetti answered. 'At least, there's no mention of it in the report from Bocchese's men.'

'The killer might have thrown it into the canal,' Vianello suggested.

'Which shows a certain premeditation, I'd say,' Griffoni added.

'Perhaps leave that sort of thinking for the prosecutor,' Brunetti said, trumping them both.

'He had a computer. Bocchese has it now,' Brunetti continued. 'I'd like to wait until I talk to the man who lives in the *palazzo*, Professore Molin. The dead man helped him walk around the city. If anyone has an idea of what he did or who his friends – or enemies – are, he's the one.'

The other two nodded in agreement.

'Any contacts in the Sri Lankan community?' Brunetti asked without much hope, then added that Anvith appeared to be the most common male Sri Lankan name.

Both shook their heads, and Brunetti knew no one. 'All right, then,' he said. 'I'll see if I can contact the Professore and agree on a time when I can go and talk to him.'

They both left to return to their offices, and Brunetti called Paola, who managed to find the university list of private phone numbers for faculty members and gave him Professore Molin's.

Years ago, Paola had read him a passage from a novel by Dickens in which the villain never tired of presenting himself as a hand-wringingly "umble man'. This was a vocal posture Brunetti had perfected over the years: there existed no person so "umble' that Brunetti could not be even more "umble'. Or, he amused himself by thinking, "umbler'.

Brunetti called the number and asked, in an "umble' voice, if he could speak to Professore Molin. When the Professore identified himself, Brunetti explained that he had been assigned the investigation of the recent crime involving someone who worked at Palazzo Zaffo dei Leoni and wondered if he could disturb il Professore by asking to speak to him about this matter, preferably at his home so that il Professore would not be troubled by being asked to come to the Questura.

Brunetti outdid himself in the use of 'Professore', giving copious thanks for any answer the Professore gave him, no matter how irrelevant or repetitive.

Brunetti's seeming humility must have struck a responsive chord with the Professore, for he consented to Signor Brunetti's passing by Palazzo Zaffo dei Leoni at eleven the following morning. The Professore explained that his class in fourteenth-century manuscript iconography did not meet until three, so he could spare the Commissario half an hour, perhaps, at eleven.

Brunetti gushed with thanks, as though he were the public fountain in Campo Santa Margherita, free to spill its freshness at the feet of Professore Molin. He said 'grazie' at least three times in the process of hanging up, feeling better with each one.

His mother had often told him that 'no one can resist flattery,' a truth he had carried with him throughout his adult life. He had always lacked the courage to ask her how life had taught her that.

20

The next morning, Brunetti rang the bell to the *palazzo* at eleven o'clock. Had he arrived early, he would have spent ten minutes walking down to Fondamenta Nuove and back; had he been late, he would no doubt have been seen as trying to usurp the customs of the upper classes.

Gloria opened the door in the wall and stood back to give him room to enter. As they approached the *palazzo*, Brunetti was careful to assure her that he would not trouble her husband in the least. She led him along the stone path to the door of the *palazzo*, which she'd left open. Inside, when she turned to take his coat, he saw that the situation was beginning to take a toll: the flesh under her eyes was slightly darker than it had been, and since she'd not bothered with make-up, her lips were pale and dry. Paola had told him that many women had given up using lipstick when wearing a mask and not resumed the habit; he doubted that this explained Gloria's look of complete exhaustion, which he saw as a sign of mourning. Brunetti was surprised at the relief he felt at seeing that Inesh would not go unmourned into that dark night. And then he remembered that Inesh did not believe there *was* a dark night and felt even greater relief.

She took his coat and hung it in a walnut wardrobe to the left of the door, then turned towards what had to be the back of the *palazzo*. 'Renato is in his study. It's the room he finds most comfortable.'

Brunetti made an assenting noise of some sort and followed her. The floors were light grey terrazzo, not in the best of shape: he could see where some of the stone pieces were missing, weakening the ability of the floor to hold together. As he noticed this, he stepped on one of the loose chips and only by force of will stopped himself from bending down to pick it up. She stopped in front of a door on the left, knocked, and waited for a voice, which soon came, saying, '*Avanti.*'

She pushed open the door and went in, but remained anchored to the handle. 'It's Commissario Brunetti, Renato,' she said.

Professore Molin sat at his desk, which was very big and very thick and helped him to look very busy by providing a surface for many books and papers. The man pushed himself to his feet and said, 'Good morning, Commissario. Right on time. That's good.'

His wife left without saying anything and closed the door silently, leaving Brunetti standing just inside the room.

'Come, come, have a seat,' said Molin.

As he approached the indicated chair, Brunetti realized he was in the company of the Noble Professore, who wore what must be the recently created coat of arms of his branch of the family on a signet ring on the small finger of his left hand. He was dressed in a jacket and tie, both of them a sober blue, the shoulders of the jacket grown too wide for him. His shirt was white, the collar stiff; he wore gold-rimmed glasses that faintly magnified his grey eyes. His hair was grey as well, and still thick. Brunetti could not remember ever having passed him on the street.

Brunetti took a seat in a straight-backed wooden chair placed in front of the desk, and Molin sat back in his. He listed a bit to the left. Thinking how much this resembled the exams he had taken at university, Brunetti removed his notebook and opened it.

'I'd like to thank you again, Professore,' he said, removing his pen from the pocket of his jacket. 'We're trying to get some idea of what sort of man this Imesh was.'

'Inesh,' Molin corrected him.

'Of course, of course,' Brunetti said and bent his head while he appeared to enter the correction in his notebook. He stared at it for a moment, then returned his attention to Molin.

Molin had folded his hands on his desk, and Brunetti, seeing the signet ring again, was put in mind of the fairy tale where the heroine is confronted by the Wicked Wolf, and was tempted to exclaim, 'Oh, what a big, big signet ring you have. To keep the lower orders in their place.'

Long experience, however, advised him to consider the problem of class and of how often his own response to wealth and power was negative. In former times, it had been jackets with leather patches on the elbows that had set him against the men wearing them, especially academics, no doubt because the other men interested in Paola were her university colleagues.

Patience intervened and, after an exchange of pleasantries, Brunetti did no more than ask, 'Could you tell me how it is he lived here, Professore?'

'He didn't live *here*, Commissario,' Molin said. 'He lived in the area behind the *palazzo*, in a converted garden house.' He turned a bit to the right and waved his arm in the general direction.

'Ah, I see,' Brunetti said. 'Thank you.' He wrote in his notebook and turned a page. 'How did that happen, Professore? If I might ask.'

Molin smiled and said, 'Of course you may ask, Commissario. It's your duty.'

Brunetti looked up and gave a surprised smile.

'My wife – whom I think you've met before – is a very warm-hearted and generous woman. She found this fellow in difficulty some years ago and offered him – quite impulsively, I must say – the garden house to live in.'

Unable to disguise his astonishment, Brunetti gave Molin a confused look and said, 'How is that possible?'

Molin nodded, as if in approval of Brunetti's reaction. 'Well might you ask, Commissario. The garden house was not being used. In fact, I have to confess it was quite a mess. So she told him he could stay there, and in return he started cleaning it out and repairing some of the things that had been neglected during the previous years.'

Brunetti nodded as if the Professore had said something very interesting and asked, 'In the years he lived here, did he ever have … visitors, or did he ever lead you to suspect that he might frequent the company of people who are, um, perhaps not the right people to let into one's home?'

Molin nodded over these questions for some time and then answered, 'There were the meetings.'

'Excuse me, Professore. I'm not sure I understand what you're referring to.'

'Occasionally, every few months, he would invite some of his compatriots into the garden house.'

'For what purpose?' Brunetti asked.

'I have no idea. Occasionally we would smell incense and could hear what might have been chanting. I assume it was some sort of religious ceremony.' Before Brunetti could say anything, Molin said, 'That's all I know about his private life.'

Brunetti wrote some things in his notebook, then flipped back a few pages and said, 'You told me, Professore, that your wife found him "in difficulty". Could you tell me a bit more?'

'My wife didn't tell you about that?' he asked, surprised.

Brunetti waved a hand, as if the remarks of his wife would not be as memorable as his, so Molin went on. 'My wife found him lying in the *calle* outside, I think it was eight years ago. He'd been beaten and left unconscious in front of our door. He said he'd been mugged and they'd taken two hundred euros he was planning to send to his family.'

Brunetti looked up quickly, his suspicions visible. 'Do you think he might have invented this, Professore?'

Molin raised his eyebrows, then said, 'No, I wouldn't go quite that far. It's sufficient that my wife found his story convincing and thought it safe to take him in and give him a place to live.' Brunetti heard the resentment percolating under the Professore's last words. After a pause, Molin added, speaking slowly and softly, 'Yet the fact that he was beaten doesn't necessarily mean he was mugged.'

'Ah,' said Brunetti, drawing out the sound; he bent over his notebook and wrote for some time. Then, in an apparent change of subject, he said, 'Your wife told me that, during recent years, you've had a certain amount of difficulty moving around the city, and this Inesh helped you keep to your schedule.'

The Dottore nodded but added nothing.

'During this time, what did you talk about?'

'Not much, really. I always had something to read while we were on the boats: student papers, sections of dissertations from the students I was advising, articles from the journals, or perhaps I took notes for articles I was preparing.' He paused to let Brunetti write that down and then said, 'He read from one of his Sinhalese books, which I took to be books about Buddhism. At any rate, they had Buddhas on their covers.' He let a moment pass and added, 'Sometimes he used his prayer beads, sat moving them in his hands.'

Brunetti watched as Molin lost the fight to stop himself making his next remark. Interest splashed across his face, Brunetti met his glance as, voice rich with the forbearance of the educated classes, Molin said, 'But people cannot be freed of their primitive beliefs, so I didn't bother to ask him about this.'

Brunetti saw fit to respond in the voice of the patient agnostic. 'Yes. I tried for years with my mother, but it was impossible.'

Molin at first graced him with a surprisingly real smile and nod, as if he, too, had suffered the primitive darkness of the peasant mind. But then he must have heard a dissonant echo somewhere, for he changed the position of his hands and looked down at them.

Brunetti smiled and said, 'I understand,' while he asked himself what had happened between the two men when they were walking. They would have shared a lot of time and contact. Why not conversation? Brunetti attributed it to Molin's sense of self.

'Did you ever talk about books?' Brunetti asked.

'Books? With Inesh?' the Professore asked, sounding as though he was surprised to learn that the man knew how to read more than his Buddhist bibles.

'Yes. He had a few books about the colonial history of Sri Lanka, as well as a few about the recent history there.'

Molin gave a patient smile and said, 'I'm afraid neither is a subject to which I could contribute.'

Or would want to, Brunetti said to himself, finishing the sentence Molin was too polite to say aloud.

'And the usual crime books.'

That caught Molin's attention.

'What about crime?'

'Thrillers and crime novels. A lot of people, it seems, use them to learn a foreign language.'

Molin's surprise had been momentary; he slid back into polite curiosity. 'Anything else?'

'Yes, as a matter of fact. He had a number of books and some pamphlets and press clippings about terrorism.'

'The Tamil Tigers,' Molin said pedantically.

'No, not at all,' Brunetti said. 'About the trouble here in the eighties.' He'd been looking at Molin when he said this and saw

him freeze. For a moment, Brunetti wondered if the man was having another stroke and he drew his feet under his chair so he'd be
ready to scramble around the desk if the other man collapsed. But
he did not. He stared at Brunetti, then managed to pull his eyes
away from him and looked down at the papers on his desk.

Molin sat like that for some time: the silence in the room
stretched out. Then he looked at the papers on his desk and
selected one. He held it up to his face, as if searching for the sig-
nature, set it down, and looked over at Brunetti.

'I'm sorry, Commissario, but I've got to make a number of
phone calls. Would it be possible for us to end this now? I don't
think I have any other information that would be of use to you.'

'Of course, of course, Professore,' Brunetti said, getting easily
to his feet and slipping his notebook into his pocket. 'I'm afraid
I've already overstayed my welcome, and I won't trouble you any
more.' In normal times, he would have gone over to shake the
Professore's hand, but now he merely nodded his head as a token
of his gratitude, thanked him again, then went to the door and
let himself out of the room, leaving the Professore with the paper
still in his hand, still tilting a bit to the side.

As Brunetti made his way to the front door, Gloria appeared
from a room on the right and waved him inside. More over-
stuffed chairs, a carpet worn bare across the centre, a window
onto the dark undulation of shapes that was the garden. She
seemed relieved to see Brunetti and asked, 'Could he help you?'
She sat at the end of a sagging sofa; Brunetti took a seat in a chair
covered with faded brocade.

'He gave me some information about the man, but he seems not
to have known him very well,' Brunetti said. 'I asked what they
talked about while they were together travelling through the city.'

She smiled and relaxed. 'I've wondered about that, as well. As
I'm sure you noticed, my husband isn't much interested in anything beyond his academic work.'

Actually, as Brunetti had noticed, Professore Molin wasn't interested in anything beyond convincing Brunetti that he had little in common with the dead man and no interest in him or what he did. 'I suppose that's an occupational hazard for a university professor,' Brunetti said easily, thinking how very different were the mental habits of his own dear wife, insatiably curious about most things, and people.

Casually, in an entirely conversational tone, he asked, 'Did you know much about him?'

'Inesh?'

Brunetti nodded.

'A bit. He told me about his sons, so I became a long-distance participant in their raising. And he'd show me photos of them and his wife.'

'Did he ever go to see them?'

'Twice. About six years ago and last year. For a month each time.' She smiled and said, 'He was never so happy as in the weeks before he went home.'

'Not after?' Brunetti asked.

She waved that idea away and said, 'Anticipation is always a joy. It's memory that's so sad.'

He considered this for some time and admitted she was right. Then it occurred to him to ask, 'How did he afford those trips? Do you know?'

'He worked. Lord, the man worked. A lot of my friends have parents or relatives that need someone to be with them during the night; Inesh had a gift for old people. He came from a culture that values them, so he'd go and sleep in their homes, in the room with the old person, and people paid him for this.'

Before he could ask, she said, 'It was a lot of nights for him, many of them sleepless. He told me it was a good chance to read. And to meditate.'

'Did he manage to pay for the trips to Sri Lanka with that?'

She waited a moment before she said, 'He didn't have rent to pay, Guido, or utilities. All he had to pay for was food and clothing.'

'And books,' Brunetti added.

'Yes, and books. I lent him many of mine over the years, in both English and Italian, and I know he bought more from Carlo in the *campo*.'

'What did he borrow from you?' Brunetti asked.

'Italian history, English novels – he loved *Great Expectations*. I remember that. He must have asked me for it three times.'

'What else?'

'Recently, he became interested in the Red Brigades and their successors,' she said, as if memory were flooding back to her. 'He asked me to explain it to him, who the members were, what sort of things they did.

'I told him as much as I remembered: the attacks, the people who disappeared, the kidnappings … ' She stopped here to consider something and then continued: 'They got an American general, and some other men were murdered, but I'd forgotten their names or even why they'd been kidnapped.' She rubbed at her face with one hand and said, 'He couldn't understand it.'

A long silence spread over them after she said this, but she broke it by saying, 'I don't understand it, either. I suppose I thought I did. Then. But no one did, really.'

'Did you ask him about the Tamil Tigers?' Brunetti finally asked.

'I never spoke of them,' Gloria said.

'Probably wise,' Brunetti answered, then added, 'I found some books about the Red Brigades on his bookshelf. And about their brief comeback in the eighties, such as it was.'

'The eighties,' she said in a far-off voice, 'when we still cared about things like justice.' She pronounced the last word with something similar to contempt. 'But no one managed to find it.'

Both of them sat silent for what seemed a long time. Finally she made a preparatory noise, the sort of thing used to preface an awkward question, or a request. 'I've had a call from the leader of the Sri Lankan community here,' she finally said. Seeing Brunetti's surprise, she explained, 'He's the one who called Inesh's wife to tell her about his death.'

Brunetti nodded but remained silent.

'She's asked him to take care of things for her,' Gloria explained hesitantly.

'What does that mean?' Brunetti asked, not unkindly.

'His ashes. She asked him to see that they were returned to Sri Lanka so that they could … ' Her voice trailed off here, and she closed her eyes. 'She's not interested in anything else. His things, that is.'

'Can she do that?' Brunetti asked, reproaching himself for not having thought of this before.

'As soon as the body's released. The cremation can be done here, and then there's a procedure for … ' She stopped here, searching for the proper word, but could find only, '… all the rest.'

Brunetti nodded, then asked, 'Why are you telling me this, Gloria?'

Her surprise was real. 'I thought you'd want to know.'

'Yes. Thank you,' was all he could think to say.

Her smile was painful to see, so, instead of continuing the conversation, Brunetti invented another appointment and got to his feet. He apologized for having to leave; she went out into the hall and took his coat from the wardrobe.

He put it on but left it unbuttoned, deciding that the weather outside would tell him what to do with the buttons. 'It was good to see you again,' he said.

'The same for me. It's good to learn that someone else hasn't changed much since student times.'

'I like to think I have,' Brunetti said, pausing to add, 'At least in some things. I suppose I hoped and thought that people wanted to do noble things and think of their fellow man.' He smiled at the memory, and at that younger person, realizing how proud he was to have had those hopes at that age, even if some had grown less attractive or reachable as he grew older.

'It all seemed so easy then, didn't it? And so clear?' she asked him.

He reached to touch her shoulder, placing his hand on it and tightening it in some sort of message of solidarity or condolence. He thanked her, said goodbye, and left the *palazzo*, telling her he'd let himself out of the garden.

As he started towards the door, the memory came to him of the press clippings and photocopies kept in the scrapbook. Perhaps he should have taken them along as 'objects of interest'. He stopped, searched his pockets and, finding that he still had the keys, turned to head back towards the garden house.

The tape on the door was coming loose in places, so he looked around inside until he found the roll of red-and-white tape. He stood in the silence. Only now, with the sunshine spilling into the room, did he feel the full peace created by the blending of colours and absence of objects. The flowers in the glass in front of the wooden statue of the Buddha had drooped a little more.

From this distance, he could see the scrapbook on the shelf and went to get it. Not now, he told himself as he was placing new strips of tape on the front door. Wait until you're back in the Questura.

21

As he started towards the door to the *calle*, it came to Brunetti to ask himself how the nuns got into their part of the garden. He had seen no second door in the wall; perhaps it was somewhere around the corner. But to go and look for it, he'd have to leave the property of the *palazzo*, with no way to get back in. He looked to the right and took four or five steps through the dank bushes, disliking the need to push some branches out of the way in order to move through them.

But finally he saw the metre-high stone wall and, on the other side, the order imposed as if by monastic rule: grass cut, trees newly trimmed, what must be the vegetable garden protected from the coming winter with a layer of leaves and straw. He approached the wall and saw, at the far end of the land, near the canal, the distinctive black habit and white veil of the Benedictine. Her curved back as she raked at the leaves and twigs told Brunetti something about her age.

Reluctant to invade their territory, he remained on the wild side of the garden and walked towards her, forced to stay close to the wall. As he got within three metres of her, he stopped and called, 'Sorella, Sorella.'

She turned towards him suddenly and could not disguise her astonishment. She stopped, stood up as straight as she could manage, and called back, '*Sì?*'

Brunetti held up both of his hands, palms towards her, and waited until she approached the wall. He stayed silent, glad that the wall was there to emphasize the fact that he was remaining on his side of it, respectful of her property.

Still holding the rake, she drew closer to the wall until they met on opposite sides. She wore the large white bib, high collar, and the full veil, so her face was a bit shadowed. Still, he saw the wrinkled skin, so much like that of an apple kept in the cellar for months. Her eyes were brown, her skin either dark or tanned by time spent outdoors.

'Good day, Sorella,' he began, then gave his compliments that her garden was so clean and orderly. As he looked at the trees behind her, lined up against the wall like suspects, he asked, unable to quell the wonder in his voice, 'Are those apricot trees?'

She turned to see which ones he meant. 'The first four are. The last two on the left are peaches.' Her voice was high but not unpleasant. From her accent, he knew she was not from the Veneto; he doubted she was Italian.

She turned back to him and said, 'Not many people would recognize them any more.'

'But surely they would,' he insisted.

'If they were country folk, they would. But not city people.' Her voice was warm and loving when she named the first group, perhaps a bit less so with the second. Then, gratuitously, 'Not many of the children in the school have ever seen a live cow.'

'It's a pity you can't have one here, isn't it?' he asked, testing her sense of humour.

She gave a sad smile. 'You can't have only one cow. It's bad for them. They get sick with loneliness.'

'Like us,' Brunetti said.

She smiled and the years went running from her face. Changing tone, she asked, 'How can I help you, Signore?'

'Did you know the Sri Lankan man who lived on this side of the wall?' he asked.

'Inesh?' she asked, sounding, for the first time, faintly nervous.

He nodded to acknowledge the name and smiled to dispel her nervousness.

'Yes, we all knew him,' she said. 'He'd help us sometimes, when we had something heavy to move or something we couldn't do.'

She used the past tense, Brunetti noticed. 'You know what happened?' he asked.

'We know that he's dead,' she answered, then added, voice bleak, 'and how.' Both of them let some time pass, and then she said, resting the head of the rake on the ground and leaning her weight on the handle, 'He was a very good man.' She suddenly reached into her black habit – perhaps a pocket? – and pulled out a string of wooden beads, separated by tiny knots, on a very thin length of string. She held it out to him, and he saw the crossed pieces of carved wood. 'He made me this.'

'Why?'

'Because we were friends. He helped us with the garden, and we gave him all the fruit he wanted. In fact, we told him he could come and pick what he liked, but he wouldn't do that: he always waited for us to give him what we had.'

'Are you the gardener?' he asked.

She paused for a moment and then said, the nervousness back in her voice, 'You ask a lot of questions, Signore.'

'Yes, I do, Sorella. That's my job.'

She took a quick breath and asked, 'Does that mean you're a policeman?'

'I'm afraid it does, Sorella,' Brunetti said, and smiled to soften any harsh response she might have.

He saw her hands tighten on the rake. 'Are you here about Sara?' she asked, this time unable to hide the nervousness.

Confused, Brunetti said, 'I'm sorry, Sorella, but I don't know anything about someone named Sara.'

She gave him a quick glance, then levelled the teeth of the rake on the ground as though she were going to continue her work. Not looking at him but not moving the rake, she asked, 'Are you telling me the truth?'

'Yes, I am. I don't know who Sara is.'

This time she pulled the rake's head towards her, stopped, and said, eyes on the ground, 'She's his dog.'

Brunetti took a while to work this one out. Finally he asked, 'Inesh's dog? I didn't know he had a dog.'

'No one was supposed to know he had a dog,' she answered. 'She followed him home one day, but he didn't let her in. The next day, she followed him again, and he let her in and fed her. And then she went and hid under the bushes. After that, she started coming over to us, and we fed her, too.' She looked up and smiled, saying, 'We eat meat. She didn't like being a vegetarian.'

Brunetti couldn't stop himself from smiling at this. 'That's very thoughtful of you all.'

She looked at the ground and said softly, 'Perhaps not of all of us, Signore.'

'What do you mean?'

'The Mother Superior. She says the rules say we can't have pets.'

'I wouldn't know,' Brunetti temporized.

'There's no harm, is there? Really? If it's doing good?' she asked in a completely conversational tone.

'No, I suppose there isn't,' Brunetti agreed. 'But what about the Mother Superior?'

'Oh, Sara's very smart. When she knows the Mother Superior is coming – dogs have a very good sense of smell – she just jumps over the wall and waits over there. On your side.' She pointed back to the *palazzo* with the head of the rake.

'And when she's gone?'

'She comes home,' she said, adding, 'It's home for her now, isn't it?'

'Yes, I suppose it is,' Brunetti confirmed.

'It's good to have a home,' the nun said in a way that caught Brunetti's attention. 'To have a place you come from.'

'Which country are you from?' he dared to ask.

'The Philippines, like some of my sisters here.' She slipped her hand back into her habit, and it emerged without the rosary.

She suddenly looked at the sky, as if seeking something from it, then said, 'You must ask me your questions now, Signore. It's almost time for Sext, and I don't want to be late for prayers.' She said it as though she were talking about being late for a party.

'Of course, Sorella,' Brunetti said. His arrival had been an impulse, but now he had to decide what might be important. He thought of something to ask. 'Did Inesh ever work in their garden?' he asked, waving his hand towards the other garden.

'Work?'

'Grow things? Plant trees? Dig?'

'Yes, every year he planted a bush or two. Down towards the end of this wall, where there's light coming in from our side. The people in the *palazzo* don't pay any attention to the garden, so he could plant what he wanted and they'd never notice.'

'Did he plant any this year?'

'He told me he was going to plant some berry bushes – I think blackcurrants – before the winter came. He planted three of them, but then he stopped, came over and said he didn't need more than three, and would I like the other two he'd bought.

'I was thinking about which of the younger sisters I could ask to dig the holes.' She looked up at him and added, 'I'm a good raker, but I'm not much of a digger any more.'

Brunetti smiled down at her: she barely reached his shoulder.

'He must have understood because he disappeared for a while and came back with two bushes and planted them for us.' She turned and pointed to some thin-branched bushes about five metres from where they were standing.

'Don't be discouraged, Signore. I know they look bedraggled,' she said. 'In springtime, they'll perk up and start growing.'

'Do you know where exactly he planted his?' Brunetti asked.

'Well, he needed some time to go and get the ones he gave us, so it could be anywhere on their side. I think he was the only one who knew his way over there.' She waved at the jungle behind Brunetti. 'I doubt I could find them,' she added, pointing with the head of the rake to a narrow path that ran off behind him. 'That one's a dead end.'

'Thank you, Sorella,' Brunetti said. 'I won't keep you from your prayers.'

'Oh, nothing would, Signore,' she said, and he believed her.

He thought of his mother and the joy it had always given him to make her happy. 'Could I ask a favour of you, Sorella?'

'Of course,' she said. 'That's one of the reasons we're here: to help one another.'

'Would you pray for my mother today?'

'Do you pray for her?'

'In my own way, yes.'

'Good. Today she'll have two people praying for her.'

'You're very kind, Sorella,' Brunetti said with absolute certainty.

'Like your mother, eh?' she asked, smiling at him, and turned away to hurry to her prayers.

Brunetti decided he did not want to get lost in the maze that was the garden of the *palazzo* and let himself out from the garden into the *calle* leading back in the direction of Campo Santa Maria Nova. When he entered the *campo*, Carlo was sitting at a table in front of the bar next door to his shop, talking with another man Brunetti thought he had seen before but could not place. On the table in front of them were two cups and saucers and three books. The saucers had been pushed to the opposite side of the table, and one of the books lay open in front of the men. Carlo took it carefully and turned a page, and then another, and then opened the book further on. He held it out to the other man, who took it from him and turned a few more pages before handing it back.

Carlo nodded, closed it and set it on top of the two others. He got up and went back into his shop, followed by the man. After a few minutes, the man emerged without the books and headed towards the bridge that led to I Miracoli.

'*Buondì*, Commissario,' Carlo said when he saw Brunetti approaching. Then, seeing the scrapbook, added, 'You found it.'

'I went back to get it, and now I'd like to ask you some questions about it.'

Carlo shot him a quick glance filled with uncertainty. However good a customer Brunetti might be, he was still a policeman.

'Don't worry, Carlo. All you did was sell it to Inesh. My interest is only in the scrapbook and what's inside it.' He was about to ask who the man Carlo had been sitting with was when it occurred to him that this was not the sort of question he could ask casually, certainly not at that moment.

Carlo said nothing, so Brunetti continued. 'You said some of the things in here came from the father of a friend.'

Carlo nodded and gave a wary smile.

'Would you tell me his name?'

'My friend or his father?' the book dealer temporized.

'Only the father. The son has nothing to do with this, and I'll make no attempt to discover who he is.'

'They'll have the same last name anyway, won't they?' Carlo asked, not sarcastically, almost whimsically, as if to suggest he thought the police could do better than this.

'I know, I know, and this is a small town.' Before Carlo could speak, Brunetti added, 'It would help me if I knew how old he was when this was made.' He held up the scrapbook.

'His name was Federico Nesi, and he died two years ago, perhaps three. He was in his sixties.' Carlo looked at Brunetti to see if this would suffice, then added the name of the bank branch of which he had been the director and said, 'He died of a heart attack.'

Brunetti held up the scrapbook: only the cover appeared to have been checked for fingerprints. 'I'd like you to take a look at this with me.' Brunetti wanted to be sure that only his fingerprints appeared on the documents inside, should that ever become important.

Carlo nodded, saying, 'Do you mind if we go inside to do this?'

'Of course not.'

For the next ten minutes, Brunetti and Carlo stood side by side in front of a desk as Brunetti unfolded document after document, careful to do so from the top-right corner.

It contained what he thought it would: manifestos with names like '*Libertà*' and '*La Voce del Popolo*', each setting out the way to a better future for Italy, if not for the whole world; precise explanations of the 'real meaning' of recent political events; a handwritten list of the names of politicians Brunetti had to struggle to remember, all their names preceded by a large black X; a small poster addressed to the workers in the petrochemical factories of Mestre, begging them to consider their health and leave their jobs. Brunetti looked up after reading this one, thinking it was true that prophets were not heard in their own time.

They continued reading through the outdated plans and hopes and threats, all aimed at a better world, all based on the belief that people would act in their own best interest if only they could be made to understand what that was.

Few of the documents bore signatures; few credible names appeared below even the most moderate suggestions or protests; anyone familiar with the 60s and 70s would see immediately that the spirit of protest had been broken, and these were the leftovers and table scraps of social protest. Achilles had retired and grown timid, not caring about the rust on his sword.

As they paged through the once strident protests, two names occurred with some frequency: 'Belisarius' and 'Aeneas'. Well, thought Brunetti, the classics were still taught then: Belisarius defended the Byzantine Empire, and Aeneas founded Rome.

Not only did Brunetti sense a strong self-regard in the writing of these two, but it seemed that both of them longed for the return of a Strong Leader. It was embarrassingly easy to understand who each of them thought suitable for the post.

At a certain point, Brunetti said, 'I think we've read enough, don't you?'

'More than enough,' Carlo agreed. Then, as Brunetti closed the book, the younger man asked, 'Did people really think like that then? I wasn't even at school yet.'

'I suppose we did,' Brunetti admitted. 'Some of us thought that things could change, or could be made to change.' He took the liberty of patting Carlo on the arm and said, 'Could I ask another favour of you?'

In a rough voice, Carlo said, slipping into a gross parody of the strongest of Giudecchino accents, 'That's what happens when the police get their hands on you. They shake you until you confess.' Then, returning to his own more gentle manner, he said, 'Of course.'

'Would you ask your friend if his father was one of these two?'

'Only if I can tell him a police officer is asking,' Carlo said.

Brunetti considered this for a moment and nodded. Then he added, 'In that case, if he's willing to say which one his father was, would you ask him about the other?'

'I'm afraid that's going too far, Commissario.'

'Yes, I suppose it is,' Brunetti said, and decided it was time to go home for lunch.

22

Lunch started as a quiet meal, but when the topic of Asian swine flu sat down among them, things quickly grew louder. By long agreement, Chiara would eat a meatless meal while the others ate what Paola had prepared for them, sometimes – but hardly always – containing meat. On this day, Paola had chosen to prepare *insalata caprese*: for Chiara, a bed of sliced tomato and sliced boiled beet covered with basil leaves and thick slices of *mozzarella di bufala*: for the others, the beet was substituted with prosciutto.

It was the ham that led Chiara to remark how the disease had recently been detected in the wild boars that had for months infested the streets of Rome. 'And it seems to be spreading north,' Chiara continued, when her mother interrupted her to say, 'Not while we're eating, Chiara.'

Chiara set her fork down softly and said, 'But it's important.'

Paola cut a slice of prosciutto in half, speared it and ate it, then a small piece of bread. 'Everything is important in some way, but some of these things don't need to be discussed at mealtimes.'

'When will I learn the difference between what we can and can't talk about at the table?' Chiara asked, hurling a bewildered look at her father, as if asking for support.

'When you're married and have children and they try to provoke you while you're eating,' Paola said, reaching out with her fork towards the platter of prosciutto. 'You'll understand then.'

Brunetti laughed. The instant he heard himself do it, he knew he'd made a mistake and had managed to offend either his wife or his daughter. Perhaps both. It would have been cowardly to turn it into a cough, so he did not. He searched for a way to compliment Paola's cooking, but there was nothing on the table that she had cooked. He settled by taking a few more slices of cheese, being careful to keep his fork far from the provocative prosciutto.

He and Raffi exchanged a glance of masculine solidarity in the face of this female petulance. Raffi, both younger and bolder than his father, picked up the platter that held what was left of the prosciutto and used his fork to slide it all onto his plate. He put his head down and, using his knife, cut it into manageable pieces and ate them one after the other, then reached for a piece of bread.

When they were finished, and without further comment, Chiara got to her feet and collected the plates of everyone at the table and took them to the sink. Her mother was at the stove, stirring the sauce, something with cauliflower and Brunetti wasn't sure what else, though certainly onion. Chiara stopped next to her mother, put her arm around her waist, and said, 'Cauliflower?'

'Yes.'

'You're the best,' Chiara said.

'Yes,' Paola repeated laconically, and Brunetti knew that lunch had been saved.

*

On his way back to the Questura, Brunetti reflected upon the return of Signorina Elettra. In her absence, he'd had a look at the programme for the conference and called a friend at the Italian office of Interpol to ask about it.

'The real cyberkillers,' his friend had said of the speakers and participants, then admitted how disappointed he'd been not to have been invited. And Signorina Elettra had left early because she found it boring. Brunetti had tried a few unsuccessful words of comfort and thanked his friend for the information, then ended the call.

'The "real" cyber killers,' Brunetti repeated to himself. Thinking about it, he realized he wasn't surprised, not really.

He went directly up to her office as soon as he arrived and found her at her desk. She was wearing red: in the midst of his pleasure at seeing her again, he barely noted the details. She glanced up from her screen and smiled.

'Ah, Commissario, you have no idea how much I've missed you all.'

'And how happy you are to be back?' he hinted.

'Well,' she said, 'it's a pleasure not to be surrounded by so many—' She broke off and turned to one of her two windows, perhaps to hunt for the correct phrase. 'So many unimaginative people.'

Brunetti came closer to her desk but said nothing. He smiled and nodded, soliciting an explanation.

'I have to admit that I was shocked at some of them,' she said, failing to disguise the power of her emotion.

'In what way?' he asked.

She gathered her thoughts and finally tried to explain. 'This was Interpol, and these were people who have been exposed, for years – in some cases decades – to the cleverest criminals working today, people who are almost impossible to discover.'

He nodded.

'And they felt themselves – at least most of them did – honestly bound by the law.'

For a moment, Brunetti wasn't sure whether she was speaking about the criminals or the headhunters. But then it dawned on him: she meant the police.

'All of them?' Brunetti asked, careful to inject a tone of surprise into his question.

She shook her head in disapproval, closing her eyes in sure distress. 'Well, not some of them, thank heaven. But certainly the major part of them spoke repeatedly of the necessity to work within what they called "the just restraints of the law". Did he see a shiver run through her body?

'Luckily, I'd watched them from the very beginning of the conference and realized that most of them were of this opinion.' She placed her hands, helpless and palm down, on her desk. 'A few said very little, or nothing, so perhaps there were some realists among them.'

'How shocking,' Brunetti whispered.

He allowed a cleansing moment to pass and then said, 'I have a few things I need your help with, Signorina: I hope they'll rid your mind of the horrors you've seen.'

Her smile was his reward, and he began to explain: Inesh's murder, the contents of the scrapbook, Belisarius and Aeneas, Federico Nesi, Inesh's books, Molin's objection to the sale of the *palazzo*. He paused and then tossed Rubini's name onto the pile. Signorina Elettra raised her eyebrows in recognition, which prompted Brunetti to add that a rumour was afoot that he was expecting to return to work soon. She had taken notes as he spoke, asking questions about people's ages and professions, if they'd been to university or not.

Brunetti was surprised when he saw how long the list turned out to be and explained that he had no idea what connections, if any, existed between or among them.

She looked up, eyes bright. 'On the first day, before things became intolerable, an overweight, middle-aged woman from Toulouse – a statistician – whom no one paid any attention to gave a very interesting talk on what she called *'"triangulation"'*,' she said, pronouncing the English word with a French accent. 'She gave us a site and the way to enter a list of names.' She paused here, face transformed, like people of faith at certain moments during the Mass. 'In a ... miraculously short time after entering the data, we would be sent a record of any and all contacts that might ever have taken place among them – at least if they exist in the files of a European bureaucracy, newspaper, company, or publication of any sort.' She held up her notes until he smiled, whereupon she said, 'I'll give these a try.'

Speaking with a seriousness he was surprised to hear in his own voice, Brunetti said, 'Didn't anyone else listen to her?'

She shook her head and waved a finger in negation. 'As I told you, Commissario, the woman was middle-aged, and stout. And she spoke in a very soft voice,' she said, leaving it to Brunetti to imagine how much attention would have been paid to such a person in a conference dominated and filled by men.

Brunetti was about to protest, but he paused in consideration for some time and then nodded in agreement and said he was very curious to see what results this system would produce.

'Ah, so am I, Commissario. I think I was the only person who bothered to write down the name of the site.' She lowered her head and waved him closer before saying in a conspiratorial voice, 'I wanted to try it out first with the staff here, but I trembled at the possibilities.'

His smile blossomed at the same time as hers. Brunetti thanked her, said once more how relieved he was to see her again, and went up to his office.

*

Only a few minutes after he arrived, Griffoni appeared at his door. 'Do you have a minute?' she asked as she came in.

'Even two,' he answered, smiling.

When she was seated, she said, 'I think I told you I asked one of my … ' as always, that brief hesitation, '… sources about Rubini.'

'Yes, when I told you he hoped to send his daughter to university in the United States.'

She smiled that he remembered and said, 'And now he's telling people that she applied to both MIT and Stanford: both accepted her, and Stanford offered her a partial scholarship.' She smiled and said, 'Girl genius, apparently.'

'One would think,' Brunetti agreed, sort of.

'She's to begin classes in January,' Griffoni said. As Brunetti waited to see if she was going to explain her interest in the girl's academic career, she added, 'She'll have to pay her living expenses, which means Rubini will have to pay them for her.' She paused, waiting to hear Brunetti's reaction.

'From what I've heard about his current situation, that's not likely,' he said, in a voice as neutral as he could make it sound. After a moment, he said, 'I'm sorry for the girl.'

Griffoni nodded a few times, smiling. 'May I reveal the happy ending?' she asked. 'From your reaction, I assume you haven't heard.'

'What?'

'That Rubini has found a solution.'

This time it was Brunetti who smiled. 'I'm not surprised about that, but I'll admit I'm curious to know what it is and how you found out.'

'From the same person,' she said, referring to her unidentified source.

'And the happy ending? What is it?'

'It seems that two art dealers in Milano have hired him.'

'Rubini?' Brunetti asked, thinking of foxes and chicken coops.

'The very one,' she said.

'To do what?'

'As it was explained to me, Rubini will arrange the return of stolen paintings. And other things.'

Rubini being Rubini, Brunetti asked, 'What's in it for him?'

Rubini being Rubini, Griffoni answered, 'Twelve per cent.'

'How does it work?'

'On the honour system,' she said.

Brunetti's head sank into his hands for a few moments, but when he removed them, he'd had time to consider this, and he said, 'I'd trust Rubini if he gave his word. But an art dealer, especially from Milan ... I don't know.' Then, almost incidentally, he added, 'Besides, what he's doing is illegal.'

As if he'd not spoken, Griffoni said, 'As it was explained to me, the service ... ' She paused, giving Brunetti the opportunity to respond to that word if he chose. When he did not, she continued, ' ... passes by word of mouth. Apparently, Rubini knows everyone in the business.'

Although this hardly needed confirmation, Brunetti nodded.

'So he uses what he already knows.' Seeing Brunetti's expression, she clarified this. 'If he knows anything. Or else he asks around, thus once he's in contact with the current owners, he asks the price and waits to see what the former owners decide.'

Brunetti poked at 'current owners', but thought it better to leave it where it was lying and instead asked, 'And if something happens, he gets twelve per cent?'

'So I've been told.'

'What happens if he doesn't manage to arrange anything, or if the price is too high?' Brunetti asked.

Griffoni must have thought Brunetti's concern was for Rubini, for she explained, 'There's no commission, but he still has a job with the gallery as an "artistic consultant". No one knows how much he gets a month, but he pays taxes on it, contributes to the pension system, and by contract has five weeks of paid vacation a year.'

'Has this service begun?' Brunetti asked.

'As with all things regarding Rubini, there are whispers. One of them is about a Tintoretto engraving that had been in a family for generations. It was returned to the owners.'

'Has anyone explained this sudden change from common thief to chief negotiator?' Brunetti asked.

'His daughter,' Griffoni said, and seeing the look of utter confusion that took over Brunetti's face, she went on. 'She was ashamed that her father had been in prison and threatened that she'd never speak to him again if he didn't stop stealing.'

'And she trusted his word when he agreed?'

Griffoni's answer was instant. 'You do.'

That ended the discussion of Rubini.

23

Returning their attention to the murder of Inesh Kavinda, Brunetti pulled out his notebook and opened it, then told Griffoni about his conversations that morning, first with Molin and then with his wife. He spoke slowly, listening attentively to what he said about the couple, knowing from long experience that many ideas or opinions were not clear to him until he was forced to speak out loud and thus perhaps hear new possibilities. Hearing himself speaking of Molin now made him realize how much he disliked the man.

'Molin tried to sound sympathetic towards Inesh. After all, he'd more or less lived with them for years. But I didn't sense that he was upset by his death or the way it happened.' He found himself thinking that this dispassion was how an employer thinks of a worker. Molin's wife, however, surely mourned Inesh's passing. As did the nun.

He told Griffoni that Gloria Forcolin had known far more about Inesh and his life, both in Italy and in Sri Lanka.

'Well, she's a woman,' Griffoni said. 'Of course she'd know.' When Brunetti stared across at her with a blank face, apparently not understanding, she said, 'Because she'd ask, Guido.' Then, in the face of his silence, she added, 'It's what we do when we're talking to people: we ask them questions and pay attention to their answers.'

'That's a bit simplistic, don't you think?' he asked, not a little offended by her remark.

It took Griffoni a moment to answer, and when she did speak, it was only to say, 'As you wish, Guido.'

Brunetti accepted the peace offering and said, looking at the final note he had taken, 'The only thing that seemed to interest him was my mentioning that Inesh had some articles and books about terrorism. In the eighties.'

Griffoni looked at him, her brows drawn together, as though she were trying to keep horror at bay. 'The train station,' she said softly, referring to the bombing in Bologna, one of the worst attacks of those wretched times.

Brunetti nodded and, not conscious at all of what they were doing, they observed a long moment of silence. 'I remember the American general who was kidnapped. But that ended without blood,' Brunetti said, then added, 'I think one of our senators was killed, but I can't remember his name.'

In an attempt to change the subject, he thought of Alvise and Brandini and asked, 'Any news about Brandini?'

'They're still on patrol together. Another two days, and then they each get assigned a different partner.' They exchanged a glance, each waiting for the other to say something.

It was Griffoni who finally decided to speak. 'They've got on fine. Vianello's in the squad room, so he hears what's being said, and it seems no one thinks they're worth talking about.'

'They aren't,' Brunetti affirmed, and he saw that Griffoni understood the wisdom contained in his remark.

Griffoni asked if he'd like to go out for a coffee; Brunetti declined, saying there were reports he had to read. This was certainly true; it was equally true that he had been putting them off for weeks. Griffoni said she'd go alone, leaving Brunetti to his files.

There were four in his in-tray. He pulled them out, set them on his desk, and started reading. Theft, assault, fraud, and impersonation.

He turned to the last and found the usual story of the dental technician who, having for years watched the dentist for whom he worked make and fit false teeth and implants – and then get paid in cash – decided he might have a try on his own. And so, with apparently minimal oversight, he snapped his fingers and three months later was treating patients in a private practice in Venice. He wasn't discovered for some time, not until a former patient of the dentist for whom he had worked recognized him and went to the trouble of photographing his diplomas and seeking to verify them with the medical authorities.

The fact the practice was abandoned, equipment and all, before the police arrived suggested that someone at the office that verified records had called to warn him.

Over the years, every time Brunetti went to see a doctor he did not know, he made a great business of looking carefully at the diplomas on the walls, sometimes even photographing them with his phone. In one case, when his turn came, he was told that the doctor had been called away for an emergency, and would the signore like to reschedule, perhaps three months from now?

The theft was boring because it was such a cliché. Returning from a vacation, people living in a fourth-floor apartment had found their home completely ransacked by a person or persons unknown who had smashed the skylight in their kitchen and searched the house thoroughly, managing to find the woman's jewels and the man's collection of Renaissance coins.

The last two were quickly read. The assault was actually a drunken brawl in a bar between two men with long records of the same offence. It was unlikely that a magistrate could be found who would consider it worth the trouble to bring a case against them, so Brunetti didn't bother to read further.

Seeing that the case of fraud had taken place on the internet, Brunetti stopped before the second paragraph, entered the name of an officer in the Guardia di Finanza in Rome, and forwarded it to him. He suddenly decided he'd had enough, shut down his computer, and left the Questura.

24

The following morning, Brunetti arrived at the Questura well before nine and decided to go directly to his office to hang up his coat and glance at his emails. As he was scrolling down through them to see the names of the senders, he wondered how it had come about that the first thing he did when he entered his office was to check them. This was, he reminded himself, the same man who mocked his children about the umbilical cord connecting them to their phones, their constant need to know who was in and who was out, and the amount of time they threw away by following the trail of celebrities whom they would never meet and who lived in places where no sane person would want to be.

Why could he not be more like Paola, who at least displayed a pro forma interest in their cyberworld, its customs and tastes? He'd tried once to compliment her on her patience, but she'd dismissed the idea, saying, 'The least we can do is glance in their direction once in a while, I suppose.'

He returned his attention to the emails: all were urgent; few were important. After a few minutes, he closed the screen and went downstairs.

He found Signorina Elettra in her office, her desk clear save for her computer screen and keyboard, plus a pile of papers in a transparent plastic folder. He turned to the windowsill and was pleased to see an immense bouquet of red roses.

She saw him studying the flowers and said, 'The Vice-Questore had them delivered.'

'It is a comfort to all of us, not only the Vice-Questore, to have you here again, Signorina,' he said, meaning it.

'You are too kind, Commissario.' Gazing up at him, she gave him a smile, and said, 'I've had time to try out the Frenchwoman's system of triangulation on the names on the list you gave me.' Then, modestly, 'I've made a few changes to her programme that allow it deeper access to the past.'

Thinking it would be impertinent to ask, Brunetti limited himself to, 'Excellent.'

Her shrug was almost invisible. 'It was merely a matter of imposing a few simple rules.' So much for the Frenchwoman's system.

She picked up the folder and passed it to him, then said, 'I took the liberty of scanning copies of everything here to Commissario Griffoni and Ispettore Vianello. I hope you don't mind.'

'Of course I don't. It saves time,' Brunetti said. He thanked her, they carried the papers back to his office, closed the door, went to his desk and began to read.

There was no introductory editorial comment from Signorina Elettra. He flipped to the back and saw that there were no concluding remarks from her, either.

Brunetti removed his jacket and hung it on the back of his chair. He was curious to learn what would be revealed by Signorina Elettra's – or the Frenchwoman's – system.

Rubini's name had popped up in Signorina Elettra's search because of his relationship with two other people whose names were mentioned. His criminal record began only after he had graduated from university with, Brunetti was astonished to discover, a degree – with the highest honours – in art history. No wonder he had usually taken the best paintings: his professors should be complimented by their student's talent.

There followed, in chronological order, his criminal record. Brunetti saw how much of his life Rubini had spent in prison or under house arrest. Rubini's obsession with theft sounded like the obsession of gamblers: playing was what counted; it didn't matter whether you won or lost, so long as you had the thrill of playing.

During his time at university, Rubini had lived at an address in Cannaregio that had to be near Fondamenta Nuove; the second year, a student enrolled in the Faculty of History, Federico Nesi, had moved in. Attached were copies of the contracts registered at the Ufficio Anagrafe. With the arrival of a second tenant, the owner had asked for a new contract in both names and a financial guarantee of the rent from their parents, sure proof the owner was in the habit of renting to university students.

Then Signorina Elettra had found that another name on Brunetti's list, Renato Molin, resident with his aunt at Palazzo Zaffo dei Leoni, had also been enrolled in the Faculty of History. In the margin, Signorina Elettra had written: 'I've attached a few things you might find interesting, among them his final undergraduate thesis, which seems at odds with a professorship in medieval Italian history.' Brunetti glanced at the reproduced title page – 'The Sheep Look Up and Are Not Fed' – which he found strangely out of place in a university with no programme in agronomy.

Brunetti ignored the rest of the title page and began reading the text. He was soon immersed in the amniotic fluid in which he had spent his first years at university. He read of 'perpetual exploitation', of the 'barriers of class and wealth', of 'repression of the poor', and the 'disregard of the ruling class for peasants and workers'. He thrilled at the passionate rhetoric, so common to his first professors, especially those teaching history and philosophy. But now, alas, he recognized the absence of clear argument or historical objectivity. He thought of the graffito he had seen on a wall: 'Capitalism = Theft'. The same hand could have written these articles, the same mind made the equation. For a moment, he wished he had read the introduction to all of this so that he would be sure which century Molin was referring to, the twentieth or the fifteenth. But when Molin's wrath failed to consider the Peasants' Revolt and passed to NATO and the Christian Democrats, Brunetti understood where he was.

He recalled, then, a remark his mother had made during his enchantment with the Better World his university friends were so sure they were going to bring about. He'd offered their small living room to his friends to use for a meeting, had spent days telling her to buy a better brand of coffee and have some beer and a few bottles of wine ready, should his friends want to drink something during the discussion.

She had stayed in the kitchen during the meeting, attentive to everything, always ready to make another coffee when asked to do so, or to open another bottle of wine when one was emptied. And his friends spoke of the way they would ensure a better life for the workers of the land, for factory workers, for all the poor peasants living under the crushing heel of capitalism.

They finally left, the five he admired the most and most wanted to impress with the purity of his belief, and his mother began to wash the glasses they'd left on the table.

'What did you think, Mamma?' he'd asked, eager that she, one of the workers of the earth, should express her admiration and respect for these young men.

She'd continued slowly washing the glasses – he remembered she always washed glasses in cold water to save money. Her silence annoyed him, for he thought it somehow disrespected the arrival of the New Order.

At his third request, she'd let the water out of the sink and began to dry her reddened hands on her apron. Finally she'd turned away from the sink and said, 'Did you notice that none of your rich friends paid any attention to me, Guido? They expected me to make them coffee and pour them wine and beer while they discussed freedom for the … peasants.' After that night, Brunetti could never hear or read that word without wincing.

'I had four years of school, Guido, so I don't understand what some of the things they said mean. But I do know they never thought to ask me what I wanted, what freedom meant to me.' Her hands were finally dry. She'd slipped her apron over her head and hung it in its place on the nail in the back of the kitchen door. 'And they didn't ask me, Guido, because I don't mean anything to them.' She'd smiled at him, but did not give him a kiss, said goodnight, and left the room.

Brunetti rubbed at his eyes, telling himself they were tired from reading on the screen for so long. When they felt better again, he returned to reading what Signorina Elettra had sent him. There was Rubini's thesis, which compared the depiction of Christ's hands in six Renaissance painters, and Nesi's, an analysis of steel production in Russia between 1939 and 1945. Neither, he thought, would contribute anything vital to the investigation of Inesh's death. She had been unable to find a copy of Molin's: only the submission form he'd signed remained.

The next piece of information she had included was the student list for a class in modern Italian history: all three of the young men were registered in the class, which was taught by Professore Giuliano Loreti.

The name burst out, leaping over decades and dragging Brunetti's memory back to the case that had brought the idea of terrorism to Venice. Professore Loreti had been a likely Christian Democrat candidate for Parliament in the forthcoming elections: from Brescia, the only son of a wealthy industrialist, already a consultant to the parliamentary commission concerned with employment law, he had, one day, simply disappeared. On the day he vanished, he had taught his class, spent the afternoon in his office, had dinner at home, told a neighbour he was going out for a drink with friends, and had never been seen again, nor was any trace of him ever found. At the time, when kidnapping was frequent and savage, his disappearance was attributed to Leftist terrorists, the inconclusive investigation based on that suspicion.

Brunetti, feeling not a little bit proud of his ability, opened Google and had a look for the late professor. He learned that Loreti had been Jesuit-educated, had studied in the United States, and was viewed, at the time of his death, as one of the bright hopes of the moribund Christian Democratic Party. Both *la Repubblica* and *Il Corriere della Sera* mentioned his glowing scholarly reputation and 'his merciless attacks on the politics of the Left'.

Brunetti glanced towards the window and considered all of this, then returned his attention to Signorina Elettra's information about Renato Molin. After completing his second year, Molin had been absent from the university for three years, only to return as a different person, his interest now shifted to medieval Italian history. He had completed his doctoral studies in six years and stayed on to begin the slow climb up the ladder of success, arriving at a full professorship only after two more decades.

Federico Nesi had devoted his first university years to the study of history and political science. He had not done well in his classes, perhaps the reason why he temporarily abandoned

the university, only to return a few years later to study econom-
ics, finishing with a master's degree in management and
banking.

His path upwards had begun with his first job, as branch
manager at a long-since dissolved bank. He had passed to
another, jumped ship a year before it too was carted off to the
bank cemetery, and died a year after retiring as director of a
still-surviving bank.

After university, there was no evidence that he had been
involved any longer with either of the other men, not even to be
photographed with one of them at an official dinner or to have
their names appear in something so small as a photo caption in
Il Gazzettino and thus subject to the power of Signorina Elettra's
lens.

Brunetti pushed his chair back and crossed his legs. Molin
had not only been both Rubini's flatmate and classmate, but also
– he was surprised to learn – witness to his wedding. Nesi
became a banker, Molin went on to a university career, and
Rubini went to prison.

Brunetti walked over to the filing cabinet on the other side
of his office and took the scrapbook he'd found among Inesh's
things. He went back to his desk and leafed through it until he
found an essay by Belisarius, the name chosen, perhaps, by a
young man with ambitions to greatness. It had obviously been
written on a typewriter and photocopied: it was visually pre-
sentable, save for some clumsy traces of erasure marks towards
the end, as though the writer had decided to make some final
changes by hand to the word 'Medieval' after he'd pulled it
from the typewriter, creating his own palimpsest. Brunetti
recognized the steep, curved double arches of the capital 'M'
that had also appeared on Molin's submission form for his
doctoral dissertation, and thus he discovered the identity of
Belisarius.

The message in the article was – however outdated – clear: the rich were kept in power by the connivance of the educated classes, who encouraged the People (Belisarius always capitalized this word) to vote into office the lickspittle frontmen of the Elite (also capitalized) who would make promises they had no intention of keeping and assure the People that their votes would bring better times and a more honest and equitable society.

It was hard, because it was embarrassing, for Brunetti to read this sort of thing, so closely did it echo the rhetoric he had found so persuasive in his first years at university. He had voted for similar types, who promised better times and a more equitable society. 'And just look at us now,' he said aloud. Hearing someone's footfall, he looked up, already embarrassed at the thought of being caught talking to himself, but it was only a uniformed officer walking by in the hallway.

His own children were avowing much the same ideas today, based on the equally idealistic vision of humanity that had animated the young Brunetti and led him to espouse certain ideas and people (always men). He'd hoped that the ideals of his generation would make the world a better place and introduce a better sort of person (always a man) to political power. Instead, the same stunted politicians (some now women) still dressed in the same expensive suits to have their turn at the trough.

He focused his eyes on the papers, turned a page, and found a short article by Professore Loreti. He began reading and recognized the same sort of argument that the Right had persisted in using until the financial system fell apart in 2008. Remove government control of pricing and markets; trust banks and the leaders of big business to do the best for clients and workers, strengthen and enforce the laws regarding illegal immigration to Italy.

Reading this, Brunetti was put in mind of the *'tris'* he'd seen on menus in restaurants that catered to tourists. Give them three types of pasta as a first dish: spaghetti with tomato sauce, lasagna, and ravioli with spinach and ricotta, all thrown together on the same plate: *'tris'*. It filled you up and staved off hunger for a while. Who would turn it down?

Finished with Professore Loreti's article, Brunetti thought he might as well do it right and so paged through the remaining papers in the scrapbook until he found a single-page manifesto, Belisarius' name at the bottom. After reading only two paragraphs, Brunetti wondered why Molin had chosen that name and not 'Samson', for he was willing to tear down the entire social and financial system of the West and stand laughing as the blocks crashed down upon his own head. And upon us all. Eliminate private ownership of all large enterprises, entrust power to the People, believe in the goodness and equality of mankind. Eliminate armies; let the People embrace one another and possess no more than the others had. Belisarius offered no advice on just how to bring all of this about, but Brunetti was certain he'd have an answer, somewhere.

Without pausing to articulate the thought, Brunetti had concluded that if Molin was Belisarius, Nesi was most likely to have been Aeneas. Nesi had abandoned the others but had taken with him these papers, which were important enough for him to keep for the rest of his life. He'd lived for a time with the others, then had floated out of their world, only to embrace the world of finance, success, wealth. Yet these were the papers that had survived.

He took out his phone and punched in Carlo's number. Brunetti wasted no time and told the book dealer that he wanted to speak to his friend, Nesi's son.

'He knew this would happen,' Carlo said. 'He knew as soon as I told him where the police had found the papers.'

'What else did he say?' Brunetti asked.

'That he doesn't like it. His father was a good man and shouldn't be dragged into this.'

'Carlo,' Brunetti began, 'how does he know that there's anything to be dragged into?'

A long silence grew out from this question. 'I suppose he'll ... ' Carlo began, and then stopped.

'Just say it, Carlo.'

'That he'll believe it's what happens when you deal with the police. They never let you go again.'

'Do you believe this?'

'Most people do.'

'I know that, but I'm not asking about "most people". I'm asking about you.'

Brunetti heard another voice, then Carlo answering, 'On the shelf towards your left. Third row from the ceiling.

'I don't believe it, Commissario,' Carlo came back to say.

'All right, then I'll ask you a favour. Could you call and tell him I want to talk to him about these papers? That's all. I'm not interested in his father, don't have any reason to ask about him. I simply want to know where his father got these papers.'

'And you want me to ask him?'

'Carlo, I don't even know who he is. He's a young man named Nesi: that's all I know. And all I want to know. About him. I want him to talk to me about his father's papers,' Brunetti repeated, coming down with special force on the last word. He let a long time pass and then asked, 'Will you ask him?'

Time spun its wheels for a bit and then another bit. 'All right,' Carlo said and broke the connection.

It was almost an hour before he called, saying, 'He doesn't like it, but he'll do it.'

'Thank you, Carlo. When and where?'

'Tomorrow. He suggested you sit on one of the benches in the *campo*. He said to tell you he'll tape it on his phone, so there's no chance of any mistakes.'

'Good idea,' Brunetti said, meaning it. 'What time?'

'High noon.'
'Sounds like that Western movie,' Brunetti said.
'What?'
'You're too young to know, Carlo.'

The next morning, Brunetti spent some time taking another look through the scrapbook he'd come to think of as still belonging to Inesh. He had the time, so he read through it again, this time more carefully. Brunetti was again embarrassed by how jejune their arguments – or what they thought were arguments – actually were. Both Aeneas and Belisarius were certainly clever, but a second reading punched holes in their assertions and allowed the false arguments to slide out: reductio ad absurdum, ad hominem, post hoc, slippery slope (especially effective when talking about immigrants). It wasn't really thinking, Brunetti realized; it was conviction or belief so strong that other opinions didn't merit consideration.

Belisarius wrote in long sentences that seemed to express complex ideas clearly but ended up in a tangle of syntax and contradiction, while Aeneas wrote more clearly but had less to say. Both, however, agreed that only violence, at this point in history, would be effective in the fight for equality.

At eleven thirty, he shut the book, put it in his briefcase, and went downstairs with it. Outside the Questura, he turned left. The *riva* – even this insignificant one in front of the Questura – was full of people walking both ways. Brunetti sensed they were tourists, although he could not explain how he knew this: it was a combination of clothing, sneakers, and an aura of uncertainty about where they might be. The most timid-looking might well have been those who realized that even if they did know where they were, it still wasn't much help.

He chose to go along Rio della Tetta, not because it was any faster but because the pink paving stones gave him such delight.

He crossed an already crowded Campo San Giovanni e Paolo and continued past the canal where Inesh's body had been found until he came down the bridge into Campo Santa Maria Nova.

Brunetti paused in front of the bar and studied the people on the benches. Some of them he excluded, either because of their age or because they looked like tourists. A young man sat on the bench directly across from Carlo's shop, a paper shopping bag beside him, preventing any attempt that might be made to take the seat. He was busy tapping a message into his phone.

Brunetti, carrying the papers in his briefcase, went and stood in front of the younger man, careful to remain an arm's length away. 'Signor Nesi?' he asked.

The young man got to his feet, stifled the attempt to extend his hand, and asked, 'Commissario Brunetti?' He was very tall and very thin with a narrow face and the nose of a medieval Spanish nobleman. His eyes were hazel, his look sudden and swift.

'Yes,' Brunetti said, then pointed to the shopping bag on the bench and asked, 'May I?'

'Of course, of course,' the young man said, moving the bag to where he had been sitting; he then sat beside it, leaving Brunetti only the end of the bench on the other side of the bag. Brunetti sat and crossed his legs, turning himself in the young man's direction and placing the briefcase on his lap.

Without preparation, which he thought unnecessary, Brunetti opened his briefcase and pulled out the scrapbook. 'I'd like to thank you for agreeing to talk to me,' he began. Without waiting for Nesi to answer, he went on: 'As Carlo's told you, I'd like to know more about these papers.' He tapped absently at them.

Nesi set the shopping bag on the pavement in front of them, switched on something on his phone, and set it carefully on the bench between them.

'Why?' the young man asked.

'Because they might be connected to a crime.'

'That happened when?'

'This week.'

'Really?' Nesi asked with great seriousness, as though he wanted to be certain of what he'd heard.

'Yes, the Sri Lankan in the canal.'

Brunetti heard him sigh and felt, even with the space between them, that Nesi's body eased and relaxed. So, too, was his voice much calmer when he asked, 'How is the murder related to the papers?'

Before he could answer, a little boy rolled past on a scooter, followed by a wildly barking dog. Bringing up the rear was a girl in her late teens, shouting, 'Briciola! Briciola! Stop that—come here.' The boy swerved to the left, into the narrow passage leading to Campo San Canzian, followed by the dog, followed by the girl, followed by their diminishing noise.

When it was quiet again, Brunetti said, 'That's what I'm trying to find out.' The investigation into Inesh's life in Venice had disclosed nothing so far: he worked, saved his money and sent it to his family in Sri Lanka. 'He apparently had no enemies and no debts, so with the common motives gone, we're left looking for anything uncommon.' Brunetti tapped at the scrapbook, saying, 'These papers are uncommon.'

Gesturing in the direction of the papers, Nesi asked, 'Do you think the motive's in there?'

Brunetti shrugged. 'It might be, but I have to find out how the papers fit in before I understand anything.'

'Fit in with what?'

'With why someone would want to kill him.' Even as he finished speaking, Brunetti realized it was as circular an explanation as he'd ever given. So he went on: 'These papers were found in the house of the man who was murdered. Your father knew one of the men living in another house on the same property. The papers date back to the time when your father and two other men were at university together.'

Brunetti leaned forward, hands clasped around the scrapbook, elbows on knees, and asked, 'Have you read what's in here?'

To Brunetti's astonishment, Nesi laughed, a real, bright laugh, nothing forced, nothing sarcastic, simply amusement. Slowly, his laughter stopped, and he turned to Brunetti. 'I'm at the same university as my father. But I'm studying Oriental languages.' Waving a hand at the scrapbook, he said, 'That's why I gave up when I read the first few pages. It all seemed like mad raving to me, but when I told Carlo about it, he said the pamphlets might be interesting to a few of his clients, so I asked him to sell them all for me.'

Brunetti turned to look at him and saw the residue of his smile.

'It was a year before he gave me ten euros for them, and I'd already forgotten about it.'

Brunetti pushed himself upright and rested against the back of the bench, and asked, 'Did your father ever say anything about what's in here?' he asked.

Nesi's smile evaporated; it was as if he'd frozen over. He folded his arms across his chest and turned to look at the leafless tree that had once stood in the centre of the small *campo*. After a long time, he said, still studying the leafless branches, 'My father was a strange man.'

'So was mine,' Brunetti said without thinking.

'Mine said – not long before he died – that he had done a terrible thing when he was young.'

Brunetti's father, swept up into the last days of the war when he wasn't even yet a teenager, had said only that he had seen terrible things done, but Brunetti saw no reason to repeat this, certainly not now.

After it became evident that Nesi was not going to speak, Brunetti asked, 'Did he say what it was?'

Nesi shook his head. 'He said it only once, really in his last days.'

'What exactly did he say?' Brunetti asked, curious, not insistent.

'That he'd done a terrible thing – only that. Then he corrected himself and said he'd only helped. He was insistent about that.' Nesi folded his hands together and went on. 'The strangest thing was that he said they did it because they were cursed.' The young man spoke with the confusion of someone raised in an age that no longer believed in curses.

'"Cursed",' Brunetti repeated with no inflection.

'Yes. He said they'd been cursed by wanting.' Nesi shook his head and said, 'Don't even ask. He didn't explain. He was filled with painkillers and didn't recognize me or my mother. But he kept saying, "We all wanted. We all wanted," but he never got to saying what it was they wanted.'

'Was he lucid?'

Nesi shrugged. 'I have no idea. He slurred everything he said, didn't know who we were. He could have been standing on a street corner, trying to talk to the people walking by.'

'I'm sorry for your pain,' Brunetti said. He got to his feet and thanked Nesi for talking to him. He thought it might be kinder to leave the young man there to gather his spirits by himself.

Brunetti turned to leave but heard Nesi say, 'I brought you the rest.' When he turned back to him, Nesi held out the shopping bag. Without thinking, Brunetti accepted it, thanked him again, and turned towards home.

25

Brunetti waited until he was home before he dared to look inside the shopping bag. He lifted it onto the kitchen table, Paola's desk being covered with notes and papers, books and magazines. The 'STANDA' logo smacked him in the face from the side of the bag. He recognized it instantly: boldly red. Standa: his mother's partner in raising her sons. The store provided, first of all, food and drink, although her boys usually drank tap water. It sold clothing: Brunetti's first pair of jeans came from Standa, as did his first pair of sneakers. He could still remember the lush feel of slipping his naked feet into the softness of the canvas shoes, bouncing on the rubber soles.

He closed his eyes and recalled not only a decade of white cotton underwear, but also his first cashmere sweater, given to him by his mother when he graduated from *liceo* with the highest grades and was accepted by the Faculty of Law at the university.

The sweater was a medium grey, the same colour that his mother's hair had by then become, and had a round neck. It was thick yet soft and supple and represented for the young Brunetti a step forward, though he had no idea in which direction. He had it still, after all these years, and wore it when they went hiking on vacation. Or sometimes he wore it around the house for the simple pleasure of remembering opening the box and seeing it and feeling cashmere for the first time.

There was no cashmere sweater in this bag, only a file of papers, the cover worn and bleached a clear blue with time and light. He pulled it out and set it on the table, moved the bag to the floor, and sat. In front of him lay a stack of papers about the thickness of a telephone book: he wondered how many people still recalled that as a measure of size. They appeared to be divided into three parts by elastic bands so old that they had died and the division could be resurrected only by finding the shrivelled end of the band and slipping a finger into the papers to follow the withered rubber to the other side. Thus he separated the papers into three sections.

The first and thickest dealt with the bombing of the Bologna train station, with newspaper and magazine articles starting from the first day and going on for a month before abruptly stopping.

The next followed the legendary kidnapping of the American general Dozier in Verona. Again, the stories came from different newspapers and were in strict chronological order. After a month, they too ended.

The last covered the disappearance of Professore Loreti and contained articles from both *Il Gazzettino* and the major national newspapers.

He remembered some of what was there: the Professore had taught his class, which that day considered the mysterious death of Air Marshal, and hero, Italo Balbo and its political repercussions. He'd then had a sandwich with a colleague, who remembered nothing unusual about Loreti's behaviour or remarks, and from there he'd said – according to his colleague – he was going home to work on an article he was writing.

The man from whom he bought his newspapers gave Loreti his copies of *Il Gazzettino* and *Il Corriere* sometime after lunch, but they had not spoken. Loreti had returned to his apartment in Castello and apparently read and took notes on a recent ministerial document concerning employment law.

His downstairs neighbour had met him on the stairs a little after suppertime – about nine – when Loreti said he was going out to meet some people for a drink. And disappeared.

When he did not teach his class the following afternoon, the university made an attempt to find him; it was not until the following day that his sister was alerted by a phone call from the university administration, asking if she had any ideas as to his whereabouts. None.

After that, events unfolded as they had learned to do during the worst years of terrorism, the years of lead: the Carabinieri entered the home of the missing person in search of him or her; that failing, they informed the Squadra Mobile, but still conducted a forensic search of the home of the missing person themselves. Depending upon the results, other agencies of the state would be contacted, or not. In the absence of signs of violence or a demand for a ransom, the disappearance was downgraded to a missing person investigation and turned over to the local police, where it would remain so long as there was no demand for money.

Given Loreti's position in society, the press had followed, panting. But they were to be disappointed by the police's failure to find any sign of what the English call 'foul play', and so the investigation had been downsized to 'missing person', whereupon the articles began to grow shorter and the pages on which they were printed further to the back of the newspapers. After a month or two, the articles followed the person into obscurity. Brunetti, who often saw things in a literary way, thought of this as a transposed simile. In the first days, the Loreti case was compared to some crime from the past. After a year, a new crime was compared to the Loreti disappearance. Over the years and generations, it had drifted into the distant past, Brunetti realized: from sensation to footnote.

He began to read about the final months and found – strangely out of place – an article from the early days of Loreti's disappearance, stating that the police were optimistic that the missing Professore would eventually be found. No evidence to support this belief was offered, and certainly its promise was never realized.

A handbreadth below the last paragraph, someone had drawn a small cross. There was nothing written. Brunetti turned the page, but there was only one final, empty sheet.

Paola found him in the kitchen when she came home about twenty minutes later, back from teaching one of the three classes she taught a week, much to the scandalized delight of her entire family. This had gone on so long that there was little fun left in teasing her about it.

She entered the kitchen, set some bags on the counter, and came over to prop her hands on his shoulders and shake them a bit. 'What are you doing in here? You know you can read in my room: the light's much better.'

Brunetti shrugged, reluctant to say her desk was covered with papers. He wouldn't have had time to tell her anyway, for Paola had seen the bag. '*Oddio*, Standa,' she exclaimed as she picked it up by the handles. 'I haven't seen one in … more than twenty years.' She put it back on the table and stepped back to gaze at it. 'No one would believe this.'

Smiling, delighted at her response to the bag, he said, 'No one would believe you're so thrilled by it.'

'I adored Standa. They had everything. Everything.' She set the bag in the centre of the table, then moved it to his left, careful to turn it so as to expose the red logo, then went to the other side and took a picture of Brunetti and the bag. 'No one I know is going to believe this.'

Paola set her phone on the table and went to the counter to start putting things away. With her back to him, she asked, 'Wherever did you get it?'

'The bag?'

'Yes.'

'Someone used it to carry papers.'

'Papers for you?'

He nodded, and when she said nothing, he realized she was not looking at him but into the cabinets. 'Yes, for me,' he said.

'What for?'

'It's about the Sri Lankan man.'

She turned to him and asked, 'The one who was killed?'

'Yes.'

'Was the bag his?'

'No. Someone kept papers in it.'

'Then why do you say they're about the Sri Lankan?'

Here it was again, but from a different person. Why indeed? Brunetti asked himself. How had these papers ended up having anything to do with the murder of Inesh?

And how was it that Nesi's father had taken such an interest in kidnapping? Brunetti was allergic to that word; it struck his guts like no other word, no other reality, put there decades ago, in Sardinia, at the beginning of his career.

He felt her arms around him and leaned back into them. Paola said, 'Just sit quietly, Guido. I'm here and it's over. Whatever you were remembering, it's over now. You're safe, we're safe, we're all safe.' And then she stopped bothering with language and made a soft crooning sound. And Brunetti sat stiffly, wanting to say that no one was safe, but was unable to speak.

Later, calmed by lunch with the kids, the raillery and jokes, the ease of communication, and his sense of Paola's uninvasive concern, Brunetti went back to her study, where the desk was still covered with stacks of papers. Maybe she did do the odd half-hour's work now and again, he mused. How else could an article of hers have appeared in something called *The Henry James Review*?

He had left his Pausanias on the sofa and opened it where he'd left off, at the description of the Parthenon. As he read, Brunetti marvelled at how Pausanias had so casually joined fact – much of it still to be seen two thousand years later – with myth. The sea was visible to Pausanias from the Acropolis, and on it had sailed Theseus, as though there existed no difference between the reality of the white marble of the temples and the imagined black sails of Theseus' ship. Brunetti closed his eyes for a moment to visualize what that ship might have looked like and woke to the sound of Paola asking, in quite an ordinary voice, if he intended to return to work that afternoon.

He did intend to go to the Questura and used the time walking there to think of what he wanted to know. The memory of his experience in Sardinia had upset him more than he realized, but it had also dislodged something in his brain, and the more he considered it, the more interesting he found it.

He lost no time when he got to his office but went straight to the official site of the Ministry of the Interior, surprised that he could access the files of his employer without subterfuge or without invoking the powers of Signorina Elettra. But, as much as he looked for information about the Ministry's plan for investigating kidnapping, he found very little. The best he came up with was a notice of a show of photographs of people who had been kidnapped, which had opened five years ago in Reggio Calabria.

He ran through the site again, finding a listing of crimes, but nowhere was mentioned 'sequestro di persona'. He thought of going down to ask Signorina Elettra, but he told himself to persist and stayed at his desk. After about a quarter of an hour, he found a document published by a magazine whose name he did not recognize.

From it he learned that from 1980 to 1984, 178 people were kidnapped in Italy. The Veneto was one of the regions most affected. He found no information about how many were rescued or returned after a ransom was paid. Nor could he find any reference to the law that immediately slams shut the assets of the relatives of kidnapped people, the better to render it impossible for them to pay a ransom.

He got up and went over to the window to study the comforting façade of the church of San Lorenzo, ever eager for Brunetti's admiring gaze. He'd read of the salacious lives of the Benedictine nuns cloistered in the attached monastery in previous centuries and the skill with which they had managed to slip out into the larger world. And good luck to them, he thought, gazing at the sky above the church.

He thought of Nesi's question, ingenuous but astute and repeated by Paola: what was the connection between the scrapbook and Inesh's death? Why was the collector of the documents interested in the disappearance of Professore Loreti? And was it Nesi who had collected them?

It was only mid-afternoon, so there was plenty of time to have another talk with Bocchese. He found the technician still at work, although the work involved a bronze miniature of a much-muscled god or demigod with a spear, not anything even remotely related to police matters. It looked as though Bocchese were trying to slip the tiny spear through the cylinder of the god's closed hand, holding the spear with a pair of rubber-headed tweezers and twisting it gently back and forth as he tried to move the cylindrical bronze shaft through the god's hand, where it seemed to be stuck. Bocchese's left hand steadied itself on the desk while it held the bottom of the spear, which was, Brunetti estimated, five or six centimetres long.

Brunetti stopped a metre from him, not wanting to create a disturbance, no matter how small, and continued to watch. After another minute, Bocchese said, 'Guido, there's a bottle of oil in my bottom-right drawer, and some cotton buds. Could you dip one in the oil and run it up and down the spear?'

Brunetti did as he was told and wiped carefully up and down the spear as Bocchese extended it towards him.

'All right,' Bocchese said. Brunetti backed away, keeping his eyes on the spear and the tweezers. Back and forth, back and forth Bocchese went, up and down, up and down, and suddenly the bottom of the spear slipped through the god's hand and slid down until it touched the metal ground at the god's feet.

Bocchese set the god, now upright on his base, in the middle of his desk. 'Beautiful, isn't he?' he asked, eyes still on the god.

'Yes, he is.' Brunetti remembered how reluctant Bocchese was ever to reveal the sources of his collection, and so said only, 'You must be very happy to have him.'

Bocchese smiled. 'Yes, I am. It took me a year to persuade the owner.'

That was more information than Brunetti had ever been offered before. He smiled and nodded, then said, 'I came to ask you a favour.'

'About work?' Bocchese asked, moving his right hand a bit closer to the statue.

'Yes, about that piece of bone in the watch pocket of the man in the canal.'

'What about it?' Bocchese asked, relaxing his hand.

'Have you identified it?'

'Rizzardi took a look. He might have written something. I was busy,' he said, lifting the statue a bit.

'Could you check?' Brunetti asked.

This, clearly, created a problem for Bocchese. He surely would not carry the statue with him when he went to the files, nor did he seem comfortable with the idea of leaving it with Brunetti. He picked up the phone and dialled a single number, then asked the voice that answered to come over for a minute.

One of his assistants was there seconds after Bocchese hung up, leaving Brunetti curious about why the chief technician didn't just shout at him to come.

Bocchese told his assistant what to look for and where to find it, then began wiping his hands with a suede cloth.

The other man was soon back, holding a small jewellery box, the sort of thing meant for an engagement ring. 'Give it to the Commissario,' Bocchese said, continuing to wipe his hands.

Brunetti thanked the man, who nodded as he passed him the box, then left. When he opened it, he saw the small piece of intact cylindrical bone, about two centimetres long and as rounded as a piece of penne, although the idea of measuring it in terms of pasta made Brunetti uncomfortable.

Brunetti pushed it to one side of the box, then the other, looking for any identification Rizzardi might have given.

When Bocchese saw what Brunetti was doing, he picked up the phone and again pushed in a single number. When it was picked up at the other end, he asked, 'What did Rizzardi say?' He listened for a moment, thanked the man, and hung up.

'It's a segment of a human finger. The doctor's taken a sample and sent it to the lab in Padova to verify his identification.'

'When will that be back?'

Bocchese raised his hands in the air, as though to ward off a mugger, and said, 'When it gets here.'

He lowered his hands and looked at the standing Brunetti. 'You're going to nag me about this, aren't you?'

'Yes.'

'If you promise not to nag me, I'll nag them and call you as soon as they call me.'

'Fair enough,' Brunetti conceded and turned to leave. 'Tell them it's really urgent.'

'They've already told me they're tired of hearing me say that.'

Brunetti ignored that and asked, 'Man or woman?'

Bocchese dialled the number again. The same voice answered and, when asked, said something loud enough for Brunetti to hear. 'Man.'

He thanked Bocchese, complimented him on the statue again, and left.

26

When he stepped out into the *calle* on Monday morning, Brunetti regretted not having worn a woollen scarf. Autumn had stopped fooling around and had apparently decided to hand things over to winter. He wasted no time on the thought of going back to the apartment to get one; instead, he buttoned his overcoat and set off in the direction of the San Tomà stop. As he turned into the *calle* that led from the *campo* down to the *imbarcadero*, he heard the sound of a vaporetto slipping into reverse and lengthened his steps. Halfway down, he passed the people coming from the boat and wondered which one it was that still idled at the boat stop: going right or left? If he ran, there was perhaps time enough to catch it, but it mattered only if it was the boat heading towards the Lido.

He took two trotting steps, but then the metallic slam of the railing that stopped entry to the boat, whichever it was, rendered the question moot. He slowed, the better to hear it, and thought he heard the boat moving off to the left, the opposite direction to the Questura. As he arrived at the *imbarcadero*, he saw that this was indeed the case: the boat he wanted was visible on the left, approaching from San Silvestro.

He took his iMob and tapped it against the sensor. The small metal bars swung open, and he walked down onto the landing to wait for his boat. Years ago, he had invented a system to try to control his impatience with the vaporetti and their matronly progress up and down the Canal Grande. How would it feel, he asked himself when particularly stressed at the thought of the time spent advancing at the vaporetto's slow pace, to be a tourist and to be seeing all of this not only for the first time but for only one euro forty? Surprisingly, it always worked to calm him down and make impatience an act of folly. Flow past the Palazzo Ducale and Cà d'Oro, slip under the Rialto or the Accademia. And he wanted not to see this? Wanted the ride to be over faster? Did he want the actors on stage – or the singers – to move faster, speak or sing faster, the sooner to get all this beauty over with? 'They'd lock me up,' he said to himself, startling the man standing next to him.

Luckily, they were just pulling into the Riva degli Schiavoni stop: Brunetti hurried to the other side to be the first person off the boat, turned right on the pavement and walked with increased speed to get away from the place of his embarrassment. After the first bridge, he allowed himself to slow down and enjoy the walk as much as he could. It was one of the broadest walkways in the city, stretching from San Marco all the way down to the Arsenal stop, where it narrowed to give more space to I Giardini. The views off to the right were long, with only small islands and the occasional boat to interrupt the sight lines that extended to the Lido and beyond.

When he walked into the Questura, he was surprised to find Vianello standing just inside the door, as if he were waiting for someone. The sobriety on his face when he saw Brunetti enforced the idea.

Without any prelude, the Ispettore said, 'I've got something to show you.'

Brunetti nodded. Vianello turned away and started towards the squad room, walking very quicky.

As they entered, Brunetti saw only two officers, both of them busy at their computers. One of them, seeing Brunetti come in, made a languid gesture; Brunetti answered with a nod. The other didn't look up.

Brunetti slowed and looked around the room but saw nothing that seemed out of place. Vianello stepped back and took his arm, leading him to the door to the changing room, where officers could change before or after work if they chose.

He opened the door and went inside. Brunetti followed him. Impatient, he finally asked, 'What is it?'

'I came in this morning to pick up a pair of shoes I forgot to take to the shoemaker yesterday. They were in my locker, but I forgot about it and left them there overnight.'

This was going nowhere, Brunetti thought.

'And I found this,' Vianello said and pulled something bright red from his pocket. At first Brunetti thought it was a silk handkerchief that someone had used to stop a bloody nose, but when Vianello opened his hand, Brunetti saw that it was a pair of very small and very red women's underpants.

He stared at them, and Vianello said, 'They were hanging from the knob on Alvise's locker.'

'Did he see them?' Brunetti asked instantly.

Vianello shook his head.

'Was anyone here?'

The Ispettore shook his head again, but something warned Brunetti he was not asking the right question.

'Tell me,' Brunetti said.

'When I was coming out into the corridor, Lieutenant Scarpa was walking towards me. And he smiled. Didn't say anything. Just smiled.'

The two friends looked at one another. Vianello tilted his head to one side and shrugged; Brunetti pulled his lips in and nodded. Then each went back to his own desk, both in possession of the same thought.

Brunetti had brought the second group of clippings along with him today, although not in the Standa bag: he did not want to arrive with a long train of people busy sharing their memories of Standa with one another.

He read the files again, straight through. During the weeks after the Bologna massacre, the number of victims rose day by day as the seriously injured succumbed to their wounds and died. The number stopped at eighty-five, but this did not factor in the suffering of the many hundreds of wounded.

Revelations and discoveries about the motive for the Bologna bombing, many of them contradictory, had been part of his youth: he grew up with the names Musumeci, Gelli, and Picciafuoco swirling around in a vapour of accusation, certainty, doubt, horror, and many other emotions, all as strong as they were conflicting. Men went to jail only to be released and then arrested again. Absolute certainty withered away in a day, and good and bad became horribly entangled with one another. If Brunetti had trouble thinking in absolutes, it might be attributed to these years and to the lack of any certainty about an event that was the major horror of his time.

Just last week, Brunetti had read of yet another trial and yet another accusation, the same old crimes and same old names: Bellini, Segatel, Catracchia. There was no solution to the crime that was not immediately called into question.

While the Bologna bombing remained in the minds of many as a still unsolved case, the kidnapping of the American NATO general was a bit like a Marx Brothers film. Kidnapped from his apartment by the Red Brigades in Verona and held for forty-two days, the general was allowed to play solitaire and forced to listen to loud music until he was rescued by an Italian special force – with the rumoured help of the Mafia – and all of his captors were arrested. During the weeks they held him prisoner, his kidnappers had never expressed interest in entering into negotiations concerning their captive's release nor bothered to ask for a ransom, apparently content to send communiqués to the American and Italian forces asserting their political views.

Given the odd leap from tragedy to slapstick, Brunetti wondered why the file on Loreti's kidnapping was stuck between the other two cases. How was it related? Because of terrorism or because of kidnapping? And how in God's name was a Sri Lankan with a human finger bone in his watch pocket related to any of this?

He went back to the window and resumed his contemplation of the façade of the church. From his first teachers, Brunetti had been taught to know and revere the saints, especially the martyrs, and so he knew San Lorenzo to be the patron saint of cooks and comedians, though he'd forgotten why. If memory served, he'd been burned to death: Brunetti was unable to find anything comic in that.

He stared at the church and the sky behind it for some time, then, deciding it was time to discuss this case in depth with his colleagues, he called both Vianello and Griffoni. The first said he was in the squad room and would come up in an hour. Griffoni was on the way back from Mestre, where she'd spent the morning in the underground firing range at the Questura there to try out the new pistol she had been issued. 'The road's blocked. I've no idea when I'll be there,' she said.

Her tone told Brunetti not to make a joke of this, and he told her they'd wait until she arrived.

27

In the meantime, a file had arrived on Brunetti's desk describing the shopping spree made the day before by a young couple who spoke Italian very well, but with a French accent. They had shopped their way around the city, buying watches about which they displayed the familiarity of collectors, using a series of fake credit cards, for all of which they had matching passports. They went around Fondaco dei Tedeschi, stopping at two shops where they acquired four watches, two IWC and two Rolex. Then, for dessert, they walked arm in arm to Piazza San Marco, and picked up – as an anniversary present from husband to wife – a Patek Philippe Calatrava, still speaking the same excellent Italian, this time with an English accent and complementing the accent with a different credit card and a British passport.

When he finished reading the report, Brunetti shook his head a few times and did not laugh. Years ago, when he was closer to the prejudices of his youth – and entirely unfamiliar with the things he thought he should despise – he would have done that, perhaps raising his fist in the air in a manifestation of solidarity with the thieves for having successfully put something over on the rich. He would no doubt have justified their behaviour as the right of the working classes to help themselves to some of the toys of the wealthy, careful to use the word 'exploitation' somewhere in that sentence.

These were ideas he'd never mentioned to his parents and, truth to tell, even though he held the proper opinions for the time of year, he never fully succeeded in convincing himself that they were true. Theft had displeased him then as much as it did now. About deceit, however, Brunetti had a far more elastic opinion. It was bad when used against him, a useful weapon when it was his turn to use it. To some it might be evidence of a moral failure. Brunetti had persuaded himself that it was merely a pragmatic survival skill.

Griffoni and Vianello arrived together more than an hour later. Before either of them could ask, Griffoni put her briefcase on Brunetti's desk, opened it, and pulled out a dark brown leather holster, which, when she opened it, presented them with the sight of a black metal handle and a promise of the pistol: slim, light, lethal.

'What is it?' Vianello asked.

Griffoni pulled what looked like an instruction booklet out of her briefcase and read, '"Beretta 92X".'

'Thank you,' Brunetti said, nodding his head at the pistol, as if to tell her there was no need to show them more.

Vianello, who carried his weapon only when in uniform, said, 'I hope you'll be very happy together.'

Griffoni smiled and slipped the holster back into her briefcase, then set it on the floor.

When they were all seated, Brunetti started to give them the information and intuitions he'd been accumulating over the last few days that might or might not have something to do with the murder of Inesh Kavinda. During the next half-hour, he even read to them passages from some of the manifestos he'd found in the scrapbook, including his favourite: 'The classes that profit from the sweat of the workers are traitors and vultures, and must be destroyed. By violence if necessary.'

When he finished, he said he'd like to talk about the disappearance of Professore Loreti, in whose class Rubini, Nesi, and Molin had been students. He asked if they had anything to add.

Griffoni surprised them both by saying, 'I don't know if it's any use, but Loreti's uncle had two children.' Seeing their expressions, she explained. 'I was stuck in traffic for half an hour, so after I read what Signorina Elettra sent, I had a look through the newspaper files to see if relatives were mentioned. There was a small piece in *Il Gazzettino* about a memorial service held by the family a year after his disappearance.' She let them consider that for a moment, then added, 'I found one of them, a retired doctor. He lives in Milano and told me he'd do anything he could to help us.'

Vianello spread both palms flat on the table in front of him and stared at them, then said, as if addressing his fingers, '*Povero Cristo*. He wasn't even forty.' He considered this and added, 'I hope he ran off with a student or his best friend's wife.'

He shook his head to free it of this and turned to Griffoni to say, 'I'm not sure this has any bearing on the case, but I think we'd be wise to remember how crazy we all were then.' Vianello paused, but neither of the others spoke. 'Think of what we'd all stopped believing in: the Left, the Right, the Church.' Then, as though he were revealing the final proof: 'How else could someone put a bomb in a train station in the mid-morning of the first Saturday of August, if they weren't crazy?'

Then, voice still tight, Vianello went on to say, 'There weren't any generals or politicians or cardinals or bankers there, just working people who wanted to take their kids on a holiday.' Brunetti suspected that somehow Vianello had left them alone in the room while his memories took him back to the Bologna bombing.

Vianello shook his head and returned to them, but brought this remark with him: 'I almost never became a policeman, you know,' he said in his usual voice. 'And I think it was because of the crazy times.'

After a long silence as they tried to make sense of this, Griffoni finally asked, 'What happened, Lorenzo?'

'I came close to having a record,' the Ispettore said, rubbing a hand across his jaw, as though he were testing to see if he'd shaved that day.

'As in "criminal record"?' Griffoni asked with what had become real curiosity.

'Yes.'

'Why?'

'Because I attacked a man the day after the bombing. Broke his glasses.'

'What?' she whispered.

'He was standing at the counter in Rosa Salva – the one near Rialto – holding up his newspaper and reading it out loud,' Vianello said, voice slowing with the force of memory, 'and when he'd finished reading out the first paragraph, he announced that the people on the Left who did things like this should all be taken out and hanged.'

Brunetti remembered hearing such remarks then, and since then. 'What did you do?'

Vianello didn't say anything for a long time, and then he began with what seemed an irrelevance. 'I was there with some friends. We used to discuss politics together, and I wanted their good opinion.'

Having said that, he went silent for a time, then resumed. 'I was standing next to him, so I grabbed his newspaper and slapped his face with it. I knocked his glasses off, and one of the lenses broke when they fell.' He paused and added a footnote. 'People still used glass lenses then.'

Brunetti waited for Griffoni, who had started the conversation, to speak. But she was silent, staring at the Ispettore.

Vianello paused, then added, 'We knew everything about politics, my friends and I. Even at eighteen, we understood it all.' He stopped then and glanced from one to the other.

When it seemed he was finished, Griffoni asked, 'What happened?'

'I'd turned eighteen a few months before, though I didn't look it, so I wasn't a minor any longer. The man started shouting, and I shouted back. The police were called, and they brought me down here and called my parents, said I'd be charged with assault. Then they sent me home and told me to come back the next day, with my parents.' Looking up, he gave a boyish smile and said, 'No one bothered to ask how old I was.'

Both nodded.

'Did you go?' Brunetti asked.

'Yes. By then the man assigned the case had spoken to the victim and asked if he'd accept an apology. And a new lens.' Vianello looked off at the wall and then back at them. 'The commissario then – Lucchin – said I had to go, with my parents, and apologize. And he told my parents to make sure I paid for the lens myself. If I did it, no charges would be brought against me.'

Brunetti remembered the Commissario's name: the story didn't surprise him. 'Did you?' he asked.

Vianello nodded and stared at the ground. 'Once I saw him without the newspaper in front of his face, I saw he was an old man. Must have been seventy.' Vianello nodded a few more times, then went on. 'And I realized it didn't matter whether I was on the right side or the wrong. I was ashamed of myself. And frightened.' The Ispettore crossed his arms and shook his head a few times. 'And it wasn't only that, that I'd committed a crime: I was ashamed that I'd hit an old man. Assault, damage to property.' He shook his head again. 'I can't tell you how frightened I was, that I'd have a criminal record for assault.' He looked across at them and said, 'I was so frightened I thought I'd cry.'

Neither of them dared to ask him if he had.

'When I apologized to him, I meant it when I told him I was sorry and that I was ashamed of myself.' Vianello looked across at them, almost as if he were asking their forgiveness too.

'I kept thinking that he might have fallen when I hit him, hurt himself, hit his head. And that I would have done it. To a man old enough to be my grandfather.' Then, with a new hoarseness in his voice, he said, 'To impress my friends and show how serious I was about politics.' He went silent for a long time; neither of them dared to speak. 'And ruin my life.'

When Vianello stopped, the silence spread out from him and enveloped the other two. The longer the silence lasted, the more difficult it was to break it. Finally Vianello got to his feet and moved his chair back to its proper place near the door and left the room. Griffoni got up too, but left her chair in front of Brunetti's desk and went back to her office.

Brunetti sat without moving for some time, aware that he had just heard something important and needed to sit quietly until it would reveal itself to him. Vianello was the best of the uniformed branch. It was not because he was Brunetti's assistant and friend, but because he was the most solid of them, swift and reliable and incapable of lying to the people he worked with.

What would he have become, Brunetti wondered, if he had injured the old man, perhaps even killed him? How does a life recover after a death? What becomes of your life if you've carelessly shoved someone else away from theirs?

He'd occasionally interviewed people who killed for a living, hitmen whose work it was to kill strangers for a fee. They were vastly different from the accidental killer, the impulsive killer, such as Vianello might have been. Death could be seen on their faces, in their eyes, almost smelled on their clothing. Brunetti had never said this aloud, but he had seen evil in their eyes, a disconnect from normal humanity, and never a sign of remorse or regret. The accidental killers, if he could call them that, were at least capable of regret, sometimes even shame. But not the pros.

Strangely enough, all of them had expected Brunetti to find them special, to respect them, perhaps, because of their courage, their abilities, their intelligence, when he could barely endure having to be in the same room with them and never allowed an interrogation to take place in his office.

His thoughts turned to the three university students living in Venice as the explosive decades of political protest were shuffling to a halt. Brunetti had come to believe that apathy and passion were points on the same line and surprisingly closer to one another than people realized. What was it Vianello had said? 'To impress my friends and show how serious I was about politics.' Hadn't they all felt that same pressure and given in to the need to conform to the newly invented rules?

Brunetti had again been saved by his mother's wisdom. Once, when trying to reveal some new truth to her, he'd mentioned that Beppe Tosatto had explained it to him, whereupon his mother had asked, 'You always said he was an idiot, and now he's explaining things to you?' And so had Guido Brunetti, at an early age, again been cleansed of the fever of political enthusiasm and restored to the healthy state of distrusting them all.

But others might not have had the benefit of her good sense and thus could rely only upon their own or that of the other eighteen-year-olds with whom they spent their time. Young people longed to change the world, regardless of the cost to themselves or others. Older people longed for the world not to change so there would be no cost to themselves.

Gazing at the closed doors of his wardrobe brought no illumination, so he went to the window, hoping that gazing at something in the distance might be more helpful. Two old men sat on the bench in front of the old people's home in the *campo*. Both wore coats perhaps thicker than was warranted by the day. One had rested his cane against their bench: both sat like statues, their faces turned towards the sun. They appeared to be talking because one or the other occasionally raised a hand in a slow gesture that was often followed by a slow nod from the other.

Would Rubini and Molin finish like this? he wondered. Or would he and Vianello? Old stories, old adventures, old desires. All four of them, however, had wives, and since men usually died younger, it was unlikely that they would end up on that bench.

'*Oddio,*' he exclaimed aloud, troubled to find himself dwelling on such things. They had been distracted by Vianello's story when they should have been thinking of the Loreti case and what it might mean. His thoughts turned to the bone Inesh had been carrying and remained there for some time.

He called Griffoni to ask her to take care of getting a DNA sample taken from Professore Loreti's uncle or from one of his two children, suggesting that she ask the cousin if his having worked as a doctor would help him get the test done quickly, perhaps in Milano.

That done, he returned to the consideration of the sky. He had learned early in his career to resist the temptation to decide on a solution when all the evidence had yet to be collected. He slid over a sheet of paper and drew five small circles and put in four of them the names of one of the participants: Molin, Rubini, Nesi, Loreti. In the fifth circle, he wrote the name 'Inesh'. He thought for a while and erased Nesi from where he was and wrote his name above an arrow half off the edge of the paper.

The only one Inesh knew was Molin, and the only one who knew everyone was Molin.

For years, Brunetti had tried to control his impatience to get things done and not to respond impulsively in certain situations. The answer was often repetition and digression, and he decided to use this technique now. He opened the second drawer of his desk and pulled out a set of keys lying at the front. Closing the drawer, he slipped the keys into his pocket, then took his coat from the wardrobe, still sorry he had forgotten to bring a scarf. He left his office and headed back towards Cannaregio, specifically to the *calle* around the corner from Palazzo Zaffo dei Leoni.

28

The small nun answered the door in the wall, recognizing him instantly. Her coat was unbuttoned today, perhaps to give her more freedom when working in the garden.

'Ah, Mr Policeman, welcome back.' Then, confused, she asked, 'Do you want to come in?'

He smiled, still standing a careful metre from the door, and said, 'If I might, Sorella.'

'We don't often have the police here,' she began, then paused and said, 'I don't know your name, Signore, and I think I might feel more comfortable if I could use a name when talking to you.'

'Guido Brunetti,' he said. 'I'm Venetian.'

A small laugh escaped her. 'Oh, I knew that well enough, Signor Brunetti.'

'Can you tell me yours?'

'Suor Benedetta,' she said. Then, surprised, she added with a small intake of breath, 'But I haven't asked you to come in. If you please.'

'Yes, I'd like to talk to you.' He looked at his watch and said, 'I hope I'm not interrupting you or keeping you from prayers.'

'No, I was in the garden,' she said, and made a great business of glancing over one shoulder, then the other, a parody of fear plastered across her face. She waved him to lower his head, which he did, and whispered to him, 'I was giving Sara her lunch. She's just finished.'

Brunetti straightened up, looked at his watch, and said, 'It's about that time, isn't it?'

'Yes.' Then, very cautiously, 'Would you like to meet her?'

'Very much.'

'Are you fond of dogs?' she asked, turning away and starting down the neatly swept path that led round the side of the convent to the large garden at the back. He nodded and said that yes, he liked them very much. At the very back, at least fifty metres away, he saw a dark shape outlined against the high brick wall that separated the garden from the canal. He turned to ask her if that was Sara, but when he looked back towards what he thought was the dog, it was gone.

'I told you she's clever,' Suor Benedetta said. She held up a hand and said, 'Just wait here, Signor Brunetti, and I'll ask her if she'd like to come and meet you.' That said, she walked slowly towards the back wall. The dog emerged from behind a large ceramic flowerpot and waggled its adoring way towards the nun. Suor Benedetta bent down even farther and spoke to the dog in a normal voice, although from a distance Brunetti could not understand what she said.

Suor Benedetta stopped, patted her knee, and the dog came closer. If she'd been a machine, she would have by now wiggled herself to pieces. The nun called Sara's name, turned and pointed towards Brunetti, and must have asked Sara what she thought of him because the dog looked towards him and made some sort of grunting noise.

'All right, *cara*, come and say hello to Signor Guido.' The nun turned and walked back towards Brunetti, setting her pace to that of a nervous dog's. Sara was medium-sized, flat-coated, and dark brown. One ear hung down, and a piece of it appeared to be missing. She was thin and placed her feet delicately. She stopped a metre from Brunetti, her tongue came out, and she surveyed him.

'What do you think, Sara?' the nun asked, as though her own opinion of Brunetti depended on what Sara decided. The dog pulled in her tongue and took three short steps towards Brunetti. He knelt on one knee and put out his hand, palm down. 'What a sweet girl you are, Sara. *Bella e brava.*' He assumed that any friend of Suor Benedetta's would be both beautiful and good.

The dog took another step closer to Brunetti and sniffed his hand. She looked up at the nun, who made a humming noise.

The noise must have decided things, for Sara licked Brunetti's hand a few times and then went over to Suor Benedetta, as if to remind her of who her heart's true love was.

Brunetti saw a three-person bench over against the wall. The nun must be in her eighties. She'd been working in the garden, and now it must be well past her lunchtime.

'Would you mind if I sat down, Sorella?' Brunetti asked. 'I've been walking all morning.'

'Oh, I should have offered you hospitality. Would you like something to drink? Water? Apple juice?' Her face was swept by guilt.

'No, Sorella, just to sit down for a bit.' He walked over to the bench and sat at one end. The dog sat in front of him. Brunetti ruffled the fur on her head, which she seemed to enjoy.

Suor Benedetta stood for a moment in a hostess-like attitude and then lowered herself onto the bench, one hand on the armrest. 'Ah' escaped her involuntarily.

When she was seated, she turned to Brunetti and asked, 'Did you come to meet Sara, or do you have other questions?'

'I'd like to ask you about your neighbours.'

'Il Dottore and his wife?' she asked, aiming her chin at the *palazzo*.

'Yes.'

'Is it also about Inesh?' she asked, and Brunetti was suddenly aware of just how bright her eyes were.

Sara got quickly to her feet and looked around, as if poked in the side by the sound of her master's name. Both of them noticed this.

'She misses him,' Suor Benedetta said. 'Now that he's gone, she's always going over the wall, trying to find him.' She put out her hand, and Sara came back and took a lick at it.

'We miss him too,' she added.

'Because he helped you?'

The nun's face tightened with confusion. 'No. Because he was good.'

Brunetti took the risk and asked, 'In contrast to your neighbour?'

His directness obviously surprised her. Lowering her eyes and folding her hands on her lap, she said, 'It's not my place to judge that, Signore.'

It came to Brunetti in a flash to ask, 'Would Sara judge your neighbour to be a good man?'

She reached out to put her hand on Sara's head and left it there, 'I can't speak for Sara either. But I can speak for this,' she said, putting her hand at the base of Sara's shorter ear. 'This happened on the other side of the wall.'

'You mean Professore Molin did that?'

Her shoulders were very narrow and hidden under her habit, a coat, and a shawl, but still Brunetti saw the shrug.

She resumed rubbing the dog's head, saying, 'Inesh left her with us once when he went back to Sri Lanka for a month.' Before he could ask, she said, 'We had a different Mother Superior then, and things were … easier for us. For Sara, too.'

'What happened?'

'She was upset because he was gone, and even though we fed her and made her a place to sleep in the toolshed, she kept going back, looking for Inesh.' She glanced up, and Brunetti nodded, encouraging her to go on. 'We could hear him sometimes ... ' she said, not having to specify whom she meant ... 'yelling at her and saying what he'd do to her if he got his hands on her.'

Again Brunetti nodded, and she must have sensed his goodwill and concern because she broke off the story to add, 'We were afraid he'd complain to the Mother Superior or to you – the police – and we'd have to give her up.'

She drew in an enormous breath of air and let it out in a sigh that was painful to hear. 'Then one day we heard him shouting and swearing at her. The bushes are so deep we can't see anything that happens over there, but we could hear her barking and then she started yipping and howling, and she came back over the wall, and that part of her ear was gone.'

'He did it?' Brunetti the policeman asked.

'I don't know, Signore. I wasn't there.' She roughened her pressure on Sara's head and said, 'And she can't tell us.' Bending down, she asked the dog, 'Can you, Sara?'

Sara, delighted with the attention, backed off a bit, then, to express her delight, ran around in circles for a while until she came back and flopped down at Suor Benedetta's feet, mouth agape, eyes closed in happiness.

'Do you know him, Sorella?' Brunetti asked in a soft voice.

'To nod to, yes. But no more than that.' Before Brunetti could ask another question, she said, 'The other sisters who have been here longer – I've been here only six years – have told me some things about him.'

'What things?'

'That he's a professor at the University, and that his wife is friendly when they meet her on the street. But they think he killed the cats.'

'What cats, Sorella?'

'It was before my time, but you learn things if you listen and pay enough attention,' she began, making Brunetti think what an asset she would be to the police.

'What did you hear?'

'The year before I came – that would be about seven years ago – one of the cats who lived in the garden – they kept the mice down – had kittens. But over there,' she said, pointing to the other property. 'The sisters who were here when I came told me that they could hear them yowling for food even over here, so they fed the cat more than usual, and she came here to eat and then went back to nurse them.' She glanced up at Brunetti, then down again. 'And then one day she didn't come, and there was no sound of the kittens.'

'Do you think … ' Brunetti began.

Her voice grew very tight and she said, 'I don't think anything, Signor Brunetti. I'm merely telling you what I was told by my fellow sisters.'

'Do you believe … ' he asked, leaving the meaning of the sentence dangling in the air, unspoken.

'I do.' No explanation given.

Brunetti nodded, bent forward and called Sara, who came to him quickly. He busied himself with her for some time, then asked, nodding towards the wall, 'Does she still go back over there?'

She shook her head. 'It's as if she knows he's not coming home again,' she said, then patted her knee. Sara abandoned Brunetti without a thought. 'Dogs know things in different ways than we do.'

Brunetti had little experience of dogs, but he certainly believed what she said.

'May I ask you another question, Sorella?'

'Of course.'

'Did your friend Inesh ever say anything about his employers?'

The nun considered this before she answered. 'He often mentioned how kind the Signora was and that he prayed for her often.'

'And her husband?' Brunetti enquired.

'He appeared not to have the same feelings.'

Brunetti laughed, knew he shouldn't have, so turned to apologize. 'It was your wording, Sorella. I have to compliment you on the elegance of what you said.'

'Thank you for that.' The nun snatched a glance at his face and returned her attention to the dog. Brunetti waited to see if she would explain. 'I spend a lot of time alone here, in the garden, and I think about conversations and what people have said and how those things could be phrased a different way to have a different effect.'

Brunetti was uncertain that she had finished but spoke anyway. 'Isn't meekness one of the virtues you're supposed to practise, Sorella?'

This time it was she who laughed aloud. 'You sound very much like my confessor.'

Good heavens, Brunetti thought, confession is still around. He remembered how humiliated he had been by it as a child and how relieved he was when he learned to lie to the priest and be judged a better person. He had spent a lot of energy since then learning to control that impulse to be perceived as a person better than he was.

'Is there anything perhaps more specific that might give me a clearer understanding of what sort of man he is?'

As he watched the nun and the dog together, Brunetti realized that if she glanced away, even for a moment, the dog would be in her lap. As it was, every stroke of the ear was matched by a small shove with her knee to keep the dog from jumping up.

She considered Brunetti's question, still patting at the dog. After some time, she put her hand together with the other and rested them on her lap. Sara, seeing that the lap was occupied, stretched out on the dry grass.

'His wife came to the door yesterday. I know, I know, but neither one of them has ever come to talk across the wall. She came to ask to speak to the Mother Superior and told her that her husband wants to clear out Inesh's home. She asked us if we knew of a charity that would want his clothing and belongings.'

So much for the tape as a way to keep people out, Brunetti thought but did not say.

'What did your Superior tell her?'

'One of the sisters has a niece who works for social services. The Mother Superior said she'd call and find out which group has most need. With all the refugees, that is.'

'Will this happen soon, Sorella?'

Her smile showed the patience that comes with long life. 'Nothing happens soon, does it, Signore? She'll call them this week and ask.'

'Did she say why they wanted to get rid of his belongings?'

She gave him a level look, as if she wondered why he wanted to know this.

'No, she didn't, Signore … ,' she began, leaving her voice in the air to let him know that she was not finished, ' … but we've heard that she's told people she wants to sell the *palazzo.*' She paused. 'And one of the sisters heard she's already spoken to someone.'

That would most likely be the hotel, Brunetti thought. He pushed himself to his feet and offered his arm to the nun. She looked up at him in surprise, as if she needed no help. But she'd been sitting in the cold on an outdoor bench, bending down to pet a dog lying in front of her, so she smiled and accepted the need to do the wise thing, latching her hand on his arm and pulling herself upright. 'Thank you,' she said.

'My pleasure, Sorella.' He bent down over Sara, who looked at him in surprise, froze in place, and made that strange sound she made when nervous. Brunetti took one step to the side and sat again on the bench. When Sara stood, he slowly extended his hand, and she came quickly to it.

'You're too tall for her, I think,' Suor Benedetta said. 'It's not a problem I have to deal with.'

Smiling, Brunetti stood slowly so as not to frighten Sara.

Suor Benedetta rested her hand on his arm and together, followed by the brown dog, they walked to the door to the *calle*. In front of it, he thanked her for her time and help and asked if he could come back in the summer for some apricots and perhaps bring his daughter along, to meet Sara. She loved dogs, he added.

The pressure of her hand tightened. 'I'll remember your mother in my prayers,' she said, reaching to open the door. He nodded and stepped outside, waiting for the sound of the closing door. After he heard it, he went round the corner, then stopped at the door to Palazzo Zaffo dei Leoni and rang the bell.

29

Brunetti stood back in the *calle*, expecting to hear footsteps on the path leading to this door. Instead, it clicked open at a command from inside the *palazzo*.

He shoved it ajar, stepped inside, and pushed the door closed, tugging at the knob on the inside to be sure it had closed properly. He walked towards the *palazzo*, looking down at the uncertain, uneven stones that paved the way.

When Brunetti looked up, he saw Gloria Forcolin standing at the front door, apparently as surprised to see Brunetti as Brunetti was to see her. At the same time, he saw Molin appear from around the back of the *palazzo*, head lowered, eyes on the uneven path, walking quite naturally in his direction.

Brunetti took a wide step to his left and started up the steps towards the woman, effectively removing himself from Molin's range of vision.

In an unnecessarily loud voice, he said, 'I'm here to speak to your husband, Signora.'

Gloria seemed entirely confused by his arrival and his voice. 'What do you want?'

'As I said,' Brunetti repeated, still speaking louder than necessary, 'to speak to your husband again. Is he here?'

She took some time to answer, but finally she said, 'He's just begun a session with his physical therapist.'

'Ah,' Brunetti said, and pulled his lips together in credible disappointment. 'How long do you think that will be?'

'At least … ' she began, and looked back at the door. Turning again to Brunetti, she said, 'At least an hour.' Another pause, and Brunetti could all but hear her preparing the phrases before she spoke them.

'I understand,' Brunetti said, this time stressing his disappointment. 'Would it be possible for me to come back tomorrow?'

Her face tightened, as happens when a person is confronted with a difficult question. 'Yes, I think so.' Then she discovered the real answer and said, 'Yes.'

He opened his mouth to thank her, but it was too late, for she had turned around and gone back into the *palazzo*, closing the door very quietly.

Brunetti turned away and walked immediately towards the garden house.

The strand of tape was still in place. He walked round to the rear of the house and checked the tape on the back door. One of the strokes of the X was out of true. He photographed the tape from a distance and then from closer up, then checked the photos to see that the signs the tape had been tampered with were visible.

Brunetti returned to the front door and unlocked it. He pushed it open, once again tearing it free from the strips of tape as he did so. Stepping over the tape, he pushed the door fully back and went in, closing it behind him. The heat was off and the place seemed colder than the outside; damper, too.

There was no longer any need to avoid contact with surfaces. Traces would have been left by many people: Inesh, his landlords, his friends, even the crime-scene technicians. The fact that physical traces of a person were found inside gave no information about when they had been left there, or why.

He was drawn by the memory of the peace on offer in the living room and went to see the Buddha. He studied the arrangement of the objects around the statue, then took his phone and found the photo he had taken the first time. Although the stones and shell had not been touched, and the withering flowers were still there, the statue was a few millimetres to the right of where it had been, a distance confirmed by the thin layer of dust missing from where the Buddha had been standing. It was unlikely that decades of training and experience had failed the crime squad on this one occasion, leading them to move things around without thought or making a note. More likely, the person who had removed the tape and entered had been rendered careless by haste and stress and had set the statue down a bit out of true.

Brunetti called up the photographs he'd taken of the books and took his phone over to the bookcase to see if the same careless hand had been used on them. Indeed, it so appeared. He held the tiny screen up to the Italian books on the shelf and began to check them against the photo one by one, if not by title, then by colour and size. When he was nearing the end of the row, he noticed that the two books encouraging violence in pursuit of political goals had been removed, thus leaving Leonardo Sciascia to have his way with Oriana Fallaci.

Seeing that potential evidence had been tampered with, Brunetti felt great relief at having thought to take the scrapbook with the pamphlets and manifestos with him. He had no idea whether it would ever be presented in a courtroom: the fact that someone had entered the house to have a look around and perhaps remove things would surely increase their interest to a judge.

He got to his feet and began to roam around the house, attentive to places where Inesh might have thought of hiding something. Because he had no idea of what might be hidden, he could not gauge size or dimension. A professional housebreaker had once told him that most people tended to hide things, mostly money – where was it, now? In high places like top shelves or low places like shoes in the closet? One or the other, but Brunetti could no longer remember which. He went into the kitchen: the thief had told him this room was most people's favourite hiding place. Brunetti had once found stolen jewellery – a diamond necklace and a ruby ring – inside a frozen turkey in the suspect's freezer.

After half an hour, he gave up trying to play detective and went back to see the Buddha again. He had no fresh flowers to leave before the statue, so he satisfied himself – and he hoped the Buddha – by rearranging the three stones and the shell in a pattern he found more satisfactory. Leaving the house, Brunetti pulled the two legs of the X into place, pressed them until they stuck to the frame, and then wrote his name on the top and bottom of both of them. Passing from the plastic tape over the wooden door frame, he walked around the house and did the same to the tape on the back door. No one who tried to open the doors would fail to understand the message. If 'Bru' didn't frighten them off, perhaps 'netti' would.

His phone buzzed, and he took it out to see who it was. It was Signorina Elettra's number.

'*Sì*,' he said.

'Were you planning to come back here?'

'Yes.'

'There are a few things you might like to read.'

'I'm near Santi Apostoli.' The calculation was automatic. 'Fifteen minutes.'

'Good,' she said and was gone.

He went directly to her office, where she was standing at the window. She had nothing in her hands: no paper, no folders, no files. She smiled when he came in and started towards her desk. He noticed she was wearing her Stan Smiths again, today the ones with the classic patch of green leather on the heel. Her jeans were a pale, faded blue but apparently new, her thin sweater the colour of hazelnut buds. He wasn't sure if she was defying the season or leaving soon for the southern hemisphere.

'What is it?' he asked,

'Bocchese gave me the computer,' she said.

'Yours?'

'No, of Signor Kavinda.' Hearing her use Inesh's surname, he was pleased with this sign of respect for the dead man: most murder victims, especially the women, ended up sounding like members of the family.

'Bocchese couldn't open it?'

'No, but it's particularly difficult when a person has to deal with certain—' Perhaps it was Brunetti's expression, patient and eager to understand, that stopped her sentence. 'Mr Kavinda's password was in Sinhalese. They didn't think of that, so nothing they tried could work.'

Signorina Elettra, he knew from long experience, was very patient with the crime team and seemed to have a special affection and regard for Bocchese because she shared his interest in miniature Renaissance bronzes, a taste not common among the people working in the Questura. It was also one of Bocchese's men who had installed the tiny listening device under the top drawer of Vice-Questore Patta's desk.

'You, instead … ?'

'I sorted that out for him, and then I found a Sinhalese translator – he teaches Modern Sinhalese Literature at the University of
Colombo.'

Signorina Elettra took a white linen handkerchief from the
pocket of her jeans and wiped invisible dust from her keyboard,
and when that was done looked up at him and said, 'I asked him
to read Mr Kavinda's emails and took the liberty of describing
his situation, his employers, his murder, and what he was reading. I asked him to translate anything he thought might be of
importance to us.'

'Into what language?' Brunetti asked.

'English.'

Brunetti nodded and asked, 'What did he find?'

'He said that he found very little. Most of the emails to his
wife were obviously meant to be read to the entire family – he
referred to many people by name, as though writing directly to
them.'

She opened her drawer and pulled out a few sheets of paper.

'This is all the translator sent. He said he could translate the
rest, but it would be a waste of our money.'

Brunetti had been curious about this and so asked, 'How is
this being paid for?'

'The usual,' she said. 'Office expense.'

'Of course.'

She handed him the papers. 'Take a look. You have more
familiarity with the people he talks about, so you'll make more
sense of what he says.'

Brunetti, hoping that this would prove to be the case, grate-
fully took the papers and went back upstairs, closing his door
when he went into the office.

He read through the emails the professor in Colombo had
translated and found nothing but praise for Gloria Forcolin, whom
Inesh called 'Madame', for her generosity and kindness. He wrote

of Molin as 'Master' and once described his anger after discovering signs of Sara's presence. Inesh had tried to make the strength of the 'Master's' response sound ridiculous, but he failed. So angry and suspicious had Molin grown at signs that an animal might be living and digging in the abandoned garden that Inesh kept her entirely out of sight and had taught her how to disappear under the aggressively lush briars or jump over the brick wall and take shelter in the convent grounds when she scented either the Master or the Madame approaching the garden house.

Two weeks before, Inesh had written to his wife that Sara's joy in digging in the garden had destroyed his peace and perhaps would make him lose his home, for she had become too familiar with the garden and no longer fled at the approach of the Master. Worse, she had found things and left them where the Master might see them, and he was very much afraid of what the Master's reaction would be if he learned what she had found. So he'd stopped feeding her and threw lumps of earth at her whenever he saw her, hoping to drive her to safety.

In the last email that the professor of modern Sinhalese literature had translated, Inesh told his wife that Sara had come back again and made such a mess that he was afraid of the Master's response, for it might now be dangerous for them to remain there. The last sentence translated read, 'It will be harder to find a new place to stay if I take her with me, but to take her with me is the only moral choice.' Brunetti set the page aside and thought about Inesh's last words, for in a sense that's what these emails were. The dog would have been responsible for having them cast out of their home, but his only moral choice was to take her with him if that happened.

Brunetti called the number Paola had found for Molin in the university staff list. He explained to Molin that he could no longer come to the *palazzo* and asked the Professore to come to the Questura to be interviewed the following morning. As Brunetti knew he would, Molin pleaded his physical state as an impediment. After a bit of back and forth, a reluctant Molin agreed that Brunetti and two *colleagues* would come to Palazzo Zaffo dei Leoni at nine to speak to him.

As soon as that was agreed, he called Signorina Elettra and asked her to send copies of the translation of Inesh's letters to both Griffoni and Vianello and to ask them to meet him in Campiello de la Cason the following morning at quarter to nine.

Thinking of little but coffee, Brunetti was still buttoning his overcoat when he walked out of the Questura, down to Sergio's bar on the corner. He realized that his real need was to be out of the Questura for a few minutes and, if nothing else, removed from thoughts of Inesh and thoughts of moral choices. Bamba, the Senegalese counterman, brought him a coffee and asked, 'Would you like something to eat, Signore?'

Casting his eye across what was on offer, Brunetti shook his head and said, 'No thanks, Bamba. The coffee's enough.' He drank it, paid, and started back to the Questura, his spirit calmed by contact with the ordinary.

Walking back to the Questura, Brunetti saw two seagulls perched on the drain of one of the houses along the canal. Still reflecting on animals, he realized he had spent most of his life hating seagulls. But now, after having watched, for three years running, a pair of them nesting on the roof of the house opposite theirs, fighting off the attacks of other gulls and raising their chicks, he found that he admired their courage and determination and was charmed beyond words by their chicks.

One of the seagulls stood on the tiles of the sloping roof, neck outstretched, violently squawking towards a twinset of surveillance cameras, one pointing to the right and, presumably, capturing the faces of people who came from that direction to enter the Questura, and one pointing to the left to do the same.

'There goes our privacy,' Brunetti muttered to himself, conscious that one reason this might happen was that Italian had never had its own word for privacy and had to borrow one from English – thus, *'La Legge sulla Privacy.'* How could you have a law about privacy if no word for the concept existed in your language? His mind busy with things like this, he passed through the door of the Questura, where he would stay until it was time to go home and return to the trivialities of life.

30

Both of them were standing in Campiello de la Cason the following morning when Brunetti arrived, causing him to wonder if it would be a good tactic for the cops to arrive late. Probably not, he decided. A man like Molin would be offended if kept waiting, flattered if they were on time.

Brunetti led the way towards Palazzo Zaffo dei Leoni, past the door to the convent and around the corner. Ahead of them, they saw motion on the ground: it turned out to be a seagull, tearing wildly at some edible remnant of what had once been a pigeon.

Frightened by their arrival, the bird grasped the remaining piece of carcass in its beak and flew to the top of the wall that faced them at the end of the *calle*.

Eyes on the bird as it continued with its meal, Griffoni asked, 'I wonder how the guys, or machines, who watch these videos will classify that?'

At a loss to understand what she was talking about, Brunetti said, 'What do you mean?'

She shot her arm out towards the still-feeding gull. 'He killed the pigeon, and now he's eating it.'

Vianello understood before Brunetti did. 'That's right. You don't notice them any more, do you?'

Glancing at his watch and seeing it was a few minutes before nine, Brunetti made no attempt to disguise his irritation. 'What are you talking about?'

This time, it was Vianello who pointed towards the gull. 'It's in front of the surveillance camera, so whoever's watching will see him eat his breakfast.' After a pause, he added, 'Disgusting.'

Brunetti thought of that other gull, that other camera. He pulled out his phone, no longer concerned with time, and punched in Signorina Elettra's number.

After only two rings, he heard her say, '*Sì*, Commissario?'

Wasting no time and deciding not to speak in code, Brunetti asked, 'Can you get into the surveillance cameras?'

'Probably,' she answered calmly, her mood responding to his. 'It depends on where. Much of the city still doesn't have them, or has them installed but not working.' She let a moment pass, then asked, 'Where are these?'

'Cannaregio, near Campiello de la Cason,' Brunetti said. 'There are two of them on a light pole where Calle Valmarana meets Calle del Tragheto. There's one that points along Calle Valmarana.'

'Just a moment, Signore,' she said, and he heard the familiar tap tap tap of her fingers on her computer. It came to Brunetti that this is what a gambler must feel when the ball goes click click click around the roulette wheel.

And then she was back, saying, 'They're working, at least in that *calle*. But coverage stops at Canale dei Santi Apostoli.' Which meant, Brunetti understood, that no camera was working in the place where Inesh had been killed.

'I'd like to know who went in or out of the door to the *palazzo* on the night Signor Kavinda was murdered.'

'What times, sir?'

Vianello had sung at about eleven. 'From eight until eleven.'

'Of course, Commissario. And then?'

'As soon as you've seen them, text me.'

'Yes, Commissario.' She was gone.

When they reached the door and he rang the bell, Brunetti looked at his watch and said, 'Only six minutes late.'

Griffoni smiled and said, 'He sounds like the sort of person who will put every one of them on our bill.'

Vianello laughed but said nothing.

A minute passed, but Brunetti resisted the temptation to ring again. He leaned towards them and said, careful to speak softly, 'This delay in answering is known as the assertion of authority. It shows who's in control, right from the beginning.'

'I'll remember that, sir,' Vianello said. Griffoni merely stood a bit straighter.

The door in the wall snapped open. Brunetti pushed it fully back and allowed the others to enter before him, then closed the door quietly and led them towards the door to the *palazzo*.

Professore Molin stood there, at the top of the steps, one hand on the door handle, the other resting on the head of his cane, tilting to the left, as was his habit. Because his hands were helping to support him, Molin did not have to offer to shake hands with the police, but he did move aside a bit to let them pass into the building.

When they were inside and Brunetti had closed the door, he turned to Molin and said, 'Professore Molin, this is my colleague, Commissario Griffoni.'

Molin nodded and said, *'Piacere.'* Griffoni repeated the word, adding 'Professore' after it.

Brunetti, turning to Vianello as though he were, perhaps, a section of the hedge that had attached itself to his sleeve, said only, 'Officer Vianello.'

Molin looked at Vianello but did not bother to nod.

He turned and, making conspicuous use of the cane, led them down the stone-paved central corridor of the ground floor and, with visible effort, up one flight of stairs to the first floor.

He paused there as if in need of a rest, and Griffoni let her eyes roam over the walls. Four chain-mail vests showing signs of wear on their leather parts and buckles hung along the corridor, swords and pikes suspended between them. There was a map of Jerusalem that Brunetti suspected to be modern because of the brightness of the paint. One end of a substantial horizontal crack in the wall peeked out from behind the right side of the map. On the opposite wall were lugubrious portraits of unhappy men and women eyeing one another with suspicion and disapproval.

Molin paused in front of the third door on the left and turned back to Griffoni and Vianello, both gazing at a portrait of a particularly sombre cardinal, the gloom of whose face seemed to have darkened even the red of his cassock.

Seeing that Molin had stopped, Griffoni turned to him, pointing to the portrait. 'Is this an ancestor of yours, Professore?'

'Perhaps better to refer to him as a relative, Claudia,' Brunetti said with the merest hint of reproach.

Looking confused, Griffoni nodded and said, 'Of course. That's what I meant: relative.' It was clear to them all that Commissario Griffoni didn't understand that ancestors left heirs, while relatives had no such obligation, and thus 'ancestor' was a compromising, however often correct, term to attribute to a cardinal.

Perhaps because she had asked about *his* family, Molin looked at her when he answered. 'It's Cardinal Giovanni Molin. He was bishop of Brescia from 1755, and he was made cardinal in 1761.'

Griffoni returned her attention to the painting. Molin continued, 'He's buried there. You can see his tomb in the Duomo Nuovo.' Brunetti waited for more, wondering if Molin had judged his words sufficient to satisfy his audience. Apparently not, for he added, 'My side of the family is descended from his younger brother.'

Griffoni nodded like a docile pupil, as if to suggest that she knew families could have two sides, and it was not possible to have an ancestor who was a cardinal.

Restored by the reference to his family, Molin took a step forward and opened the door to what proved to be the sitting room, limped in and held it open while the others entered, then closed it quietly. He indicated a sofa where they could put their coats, then crossed the room slowly and took his place on a wooden chair with arms and a padded seat. From it, he waved them to three straight-backed wooden chairs that stood in a semicircle in front of his own. The room was even gloomier than the hallway, the walls more burdened with prints and paintings.

Impervious to the snub, they took their places, Griffoni in the middle.

Brunetti took out his notebook, opened it, and thumbed through to the first empty page. That found, he folded the book open and placed it on his right thigh. While he was doing this, Vianello had taken his phone from his uniform jacket and also placed it on his right thigh. Vianello switched it to 'record', then raised it to his mouth to give the date, and place, and name of the person being questioned, as well as the name and rank of the police in attendance. That done, he turned to Brunetti and said, 'You can start anytime now, Commissario,' before returning the telephone to his knee.

Dispensing with any formality or politeness, Brunetti began. 'Professore, we are here because it is difficult for you to come to the Questura. This is, nonetheless, a formal interview and is – as you see – being recorded. We are here to inquire into the death of Inesh Kavinda, a Sri Lankan who had, for a period of about eight years, been living in the garden house on this property, at the rear of your home, Palazzo Zaffo dei Leoni.

'Signor Kavinda was murdered, and so we would like to know what you can tell us about your contact with him during the last months of his life.'

Molin drew in a deep breath to suggest just how tired he was of being troubled about this matter. 'One could see it as a problem of logistics, I suppose, of getting something from one place to another,' he surprised them all by answering. He gave a small laugh to indicate that he was joking and continued. 'In this case, I am the something, and Signor Kavinda was the person who helped move me from place to place. In short, Signori, he came with me whenever I left home and held my arm when it was necessary.'

'Because of the stroke you had some time ago?' Brunetti asked.

Molin nodded, and Brunetti said, 'I'm sorry, Professore, but you have to speak. Because of the recording.'

Molin looked at him, surprised for a moment, but then understood and said, 'Of course.' He added, 'Yes, because of my stroke. My left side is weakened, and I sometimes fall.' He raised his right hand and waved something away, then lowered it to his lap and waited for the next question.

It came. 'Do you remember what you did on the evening of Signor Kavinda's death?'

Molin nodded and said, 'We went for our usual walk.'

'Which was?'

'Down towards Fondamenta Nuove. There are only two bridges, and I usually don't have much trouble with them.'

Brunetti closed his eyes and followed the path of the two men, past the church of the Gesuiti and out onto the Fondamenta Nuove.

'That's quite a walk,' Vianello surprised him by interrupting, turning to smile at Molin. 'The distance, I mean,' he explained, his admiration audible.

'If I do it every night … ' Molin began, then veered to, 'One of my doctoral students comes now, every evening, so we can discuss his dissertation: the Siege of Bari.'

'Did that happen during the war?' Griffoni asked, startling Molin by interrupting him. He looked so surprised, he must have forgotten about her.

'Sieges always happen during wars,' Molin said and then, like someone who cannot resist eating the last cream pastry on the platter, added, 'Dottoressa.'

'I meant the last one, 1944,' she said, as if she'd had to think about the date.

'No, Dottoressa, 1068. It lasted three years.'

Griffoni closed her mouth, lowered her head, and gave every appearance of having been shamed. Brunetti sneaked a glance at Molin's face and saw his delight in having put the woman in her place.

Silence spread in the room; from outside came what sounded like the shouting of children, boys rough-housing and yipping with excitement.

Trying to move the conversation away from Griffoni's ignorance, Brunetti asked, 'Do you still go for the same walk every night?'

Molin shook his head. 'No. We go to Strada Nuova as far as San Felice.'

As if to redeem herself from having been so foolish, Griffoni said, 'It's about the same distance, I think, but the bridge is much bigger.'

Gracious in victory, Molin smiled at her and nodded.

Brunetti's phone pinged out the news that a message had arrived.

31

All three did their best to ignore the sound. Although both Vianello and Griffoni controlled their impulse to look at Brunetti's phone, Molin sensed something. His glance ran across them, like a spotlight searching for a guilty face at the scene of a crime. Vianello cleared his throat, and Griffoni brushed some lint from her sleeve. This succeeded in distracting Molin, and Brunetti read the message.

'Twenty-one forty-six. Two men emerge and turn left into Calle Valmarana: tall man, perhaps sixty – limping and walking with cane – and heavy-set, dark-skinned man. They walk arm in arm to corner and turn left into Calle del Tragheto.

'Twenty-two thirty-three. Man with cane but not using it turns into Calle Valmarana from Calle del Tragheto and walks quickly to door. Takes keys from his pocket and opens door. Goes inside and closes door.'

Brunetti slipped his phone into his pocket and, smiling at Professore Molin, said, 'In general, Professore, how would you describe your relationship with Signor Kavinda?'

Molin tilted his chin, as one does on hearing a strange sound. 'I'm not sure I understand your question, Commissario.'

'How did you get on with him? In what manner did you address one another? Did you address him as *tu* or as *'lei*?'

The question so surprised the Professore that he answered without thinking. '*Tu*?' he repeated. 'With a servant?'

The room fell silent, although not for the same reason in every person. From outside, the noise of the boys romping around was interrupted by a woman's voice shouting, no doubt trying to get them to stop and come home.

Ignoring the yipping from the kids, Brunetti spoke a bit louder. 'I thought, perhaps, after so many years ... well, that there might have developed a certain rapport.' When Molin remained without words, Brunetti said, as if excusing a vulgarity, 'It sometimes happens.' Apparently not in Professore Molin's world.

With no sense that anyone would find his surprise at the question unusual, Molin proceeded. 'He was from a part of the world where social classes are ... less flexible, shall we say, than they are here, Commissario. So people know how to deal with every situation because there are rules.' He sat up straighter in his chair. 'We both obeyed those rules.'

'They know their place, one might say?' Brunetti asked, an inquisitive smile on his face.

Molin allowed his smile to serve as his answer, but then, remembering the microphone, added, 'Yes.'

'Did you ever talk with him about, perhaps, his country, or his religion, or even how he learned to do the repairs to your building?'

Before answering, Molin looked at Vianello and Griffoni, as if asking for their help. 'I'm not interested in those subjects,' he said. 'I see no reason why I should talk about them.'

'A waste of time, surely,' Griffoni agreed.

'Exactly.'

'Could you explain to us why you forbade the late Signor Kavinda to use your garden?' Brunetti asked.

'Who ... ' Molin began, but appeared to change the question before it emerged fully. 'Who'd do something like that?'

Brunetti's smile was indulgent as he waited for Molin to recall having done just this. When he remained silent, Brunetti decided to give a not particularly delicate nudge. 'It seems you did, Professore.'

'Who'd tell you something like that?'

'Someone who was told it by Signor Kavinda,' Brunetti replied calmly. Then, smiling amiably, he added, 'And perhaps your wife will recall having been told to stay out of it.'

'My wife is not interested in such things,' Molin boasted.

'Nor you, I imagine,' Brunetti said.

The Professore gave a huff of contempt. 'Of course not.' That was meant to end the discussion. Molin pushed himself up higher in his chair and asked, 'Are you finished?'

Brunetti folded his arms and looked reflectively out the window. He saw a tall pine tree that was serving as host to some sort of invasive ivy that had already reached the top, turned, and had grown halfway down again, this time on top of itself. Brunetti was tempted to observe that years of neglect were evident from where he sat, but he resisted the impulse, glanced at Molin and said, 'That depends, Professore, on the answers we get to some other questions.'

'Such as?' Molin demanded, all pretence of patience hurled away.

'Such as the change in your political sympathies,' Brunetti said.

'My political sympathies – as you call them, Commissario – are my own business.'

'But they weren't, not years ago,' Brunetti observed. 'You were quite active in expressing them.'

'How? When?'

'When you put up manifestos in this city,' Brunetti said, assuming that the posters he'd found in the scrapbook had also been on display in the city. 'You wanted to show them around to anyone who could see.'

'What sort of manifestos?'

Brunetti paused and picked up his notebook. He flipped through the pages. Finally he found what he seemed to have been searching for, pressed the pages backwards, and read: "The classes that profit from the sweat of the workers are traitors and vultures, and must be destroyed. By violence if necessary." He turned a page slowly, glanced down the lines, turned another page. In a very pedantic gesture, he moved the book a bit farther away, perhaps the better to see the truth. "Unless workers rip them from their backs and destroy them, the ruling class will destroy not only the worker but his children and his children's children."

He looked across at Molin, closed the notebook, and held it on his palm as though by moving it up and down he could weigh it. 'Sound familiar, Professore?'

Molin looked at Brunetti, then at Griffoni and then at Vianello, as if hoping to find a small crevasse between them into which he could squeeze himself. 'I don't …' Molin began and then said, voice filled with what he tried to make seem like determination, 'I want to speak to a lawyer.' His voice had the sound of ashes.

Brunetti told Molin that he had the right to make the call privately, whereupon Molin left them in the room and went quickly into the corridor to make his call. Without a warrant from a magistrate, Brunetti preferred not to arrest Molin, and he knew it would take him some time to assemble the various discoveries he'd made into a persuasive case against the man.

At least the yelling and shouting had stopped, and Brunetti could think more clearly. Unfortunately, those thoughts were the ones he might well have had before: that night Molin could easily have dismissed Kavinda before they got to the door, saying he'd like to try to walk unaided. There was no physical evidence connecting Molin to the murder: the knife could be at the bottom of any of the canals between Rio de la Panada and Palazzo Zaffo dei Leoni. And Loreti could easily have run off with the cleaning lady.

After about ten minutes, Molin returned to the room, looking calm, but emitting the weak residue of excitement. He went back to his seat and only then noticed that he had, in his haste, forgotten to take his cane with him.

'I've spoken to my lawyer, and he's told me that I am under no obligation to continue to speak to you, so, if you don't mind, I'll thank you to get out of my home.'

That was certainly clear enough, Brunetti thought. He stood, followed by the others. Molin, remembering his cane, picked it up and walked behind them. As they approached the front door, they heard the boys shouting again; this time it seemed to be coming from the rear of the *palazzo*.

Molin yanked at the front door and pulled it open: the noise grew louder. It was sudden, short, frequent and no longer sounded like the shouts of boys but the barking of a dog.

Leaving the others on the steps, Brunetti hurried through the branch-filled tunnel to the wall separating the two properties. It was easy to spot Suor Benedetta in her black habit. She stood only a few metres from the wall, calling repeatedly to a madly barking Sara.

The dog, not far from the bench on which Suor Benedetta liked to take her rest, was having the time of her life: tilted forward on her front paws, she somehow managed to spring straight up into the air and land in the same position, barking her head off with uncontainable joy. Her tail was facing Brunetti, so he could not see what it was that had so filled her with happiness. And noise.

'Stop that, Sara. Stop it. Bad dog, bad dog.' The old nun's commands were drowned out by Sara's mad noise.

Each phrase could have been a caress to the dog, who jumped higher still, landing with her front paws thudding down in the same place. Brunetti noticed a thin white stick in front of her, targeted again and again on every landing.

'Sara, stop that. Stop that.' Suor Benedetta's orders were useless. Brunetti decided to try surprise. He continued in the direction of the still-mad dog, placing his feet softly and carefully. When he reached the wall, he was only a few metres from her; he leaned over, bracing himself on his hands, much in the manner of the vaulting dog, and shouted, 'Sara, Sara, be quiet. Stop it. Sit.'

He might as well have shot her. The barking stopped, and she froze, didn't even dare to look at the man whose voice she had obeyed. She was sitting on her tail, whining with fear.

Brunetti scrambled over the wall and went to the nun, whose face was red and frozen. He led her to the bench and helped her sit. He didn't turn to the dog until then. But Sara was paralysed, mouth open and slavering. He could see her spit on the ground.

'Are you all right, Sorella?' Brunetti asked, squatting down in front of her.

She nodded, unable to speak.

'What happened?' he asked, then took her right hand in his. He squeezed it softly. 'It's all right now, Sorella. She's stopped. Now tell me what happened, please.'

The old woman's mouth opened, but she seemed unable to speak. He squeezed her hand again and said, 'It's all over now, Sorella. Everything's fine.' He was aware of how very much it was like speaking to a frightened child.

'I, I, I brought her out to feed her,' she finally managed to say. Taking a deep breath, she went on. 'She'd learned to be very quiet. But I'd forgotten her water bowl. So I put the food down and she started to eat, and I went back inside to get the bowl.

'I was still inside when she started to bark, like she'd suddenly gone mad. She was on your side of the wall and barking like a crazy thing.' She shook her head at the memory. 'She's never done that before.' Her breathing slowed.

Hearing a voice behind him, Brunetti turned and saw the other four emerging from the tunnel of briars and thorns. They walked a few steps towards the low wall and stopped. Sara was still sitting, but her tail was free and waving back and forth.

'And then I saw it,' the nun continued, and Brunetti returned his attention to her. 'Just like the other time. She'd brought me something. But this was bigger, and I saw what it was.' She looked up at Brunetti, who saw that she was crying, tears running down her face. 'God have mercy on his soul,' she said and looked down at the ground.

Brunetti knew, but he told himself he did not. 'Are you all right, Sorella?'

She nodded.

He shoved himself to his feet, looked over, and seeing Vianello take a step towards him, held up his hand like a school traffic warden to stop him.

He took two steps towards the dog, who thought about getting up to approach him.

'No,' he said fiercely, and the dog went into hiding by lying down and covering her eyes with her paws.

He drew closer to her and saw what he knew was there. 'Sara,' he said. 'Good dog.' He patted his knee, saying, 'Good girl. Come here.'

Tentatively, worried, she lifted one paw and then the other and, careful to keep herself very small, crawled the few steps to come to his side. He kept his eyes on her, and when he saw her at his side, he said, 'Sit.' She did.

It was only then that he permitted himself to look at the place where Sara had been playing with what she'd dug up in the garden on the other side of the wall. He wasn't sure if it was a leg bone or an arm bone, but he knew it was a human bone.

32

After that, it was all relatively simple. Brunetti called the Questura and asked that the crime squad return to Palazzo Zaffo dei Leoni with a search warrant and that two extra officers be sent in a separate boat. Yes, he was there and would wait for them. He suggested to Suor Benedetta that she take the still-terrified Sara inside with her and, if the Mother Superior objected, she was to say that it was an order from the police. Then he returned to the other side of the wall.

He told Professore Molin that he was not allowed to leave until two officers arrived, who would take him back to the Questura. Further, Brunetti warned him that whatever he said could be used as evidence in any legal process against him, as would anything found during the search of his property. He asked his wife to remain in the garden until the boat came for her husband.

'And then?' she asked numbly.

This had broken her. Brunetti saw it when he looked at her face and saw the submission of her posture: bent forward, hands moving independently, eyes on the ground. Using slow sidesteps, she walked to the wall and lowered herself onto it, pressing her hands flat on either side, as if she already knew she would need their help when the time came to stand again. She lowered her head, allowing her shoulders to collapse, and sat silently, staring at the grass under her feet.

Molin, on the other hand, had stiffened, as if in response to an expected attack. Was he, like the medieval residents of Bari, preparing himself to resist the siege? Brunetti could all but see him laying in stores of food and drink, searching for his bow and arrow, his armour, his sword. As Brunetti watched him, Molin looked around the garden as if seeking the heavy stones that he could carry to the ramparts, eventually to hurl down upon his attackers. Each time Brunetti looked at him, Molin seemed to have grown harder and more compact.

But then, as Brunetti watched, he saw Molin look across the wall to the smooth, white bone, and at the sight, the Professore suddenly changed course. He grew smaller and curved forward, took a few fumbling steps and poked his cane into the thick grass and the underlying loam. As if in need of an anchor, he put his other hand atop the one already grasping the handle and allowed himself to tremble a bit.

He looked towards his wife, perhaps to assess how much room there might be for him beside her. His wife, still attuned to what had once been their marriage, raised her head and stared at him. Brunetti was chilled by what he saw in her face. Apparently so was her husband, for he lowered his head and freed his cane, then swung it in a wide arc and used its momentum to pull himself sideways until he was looking away from the bone but was himself still attached to the cane.

Brunetti had taken a vow of silence and stood there, calm yet attentive. He knew that this was the time of greatest risk, both for the accused and the accuser, a time when both of them had to control their impulses and remain silent. Years of experience had taught Brunetti how to lock his tongue and remove all expression from his stance or face or even – he sometimes thought – from the beating of his pulse.

Molin muttered something and then nodded to himself in affirmation. Knowing it would provoke Molin into repeating what he had said, Brunetti grew even stiller than Sara had; if he had had a tail, he would have sat on it. Molin had no idea of how quickly he was panting.

'*È stato Nesi*,' Molin said. 'It was Nesi.'

Brunetti had decided to unfreeze only at the next repetition, which came. '*È stato Nesi.*'

Had Molin spent the last few decades preparing for this moment and decided that Nesi, dead for years, was to be presented as Loreti's killer? Rubini was still alive and so might contest the accusation, so better for Molin – at least for now – not to name him, only poor, defenceless Nesi. Not until a wall was breached, or one of the corner towers crumbled, would it be necessary to surrender.

This was only the beginning of what happened during what Brunetti could not stop himself, later, from thinking of as the siege of Palazzo Zaffo dei Leoni. It did not take three years to break through the walls, as with Bari, nor even three months. The rest of Loreti's remains were soon found, buried in a recently disturbed grave in the very centre of the vast thicket of bushes and weeds that took up so much of the garden of the *palazzo*. The dead man's identity was confirmed by the DNA test of his cousin that Griffoni had initiated; the pathology lab in Padova also confirmed that the bones had been buried at about the time of his disappearance. The exact cause of death could never be determined: the forensic pathologist spoke only of possibilities, all of them unpleasant.

Molin, in his statement – he never referred to a 'confession' – blamed everything on Nesi, insisting that Nesi was the one who wanted to put their bold talk into action, who had invited Loreti to come and have a drink at his friend's *palazzo*, and was the one who had stabbed their teacher to death. Loreti had brought it upon himself by resisting their attempt to force him to the garden house, where they had planned to hold him prisoner until a ransom was paid.

Hearing this during their first interrogation, Brunetti had been unable to stop himself from responding, 'Like the Ukrainians?' at which point Molin, surprised, responded, 'Exactly,' before he thought about what he'd said.

A search of Nesi's house, where his wife and son still lived, uncovered nothing: no secret diary, no voice from beyond the grave, no sign of repentance beyond his confession to his son that he had 'done a terrible thing'.

Rubini, called in for questioning, maintained that he had no idea what Brunetti was talking about. He'd lost all faith in politics and could no longer remember why he'd ever cared. If he cared for anything, he maintained, it was beauty and his family. He could not be moved from that position, and there was no evidence, other than Molin's unsubstantiated claim, that he had been aware of their plans to kidnap Loreti. There were, furthermore, documents in the files of the university registering his six-month study grant in Cuba, which had begun the month before Loreti's disappearance and ended five months later, when the story was old news.

Molin had, by accusing Nesi, acknowledged that he himself had been an accomplice to the murder, and this proved sufficient to convict him.

In the second trial, for the murder of Inesh Kavinda, the lack of a confession and the presence of nothing stronger than circumstantial evidence failed to persuade the judges. Although Molin had originally claimed to have returned to the *palazzo* with Inesh on the night of his murder, this was proven to be false by the surveillance videos. Molin said he must have con-fused the dates. After all, they'd been taking the same walk for months, so it would be easy for him to confound the days. Besides, Inesh often left him at Campiello de la Cason, so it was perfectly normal for him to return home alone.

As to motive, at his death Kavinda had been in possession of a fragment of bone that was identified as belonging to Professore Loreti, the remainder of whose body was found in the garden of the *palazzo* that was then and now in the possession of the accused. The judges failed to place great importance on this.

After considering the evidence, the judges decided that it was insufficient to support the accusation that Professore Molin had murdered Signor Kavinda. He remained, however, under house arrest while the court considered his appeal in the other murder case. At this point, the Consulta Araldica reached a decision and rejected Molin's claim to nobility, so that case, at least, was closed.

Brunetti had no doubt about who had murdered Inesh, for whom he had come to feel great sympathy, and thus was able to accept the conviction he could get rather than regret the loss of the one he wanted.

Molin's wife returned to her father's home, leaving Molin to care for the *palazzo* by himself during his house arrest. He found no one capable of discovering the source of the crack in the first floor wall, now a hand's breadth wide, nor of the leaks in the attic. His legal costs for the two trials were enormous, leaving him no choice but to sell the *palazzo*. His wife agreed, and a hotel company quickly made contact with them. But here, like the vil-lain in a fairy tale, intervened the Soprintendenza di Belle Arti, ruling that no sale could be considered without the presentation by the purchasers of an approved plan of restoration. Both of those submitted by the hotel company have been rejected.

And so the *palazzo* sits there still, unsold, unsellable. The bushes and brambles, ivy and vines, have begun to devour the garden house, and even the briar-lined tunnels are astir with rampant growth.

The only one to gain anything from all of this is Sara, who now has the freedom to dig wherever she pleases in the garden of the *palazzo*. She has been further graced by the arrival of a new Mother Superior, a woman whose attitude towards animals is far more Franciscan than Benedictine and who has granted Sara free run of the convent's garden. This suits Sara, who continues to commute undisturbed from one garden to another. Like the aristocrats of former centuries, she is thus able to enjoy both the formal order and neatness of her city residence and the untamed excess of nature in her country estate. In the manner of Saint Francis, she considers humans to be her brothers and sisters, and thus she passes her days in harmony with both nature and mankind.